THE ARCANE ART OF FOLDING SHEETS

The Arcane Art of Folding Sheets

IRENE GEORGE

IG Publishing

About Irene George

Irene George grew up in country Australia in a family where tall tales and yarns were prized currency. She writes about women, family secrets and becoming who you were meant to be. Irene lives in Sydney with her husband and their lagotto, Paolo.

Her first published work is *Grafted. A Novel.*

Chapter 1

One step removed but it is a steep step, slippery with the moss of good intentions. True there are optimistic interludes: moments in childhood when they reach for your hand and as teenagers when they confide a painful secret or ask advice. But for all the times in between and for those who start late we are the wife of the father. The brothers - and sisters-in-law eventually gain legitimacy when they become parents themselves. Villain of the fairytale and interloper in the happy family, building better relationships with my stepdaughters sometimes felt out of reach.

I kept my eyes closed, determined to clear the dark thoughts I had indulged after a dream-filled sleep. I did not want Rob to read the rancour that lingered.

'Damn, didn't see that pothole. Did I wake you?', Rob was looking straight ahead, eyes squinting against the curtain of rain.

I shook my head and stretched my shoulders back into the car seat. 'How long was I asleep? Sorry, I haven't been very good company. Do you want me to drive for a while?'

'No, no, we're almost there and the rain's easing', Rob gave a quick smile. 'You must have been tired.

It was true, I was exhausted but so was he. 'I don't remember anything after Newcastle. You should have woken me'.

We were the first to arrive at the holiday house with its naked winter garden and muddy path. The last house was several kilometers further up the ridge but one glimpse of the sea dispelled any disquiet about the isolation. It was bleak now with the rain, matching my earlier mood, but it promised to sparkle the minute the sun broke through.

'I'll check if there's some firewood cut and get this going. It feels like there's been no one here for a while', Rob said pulling a jumper over his head and inspecting the open hearth. The bedrooms were icy. No need to unpack until the place had warmed up, I made us a cup of tea from the mountain of provisions we had brought. I had baked as usual and, naturally made far too much, 'You'd think we were staying for three weeks and Cleo and Marco always bring heaps of treats'.

'And too much wine'. Rob wasn't much of a drinker and thought their hedonistic lifestyle extreme.

'They like to be generous, that's all. Relax and enjoy the weekend. It won't hurt to let our hair down for a few days after the last month'.

'That's the third time you've said something like that since we got into the car', Rob said through tight lips.

'Well you must admit, it has been pretty intense. From the time Marjorie was diagnosed you have been on-call for her and the girls, not to mention helping navigate all the medical stuff'.

'I owed her that and the girls needed me. I'm all they have now besides each other'.

'Of course, I'm not criticizing just saying it's okay to take some time for ourselves', I held onto the next thought, chastising myself for not being a better person.

It had been a long month, on the back of many long months as Marjorie's health worsened and the girls became more frightened, more dependent on their father. On the face of it our life had gone on as normal; working, having the girls for dinner, seeing friends, but things had been strained. Toothpaste on the bathroom sink, foot marks on a newly washed floor—it took very little for my anger to boil over from the low roil it was set on for much of that time.

'Come and have some tea while it's hot. The fire is looking good, thanks for getting that going so quickly', I said rubbing my hands unconsciously even though I wasn't cold anymore. Rob touched the top of my head as he came to sit beside me, 'Any cake?'

I had started to cut slices of the cinnamon butter cake as Cleo and Marco arrived in a skid of gravel in their orange sports car, all gloves, beanies and chapped cheeks, their glamour a counter to the freeze.

'Gracious, it's so cold', Cleo ran inside while Marco unpacked the car. 'I was just saying, I hope there is an open fire, so much cozier in here'. Her arms were full of wildflowers, 'For your anniversary. I thought something rustic would suit this place'.

'Oh they are gorgeous and you're a honey. Thank you. It's been so hectic I didn't even get a card for Rob. You are showing me up. I've just made tea, I'll get you a cup'.

'I was going to suggest champagne but yes a sensible cup of tea would be lovely', Cleo looked mischievously at Rob, daring him to object. His response was to announce he would see if Marco needed a hand as he disappeared outside.

'You should always celebrate anniversaries', Cleo counselled. 'It's important to find a moment to appreciate each other'. It was as if she had read my thoughts from minutes ago but she went on oblivious, 'For our last anniversary Marco took me to the awful Thai restaurant where we first dated. It was sweet but we were both sick next day with food poisoning'. She chuckled before her face turned serious.

'But tell me Nell, how has it been?' Cleo drew out the last word as she sat opposite me on a kitchen stool, holding my gaze. I had hoped to avoid the inquisition until tomorrow but Cleo god bless was never one to wait.

'Tough. Rob is holding up and being strong for the girls but he is grieving. You aren't married to someone so long without having a deep connection. He hasn't talked to me as much as I'd like. He's gone into his shell'.

'And you, what about you?'

My eyes watered and I had to swallow hard to stop the rising well, 'You are the first person who has asked. I'm fine, tired and a bit stressed but it's not my grief'.

'No? It must be awful being on the outside. Let Rob work through his unfinished business with Marjorie but don't let it come between you two'.

'You know me too well. I feel so hurt by his distance even though I can rationalize it all. The girls, Paige mainly, have been vile lately. I know she thinks that I was the cause of Marjorie's illness, that all the stress and heartache activated those mutant cells'.

'You know that is ridiculous. Blaming you is a way to shield herself, to build a wall around her anger. Probably it's Rob that she is angry with but she needs her dad right now'.

'I know, I know. Hopefully a few days relaxation will give me perspective and some time for us to reconnect'.

Cleo was frowning, 'You two are okay, aren't you?'

'Yes, yes, frazzled and wrung out, that's all'.

Satisfied for the time being, Cleo relented, 'Let's see what those two are doing outside. It shouldn't take this long to empty the car'.

'Good idea', I said distractedly looking for a vase to fill, silently thanking Cleo for her head-on approach. I had not known I needed to say those things out loud but now I could look at the words more dispassionately and hopefully begin to move past the hurt.

'As I thought, gas-bagging out here in the freezing cold'. Cleo picked up a small bag, leading by example. 'Come on boys, time to start this holiday and right now that would be best indoors'.

Rob and Marco looked to the sky as renewed splashes of a cold rain whipped around their faces. The incoming tide brought a confused sea closer to the cottage walls, its spray mixing with the rain that was falling in earnest by the time Marco pulled the kitchen door closed behind him. A wind from the south shook the old windows with the promise of a drafty evening.

Over the past few years, Rob and Marco had become friends. Opposites in many ways they liked each other and found plenty to talk about. Rob was a social worker by training, now CEO of a men's charity and Marco owned a small bistro in a wealthy part of the city where well-heeled locals found respite from their own kitchens. Luckily, Rob's other passion was food and Marco was curious, a real people-person. They sat companionably, fiddling with the fire from time to time while Cleo had a shower to warm up and I unpacked.

I first met Rob at the hospital where I worked in the Emergency Department. He had been called down to see a young man who had been assaulted by two of his boarding school mates. His quiet acceptance had disarmed the young man sufficiently for him to open up about what had really happened. I remember thinking he was the kindest person I had ever seen in that moment.

It was a couple of years before we dated. I was with someone else for a while and he seemed absorbed in his work. One Christmas, he came to the work Christmas party. I'd had a drink or two and flirted a bit but he left early and I thought I'd frightened him off. So two weeks later when we were both on night shift on New Year's Eve I was surprised when he came looking for me.

'Quiet night?', he'd asked.

'Surprisingly, but it's early yet. The pubs don't close for another few hours, that's when the trouble usually starts'.

'I've had one suicide attempt, young girl discharged too soon from the psych unit, but there's been nothing for a while.

Actually, the reason I was looking for you was to ask if you are free for breakfast. I thought we could celebrate the New Year together at the end of the shift if you are free?'

I remember making some inane comment about being on evenings again the next day before accepting his offer and the little buzz of excitement that had stayed with me for the rest of the night. That first date had led to us seeing each other regularly for coffee or a drink after work. Eventually Rob told me he was married which explained the excruciating pace of our relationship. I was devastated, I didn't go out with married men, that would be a betrayal of the sisterhood, yet I thought about him all the time.

Two days after his revelation, he called to ask me to meet him for dinner. Against my better judgement I went. I planned to say we couldn't see each other again until he told me he was leaving Marjorie and that he wanted to keep seeing me. Apparently, the separation had been a long time coming but now that his children were grown up, both in their twenties he said it was time to take the leap. He made it clear that he wasn't leaving his wife for me but that having spent time together had strengthened his resolve that he couldn't stay in the marriage. It was his way of saying 'no pressure'.

I was a secret for a long time before he introduced me to his daughters, Paige and Caroline, and although I didn't push, I hated knowing that he was ashamed of us. When we finally did meet, they quickly calculated that I had been around since the separation and assumed it was my doing. It was a tough time.

'All unpacked', Cleo declared wrenching me back to the present. She was looking cozy in a designer tracksuit and sheepskin boots, her face rosy from the shower devoid of the makeup she normally wore, her wild curls still damp. 'Rob, this fire needs another log and you are the man with the knack'.

'Sure you just don't want to ruin your nails?' It was the most jovial Rob had sounded in weeks.

The light faded early which was all the excuse Marco needed to declare cocktail hour. Cleo was setting up some music with a small Bluetooth speaker, 'I have replicated some of my old mix-tapes', she looked very pleased with herself as she started the playlist of old favourites from our twenties and thirties.

Marco turned up the volume on the Style Council, all the while impersonating a Las Vegas barman and telling us about a regular client who had become addicted to Botox. We were all laughing as he described the woman's constant look of surprise and fish pout.

'Why would you do it?' I wondered. 'Not that I'm in love with these wrinkles but at least they are mine'.

'I might consider a facelift, never say never', Cleo surprised me, she had always been more down to earth than that. 'Have to keep youthful for my lovely Marco'.

'That's right, I'm the baby here', he laughed.

'Ha, especially as his clientele sound so glamorous'.

'You know Bella, our youngest asked me about Botox recently. She was thinking about it and she is barely thirty. She's already had some sort of needling thing apparently'. Cleo said.

Marco looked horrified, 'I didn't know that. Why do the kids tell you everything? I hope you told her not to do it'.

'Of course I did and they tell me stuff because I ask. Besides, they know I'm not going to explode if I disagree with them before launching into a long diatribe'.

'Ah, yes, you could have something there', Marco placed his hand on top of hers. 'You know Nell, the kids adore Cleo. They know how lucky they are to have her sorting me out'. He was laughing but his eyes were sincere.

I felt a twinge of envy as Rob looked away to study the darkness outside and was relieved when Marco changed the subject. His old German shepherd, Rex, was almost immobile these day and they would have to put the poor boy out of his misery soon. 'He's had arthritis for a while and now he has these tumors on his back that make him cry if he knocks them'

'I'm not sure what we would do if Lucca had something serious. It sounds like he's in a lot of pain though', I offered.

'That's the thing, the vet says it's hard to tell with dogs. He doesn't whine that much but he is incontinent and he mopes around the house', Marco's eyes were sad now. 'The house will be empty without him. I love that shaggy bag of bones but his time has come. We'll spend next week spoiling him, heaps of treats, and then the vet says we can do it at home. I was at school with Peter and he says he can be flexible about letting us do it ourselves even.

Cleo gave Marcus a hug from behind, 'I love the old fellow, even when he used to chew my shoes although it has been a long time since he was that frisky'. No one felt the need to talk for a while, ostensibly concentrating on our drinks and the refreshed flames in the hearth.

'Did Marjorie ever consider ending things earlier, when the pain became bad?' All eyes darted to Marco's face, Cleo coughed and I stood up to fiddle with something on the kitchen bench.

Rob 's voice was level, unhurried, 'She did ask for more morphine right at the end but no she was in no hurry to go early. Every moment with the girls was precious to her, maybe more so because she had almost left them twice before in the pit of her depressive episodes'.

Marco nodded, 'At least she knew she wouldn't be a burden to anyone. That would be the worst, having a stroke or some-thing, being helpless and knowing that you were a blight on everyone you loved'.

'I always thought those previous attempts at suicide were half-hearted as well. She never took quite enough of the vari-ous pharmaceutical cocktails she tried, more a cry for help than wanting to end it all', Rob was thinking back to when the girls were young.

Cleo and I exchanged glances and in unspoken agreement wandered over to the windows to admire the sea. 'Ouch, sorry. Marco has two left feet'. I shook my head. 'No, I think we are both sick of people tip-toeing around us, afraid of being inconsiderate. The honesty and random free-association is refreshing'.

'Refreshing is one word for it', Cleo hugged me and gave her husband a warm smile. He was deep in conversation with Rob about football—Marco could never be accused of dwelling on dark thoughts for too long. It did not take Cleo long either to move onto a brighter subject, 'Have you heard from Pippa lately. I've been meaning to message her'.

My face softened remembering our mutual friend, 'She called a couple of weeks ago, sounding fabulous as usual. She's been super busy renovating her apartment in Paris while she holidays down in Périgord'.

'Is she still painting? Last time I saw her she had taken up watercolours and they were amazing'.

'She said she has been offered an exhibition in a few weeks in a little gallery in Sarlat—so fantastic for her. And the exciting news for us is she is planning a visit directly after the exhibition closes'.

'It must be three years since I saw her, last time Marco and I were in France'.

'Yes, too long. It will be so great to catch up again, just the three of us'. She is coming for the wedding of one of the kids. I was surprised Gary allowed it but maybe he didn't have any say in it. Could be awkward'.

'Of, you know Pippa, ever the peacemaker. I'm sure she'll have sorted out how to handle it'.

Later as I closed my eyes under the warm stream of water, I was grateful everyone had been ready for an early night. Cleo, my best friend since our twenties when we were young nurses and ever the night owl had presumably taken pity on the rest of us. She was the daredevil who had egged on Pippa and me to join in escapades that promised to end badly yet surprisingly rarely did. The life of the party, every young doctor's favourite, she was the darling of every older patient as well.

I was never jealous of that popularity, that sheer presence. Like everyone else I welcomed the warm glow that she brought with her. In truth I had no desire to be as visible as Cleo, preferring to don the mask of calm professionalism, respected if not immediately loved. I prided myself on being the one who would come through in a tricky situation, keeping my head when the world went mad or Cleo inadvertently set it off its axis. Little wonder I ended up specializing in Emergency—the order in the chaos.

Cleo took the route to midwifery, loving to help frightened first timers. Although she had never had a child, her empathy and humour wrapped around the women like a warm bath. Creating safe spaces, free of judgement was Cleo's specialty and we all adored her for it. When we were young, I saw how men were drawn to that quality. She made them feel strong and capable, like they could never disappoint her even when the reality was overtly different. In the last few years she had achieved the same with Marco's three children. The two boys had been easy. Bella, the youngest had taken more time but now she called Cleo, M2, code for Mum number 2.

Pippa by contrast was the quiet one, the clever one in our gang of three. She had finished nursing with us but decided after a few years of working to go back to university to study French and linguistics. That was where she met Gary, one of her lecturers and a newly widowed father of two small girls. I remember counselling caution when she told me she and Gary were moving in together after only a few weeks of dating but for over ten years they were absolutely solid. Pippa was in love with everything about their life, including instant motherhood and we saw less of her as she gave herself over to her new roles.

I remembered how I had missed her in those early days. It was like she had become serious, a proper grown-up overnight and I was still working out what my life was all about. I was envious but at the same time felt betrayed to have been overlooked for someone else. Stupid, of course and horribly self-centred.

I knew that same selfishness was at the heart of the difficulty I had with how Rob had helped Marjorie, embarrassing not to have grown out of it. The night sky shone with stars now that the storm had cleared and I opened the window, pulling my robe tight and taking care the draft would not reach Rob who had followed me into the shower. The moon was the slimmest slither of silver but the Milky Way dazzled with its spiral of crowded light. Rob was a keen stargazer and he had taught me the names of the lesser known constellations but Orion remained my favourite. My father had liked to point it out as we sat around a fire on family camping trips, toasting marshmallows, burning tongues on the charred sweet, begging to stay up for ten more minutes. Rob must have shown the night sky to his daughters, presumably to Marjorie before that —treasured moments but not unique ones.

I turned then, he was toweling his hair and watching me from the doorway, 'Nice night. You were right, it's good to slow down for a few days. You were quieter than usual, is everything good?'

I shook my head, whether to clear it or reassure Rob that I was fine, even I wasn't sure. 'All good, enjoying winding down. It was a long drive and then those two have more stamina than me'.

'Know what you mean, Cleo would be still going if we hadn't called it a night'. For the first time in weeks he rubbed my shoulders, feeling the tension ease under his thumbs. 'I've been so self-absorbed lately and you have been fantastic even when you must have been feeling left out. Love you Nell'.

'Love you too. It has been a tough time but we are here for each other that's what's important'. I squeezed his hands on my shoulders and the smile in his eyes was all I needed.

My dream-addled afternoon nap in the car seemed like a bad idea when I was still lying awake listening to Rob's snoring reach its crescendo. Hard to believe we had been married eight years—it felt both a moment and a lifetime ago. I had never had the courage to talk to Marjorie about our intimately estranged relationship, planted in each other's worlds with no direct communication. I knew she had battled extreme highs and lows for years. She first attempted suicide when Paige was barely five and in the early days, I worried my presence could send her over that precipice again. It was a relief when Caroline reported after her mother's sixtieth birthday celebrations a year earlier that she had reached a turning point, ready to move on to a new life without Rob.

As for the girls, I had pursued various relationships with Paige and Caroline: older friend, aunt, parent. I never presumed acceptance which was as well because little was forthcoming. Rob said I should give them time, let them get to know me but I had long given up hope of anything changing.

Cleo had laughed when I told her, over a glass of wine, my theory that stepmothers personify a family's secrets and shames. Unlike Rob, she didn't recommend that I give them time, rather that I get over myself and be there for them. They were bound to say things they didn't mean, I was the adult and shouldn't take it to heart. I wanted to point out that they were also adults in their twenties at that time but that would have been mean-spirited.

Marco and his ex- had split up when his kids were teenagers because of Marco's constant affairs. There was nothing to suggest he was a reformed character when he and Cleo met years later and she married him with her eyes open. I suspected he may have continued to stray from time to time but I never heard her say one word about any problems in their marriage. I on the other hand seemed to be constantly carping at Rob for running to Marjorie's rescue every time a tap washer needed fixing or the car was making a worrying noise. The saint and the fish wife.

Chapter 2

Sun streamed into the kitchen warming the side of the room where I sat over coffee and toast. The wind had not dropped but there was talk of a bush walk later when the air had warmed up. Last night's storm had left the grey seas a study of adolescent fury, unsure of its next move once it had flung itself onto the rocks. Marco's good morning was bright as he busied himself making more coffee. Cleo was yet to appear and Rob was out for a run but the quiet time of day was over for now.

A forgotten memory from a few weeks ago nagged at me. I'd seen Marco at the hospital and I had been meaning to mention it ever since. He was wearing the same red shirt as today and I had wondered if he'd had an appointment for tests of some kind. We were all getting older, even super fit Rob was taking blood pressure tablets. Accepting a coffee top-up, I said, 'I think I saw you at the hospital a while ago. I hope everything is okay'.

Marco was facing away from me but shrugged, I haven't been to the hospital in ages. Not since Cleo worked there'. Cleo had retired from midwifery after they married, saying the hours did not suit family life, especially when Marco's evenings were taken up with the bistro. She worked a couple of days a week for a pathology company now, repetitive tasks but easy.

'Funny, I could have sworn it was you and that you were wearing the same shirt you have on now'.

'Must be my twin and he must have great taste as well', Marco made a bad attempt at a wink and I heard him repeating the story to Cleo later, telling her how funny it was. His dark Mediterranean looks were distinctive but I had been pretty stressed that week. What with Marjorie's prognosis and Rob never home, I must have been mistaken which made me wonder about my decision making at work over the last few weeks when I'd been on automatic pilot. No one had said anything directly but the Director of Emergency did suggest I must be due for a break. It was probably his way of telling me I was sub par at the moment. My cheeks reddened with the realization that the team had been carrying me, saying nothing but all too aware that I wasn't my usual self.

'Enough of this lounging around', Cleo bounced around the kitchen, 'Time for a walk while the weather is good'. Rob was back from his run and had changed into warmer clothes but was keen for more physical activity and even Marco was pulling on his walking shoes. 'Oh well, there will be more coffee later', I laughed, 'Let's go'.

The wind tangled my hair, so that I had to coil it into a knot to keep it out of my eyes and the sand was stinging my face. I walked beside Marco but the gusting wind carried our words away as soon as they were spoken. 'Who needs a beautician for dermabrasion', Cleo turned back to yell in my ear but soon she was leading us away from the beach along a forest trail.

After holding every muscle rigid in the wind, the release when the battering stopped was pure balm. Rob and Cleo were powering ahead, determined to work off last night's chocolate dessert but I was happy to dawdle along with Marco who was photographing every dripping rock, every glistening fern. He was bent down over a fungus of some kind, gaudy orange against the leaf litter. 'What do you do with all these photos?' I wondered aloud.

Marco looked up, 'Most of them won't be good, especially today because it's hard to focus in this light, but a few will make it onto my photography website. It's a hobby, nothing serious but I enjoy the precision of it. When I take a photo, I have to slow down, take notice before I react, a novelty for me you must admit', his chuckle was self conscious but without embarrassment. This was a more reflective Marco than I typically saw, maybe it was the part of himself usually reserved for Cleo. It made me like him more.

Happy with his photo we resumed walking. 'You know this morning when you said you saw me at the hospital?' He was looking straight ahead, his voice lowered and he slowed the pace, 'I didn't want to discuss it then in case Cleo came in but yes, I was at the hospital. I've noticed some weakness in my right hand recently and I thought it might be carpel tunnel so I wanted to have it checked out'.

'Oh, I see and you didn't want Cleo to know?'.

'You know how she worries, she'd have me seeing a neurologist or some other fancy doctor for a battery of MRIs and CAT scans until I glow in the dark'. The words were light but the tone hadn't changed.

'Was it? Carpel tunnel I mean'.

'Apparently not but it seems to be improving so I was panicking about nothing'.

'Well so long as it's getting better'.

'It is and if you could not mention it to Cleo...I'd be grateful'.

'Sure', I said but my arm nettled uncomfortably. I was never happy keeping secrets, partly because I was so bad at it and Cleo of all people could wheedle anything out of me.

Luckily, we caught up with Rob and Cleo a few minutes later. 'What have you two been doing back there'?', Cleo's eyes were teasing us.

'Minutely investigating and photographing a very orange fungus', I said.

'Oh Marco, you are such a bore with that camera', Cleo was laughing again and his gentle smirk took no offence.

'We are almost at the end of the trail', Rob thankfully had been keeping tabs on where we were. 'I'm pretty sure if we walk a kilometre further up the road there is a café. Maybe lunch?'

It was cold again as we moved out of the trees into the wind. The sun felt thinner as though ready to repeat the storm of the previous evening. A quick stop for lunch before we force-marched back to the cabin to warm up seemed like the best plan but I hadn't counted on Cleo's ability to toss a hand grenade when least expected.

'So Rob', she said as our toasted sandwiches arrived, 'Tell us, how are you and the girls coping with Marjorie's death?'

He made some sort of low rumbling sound and I studied the inside of my sandwich. Only Marco seemed unperturbed, eating so noisily I wanted to slap his face.

'You know talking can be good therapy', she continued without the slightest hesitation.

'Cleo, Rob's a social worker remember! I think he knows how to deal with loss', my hackles were up and my voice testier than I intended. It seemed to prod Rod back to life.

'How do you think it has been? It's been fucking shit', he started and the river that had been building in pressure, breached its flood gates.

'Marjorie and I had history. We shared two beautiful daughters, some of my happiest times were with the three of them. I feel guilty and angry but I can't show that to the girls I have to be there for them'. He sounded spent and my heart broke. There was no space for that jealous petty voice struggling for attention and yet I couldn't quieten it entirely.

Cleo had tears in her eyes and her voice was gentler, 'The girls must be struggling. I know they adored their Mum'.

'They are incredibly sad. They blame me and Nell thinks they blame her too', Rob didn't meet my eye as he said what we both knew but had not spoken. 'Maybe they are right, stress and bitterness are poison and Marjorie had a lot of both'.

Cleo was watching both of us, even Marco had stopped eating. I had the feeling I was expected to respond, to say something—something trite—contrite. A bubble of anger pushed aside, the benign words I thought I would say. 'Poison of her own making. She made choices too, let's be honest. And this theory that stress caused her cancer ...' I stopped wishing I could press replay.

I hated myself for the grimace on Rob's face, the churn in my stomach a mix of remorse and anxiety. Cleo started to say something about it being better to clear the air but no one was listening. Rob had his legs crossed and arms folded so that he resembled a twisted tree bent on protecting its inner core. Marco stumbled as he got up to pay the bill and we all envied him that moment of escape to normality.

The walk back to the cabin was a silent trudge. We were all minding our own thoughts, holding tight against the wind and the strain from the lunch conversation. I should have broken the tension, grabbed hold of Rob's hand or at least walked alongside him. I didn't, not ready yet to let go of my own sense of unfairness. The others dispersed inside quickly when we arrived at the cottage but I elected to sit outside on the deck, claiming I wanted to enjoy the view a while longer.

Alone on the deck, wrapped in a down jacket, watching waves crash over the rocks I wished I could subject myself to the same lashing. Those hasty words had cast a pall that the others were trying to dispel with long afternoon naps. My brain had been like a simmering cauldron these past months—I should go inside and apologise to Rob. Just a few more minutes of punishing cold I told myself, not noticing that he was coming from the kitchen.

'You must need to thaw out', he said sitting in the wicker chair next to mine and handing me a cup of hot chocolate, 'Happy anniversary beautiful wife'.

I gave a small smile that was tight with regret. 'Sorry. That outburst. I shouldn't have said what I did. Especially not in front of Cleo and Marcus'.

Rob covered my free hand with his, not replying, focused on the sea. When I started to speak again, he shook his head slowly. He was hollowed out. Acrid panic welled up as I realized I had shaken his trust. I had met his misery with anger, craven self-pity that bore out his daughters' poor opinion of me. It was our day to appreciate each other and I had ruined everything.

Rob spoke so quietly that I had to lean closer to hear him over the wind and waves. 'You have a right to be angry. This whole business is stressful for all of us and I've left you to deal with it alone while I look after the girls ... and myself. Transferring my guilt to you was unfair'. He continued to look out to sea but his fingers wrapped around my hand with the faintest squeeze.

'I should have told you how I was feeling', he continued. 'It's not that I regret the divorce in any way. You and I are happier than Marjorie and I ever were, even in the beginning when the girls were babies but history shapes us and memory can be cruel'. He stopped and for once I stayed quiet letting him form his next words. 'Those times when we were together as a family were precious, unrepeatable. It's almost like I'm grieving the loss of those times because now that Marjorie is gone no one else shares those memories. The girls were too young and so that leaves me...well, I feel kind of alone'. He stopped abruptly, wincing and biting his lip.

I started to shiver violently, whether from the cold or emotion I was uncertain. 'Time to go inside', Rob continued, muffling my trembling shoulders with his arm. 'I love you, you know that and thanks to you I know that these feelings will pass. Let's swap this chocolate for a glass of red'. Rob rarely apologized in words, this was the closest he was likely to come. His way of showing regret was through deeds and as much as I would have liked to hear him say *sorry,* I knew that would not happen.

'Love you too', I said, grateful that we were back to normal, yet with a niggling fear that would come back to me in the middle of the night that something had been permanently undone.

Cleo looked relieved to see us sitting together as she emerged from her siesta. 'Marcus is still sleeping. He has been tired the past few weeks, must be his age catching up with him', a gentle laugh softened the words. 'I have been trying to convince him that we should think about selling the bistro. It won't be a quick sale and Marco will insist on getting a good price'.

'Is he ready to retire?' I asked. 'You both seem so full of life'.

'Well he would never admit it but yes, I think the bistro is starting to be too much for him. It's 24/7 and every week there is a crisis. Last week the chef resigned in a fury and then after we frantically found someone to replace him at short notice he waltzed in the next day as if nothing had happened'.

'I worry that when I retire, I will be bored without the day to day challenges of work,' Rob, frowned trying to imagine what that life might be like as he poked at the fire.

'Like I said, he seems tired lately and I've noticed some slips in memory which is not like him. Too much on his plate! Besides, we want to still be young enough to travel while we have the time to enjoy ourselves', Cleo's tone was determined. I smiled at my friend, knowing that once her mind was made up there were few who could change her course.

'Good luck convincing Marco is all I can say', I grinned at the jut of her jaw and went to top up our glasses'.

'Convincing Marco of what?' he asked, a deep baritone in the doorway, hair mussed, stubble-faced.

'Cleo is trying to convince us all that we should retire early, enjoy our best years while we can', Rob said. 'Could be something in it you know. Marjorie always planned a big European holiday after she retired and then it was too late'.

'You can only travel for a few weeks a year. What would you do with the rest of the time? Baby sit grandchildren? No thank you. I'd rather be dead'. Marcus was dismissive of this premature exploration of old age. 'But I have been thinking, the four of us should have a holiday, somewhere exotic. A splurge to celebrate friendship'.

'What a great idea', Cleo was instantly diverted. 'We could go to Guatemala, I've always wanted to see Central America'.

'Or Paris, London, New York', I offered, declaring my big city preferences.

'Hiking in Switzerland has always been on my list. Japan too, there are supposed to be some amazing walks up north', Rob thinking of a more physical alternative as ever.

'Hmm could be more difficult than I imagined', Marco grinned at our enthusiastic if divergent responses.

Rob booted up his laptop so they could search out the possibilities of African safaris as a compromise we could all agree on, while Marco prepared an Italian feast in the little kitchen. He was full flight into a favourite aria when we were all startled by the crash of glass against the tiles.

'Fuck, fuck, fuck!'

'Are you okay?' Cleo jumped up to inspect the damage.

'I'm fine but there is glass and salad everywhere. I'm such a clutz lately. Leave it, I'll clean it up'. Marco was already gingerly picking up pieces of glass. 'Please Cleo, just do as I ask and bloody leave this to me', he shooed Cleo out of the kitchen. She walked back over to the sofa shaking her head and mouthing her own expletives.

Rob and I glanced at each other and while he took refuge in more web searches, I pretended to skim the country living magazine I had found on the coffee table. Typically, Cleo did not remain cross for long and when Marco returned to us, she was already telling us their big news.

'We aren't supposed to tell anyone yet but you guys are family. Joe and Becky are expecting!'

'Oh that's wonderful. Ah, that's why Marco was talking about babysitting before. How long along are they?'

'Almost three months. They're due late January'.

'Poor Becky, could be an uncomfortable summer. We may not be far behind you in the grandparent business. Rob was talking to Caroline and she and her partner are thinking about having a baby'.

'Wow, that's great. With a sperm donor?' Cleo asked.

'Cristiane does have a brother but they are investigating surrogacy too. I don't think it's legal in France but Cristiane is Canadian so maybe there it's possible? '

'When do they go back to Paris?'

'They left last week, Caroline had a concert coming up and there wasn't anything else to do here now. Paige will miss her'.

'What's Cristiane like?'

'Nice actually, normal, easy to talk to. She's in another orchestra, an oboist'.

'And Paige, anyone special?', Cleo asked.

'I wish. It might smooth out some of those brusque edges. Rob said she was seeing someone before Marjorie was diagnosed but then she called it off. Wanted to be there for her Mum'.

'How do you feel about being a grandma? I changed the subject.

'Penelope Saunders, I will not be a grandma? I will be Nonna Cleo if you don't mind'.

'Uh oh, was that a button I pressed? Haven't been called Penelope since my dad died'. I laughed at Cleo's wrinkled nose as I went to check my phone for messages in the other room. Only two people had ever called me Penelope, my dad and an early boyfriend who told me it suited me. He was studying ancient Greek and according to him she is a symbol of fidelity— and look where I ended up.

The voice mail messages from the Director of Nursing were not what I was expecting. Three of them, asking me to call her as soon as possible. My heart sank, I needed every hour of this short break. Hitting the reply button, I sat on the edge of the bed, absently massaging the left side of my neck as I waited for the connection.

Kate Syms was a thoroughly modern director of nursing, nothing like the crusty old matrons I had started my career with and so I was surprised by the clipped, impatient voice that answered.

'Nell, finally. Where have you been? We need you here first thing in the morning. There's a situation. Something that I'd rather not discuss over the phone'.

' I'm up the coast, a good three hours away. I can be there by ten if we leave here early. Can't you tell me anything over the phone'.

'Let's just say its serious and the police are involved. Everyone will need to be interviewed in the morning'. Kate left no margin for further conversation, hanging up without even saying goodbye.

I sat heavily on the bed and rubbed at my temples. What could it be about? If the police was involved it must be serious. There was no good case scenario and surely, none of my team was involved in anything illegal, all so competent and dedicated. I tried to think if anyone had had dramas in their personal life or been unwell recently but given my own stress levels, I knew I may have missed warning signs. Guilt crept like a burn up my neck. Had I slipped up, not been there for one of my people when they needed me?

An early start had not been in our plans. I pulled my hands through my hair and composed my face before I rejoined the others. 'Sorry Rob, that was work. We'll have to leave early tomorrow, they need me in by ten o'clock, something urgent that I can't deal with remotely'. My smile was wan but he nodded easily and Cleo only glanced up from her holiday searches long enough to say, "Better you than me. I'm planning one last sleep-in'.

'Where's Marco?'

'I thought he went out to the car for something but I can hear the shower running so must be planning to relax before dinner'.

'Shall we take an anniversary walk along the beach', I asked Rob, reaching for his hand. Twilight had passed and the moon did not offer any promise against the quickly falling darkness but I craved quiet time together.

Cleo waved us off, happy to stay snuggled in front of the fire. 'Don't freeze out there'.

The wind and our feet squeaking against the sand drove away the last vestige of fireside doziness. I pulled myself in under Rob's arm, grateful for the silent intimacy that was too important to risk with the foolishness I had allowed to brew over the past weeks. We were halfway back to the cottage, having turned around at the headland before I spoke, 'We should have Paige over for dinner this week, maybe Thursday if she is free. I can cook curry'.

Rob stopped and turned to face me, 'Thank you. I would like that'. There were tears in his eyes but he smiled warmly and I hoped that I had undone some of the damage my rash words had wrought earlier.

'I will text her when we get back to the house', I continued, to which Rob cocked an eyebrow. 'I know you are usually the point of contact but if I am going to have a good relationship with her it has to be as me, not only as us'. Rob squeezed me and kissed the top of my head.

Chapter 3

It was almost ten thirty when I knocked on Kate's door. 'Thanks for coming in on your day off', she sounded slightly more relaxed than the previous evening. 'The police and health department people are due in at eleven thirty. What I really need from you are the rosters from the past month; sick days, holidays as well as who was here'.

'No problem', I started to head towards the door.

'No, not at your desk. I have set you up in here so that you have privacy', Kate was more than one step ahead of me. I needed to get my head around this situation.

As I had suspected narcotics appeared to have been stolen. Over the next hour I printed out copies of rosters and time sheets. The drug register was already in Kate's office so I could see who had signed for morphine and fentanyl on those shifts. There was nothing remarkable at first view but perhaps when these records were matched with patient records it would be more obvious. Fiona the ward pharmacist was doing that analysis at another table and I hoped she would have some answers for the police.

The Department of Health officials arrived first and they were only interested in talking with Kate and Fiona. I felt at a disadvantage on the other side of the closed door and was pleased when the police arrived to start their investigation. Kate gave them all the printouts and whatever material Fiona had found.

The detective gave nothing away as I was ushered into the interview room after they had spent a long time with Kate. He sat down heavily, having introduced himself, and I tried to unsee the belly hair protruding from his gaping shirt. His colleague, a much younger woman didn't speak but her gaze never left my face.

My hands started to feel clammy as I described my role and what I knew about my team. 'I've been working in the Emergency here for more than twenty years. We're a close team, good people who work hard'. I was speaking too quickly, clipped words falling over each other. I took a deep breathe, 'We've never had a problem like this before as far as I know. It's hard to believe it would have been deliberate'. I paused as the detective raised an eyebrow.

'We can see from the information the hospital has provided that you are one of only three people who was working on all the shifts when drugs appear to have gone missing. What do you think of that?'

The sudden change of tempo threw me. 'Ah, I didn't know that. I was working a lot so that I could have the last few days off', my voice was halting.

'I understand it has been a difficult time for you. It must have been hard seeing a family member in so much pain and suffering'.

'I assume you mean my husband's ex-wife? It has been difficult but only because I have been supporting my husband and his daughters. I didn't really have a relationship with Marjorie'.

'I see. And how would you describe your own mental health over the past couple of months? Your colleagues said they have been worried about you'.

'It has been intense and stressful, that's all. I've had a lot on my plate but I do not believe my work has suffered. If anything my empathy for patients has been heightened'.

'And your team, are you as close to them as usual'.

'I've been asking myself the same question, worried I could have missed something unusual but I've wracked my brain and nothing seemed out of the ordinary', my voice was firmer now.

'Anything else you would like to tell us', the detective was shuffling his papers to indicate we were coming to the end of the interview.

'Nothing I can think of'.

'Hmm, well here is my card, if you do recall something please call me. That's all we need for now but we will be in touch again when we have finished this round of interviews'. There was no warmth in his voice and he was looking at his computer as I gathered my things. He did not even look up when I stumbled over his briefcase in my haste to leave.

Kate and Fiona were nowhere to be seen as I came back to the office. I had held onto the adrenaline during the interview but my heart raced and hands trembled as I sat in front of the rosters I'd been studying earlier. Was I really a suspect? Ridiculous. Yet anxiety unleashed doubts, cultivated feelings of guilt—no matter if they were well founded or not. I spanned my forehead with a hand and tried to rerun the interview in my mind.

One of three people he had said, I pulled the rosters closer and started a new spreadsheet. I still didn't know what dates the drugs had gone missing but I could see all the people who had worked three or more shifts with me. I worked quickly but it soon became obvious almost all of the team had worked a lot more than three shifts with me. Of course, I should have realized, I shook my head. What set those three shifts apart? I didn't have the names of all the agency nurses on this sheet, it could be someone who worked irregularly on the ward. I had only worked a handful of night shifts so that was also a possibility.

'How was the interview?' my head jerked up at the unexpected interruption. Kate was smiling but she was fiddling with something in her hand and I felt my breath tighten again.

'Okay, I...I think', good heavens I was stammering. 'They told me that I was one of only three people rostered on when the drugs were stolen', my rising intonation begged an answer to the unspoken question.

'Yes', she paused. 'Look I think it's best if you take a couple of days leave until this is sorted out'.

'You don't believe I did it?' I tried to keep my tone even as I found Kate's eyes.

'It's not a judgement. You have been through a lot lately, give yourself a break'.

'Everyone will assume I did it if I take leave. No I would rather come in tomorrow after my planned break', I hesitated as another thought struck me. 'I assume I have a choice?'

'Yes, but my advice is to take an extra day or two. Talk to your family about it and text me later'.

I stood slowly aware of every muscle in my neck and back, if only a massage could resolve that tension. Rob would be at home, probably clearing his emails and I felt a sudden urgency to be with him, to hear his reassurance, to know he believed me.

'Okay, I will send you a message later this afternoon', my voice was flat as I concentrated on picking up my bag.

'Speak soon, and Nell', Kate waited for me to make eye contact, 'Don't over think things. The police will get to the bottom of who is responsible'.

I nodded but shutting down the negative thoughts would be tricky. I didn't remember the drive home, my mind felt like it was shutting down and I realized I had started to hyperventilate. I stopped a few streets short of home to recover, only to burst into tears. Confused, worried, scared even—these were not emotions that sat well with my usual no-nonsense approach.

Gulping back the new tears that threatened, I berated myself for not being stronger. I wiped roughly at my face with a handful of tissues that I'd pulled from the glove box, strewing its contents onto the car floor. With eyes closed, I willed myself to breathe more slowly, hoping my pulse rate would follow. Slowly I started to feel normal, well almost normal.

This must be what a panic attack feels like, I thought as I carefully retrieved the paraphernalia from the floor and stacked it into the glove box. It would be alright. I could drive home now and Rob's good sense was all I needed to calm down.

A guttural sound escaped my lips, quickly followed by a run of expletives a few minutes later as I pulled into our drive. Paige's car! I did not need this today.

Taking a deep breath I smoothed my hair and prepared to make civil conversation until I could be alone with Rob. I prayed it would be a fleeting visit as I climbed the stairs and pushed open the door.

'Where is Dad?' Paige asked. She was wearing an expensive suit but her face was red, presumably from the sharp wind outside.

'Isn't he here? He didn't mention anything about going out'.

Paige was sitting at the kitchen table looking at her phone but she was perched on the edge of the chair, flicking her hair distractedly. 'I doubt he'll be long', I offered, surprised myself that he had not responded to the text I had sent as I was leaving the hospital.

'Actually, it was you I wanted to see. I'm hoping you can help me with...,'she searched for the right words, 'a personal issue'. I waited for her to continue, a faint sense of dread building that this was about our relationship. Better to hear this standing up I figured.

'I'm pregnant', her voice had dropped an octave and quickly became a hoarse torrent. 'It's okay, I am having a termination this week. Would you come with me? I don't want Dad to know'. That small voice, those downcast eyes at odds with the Paige I normally encountered. The highly polished legal professional was missing but her sheer toughness was still there, determinedly wrenching back control if only through the pressured speed of her speech.

'Of course I will come', I kept my voice low and sat heavily in the chair opposite her. 'Do you want to talk about it?'

There was no doubt in the shake of her head but her hunched shoulders filled me with sadness. No one deserved to have to face this so soon after her mother's death. The abrupt way she had approached the conversation told me more about her state of mind than anything she said.

'It's at ten o'clock Wednesday at that big clinic in the city. I saw the doctor there this morning and I have to go back for a counselling session tomorrow but I won't change my mind'.

'I doubt they will try to make you change your mind, more likely help you work through any questions you have and let you know about emotional support services for afterwards'.

Paige brought her head up sharply. 'You think I will regret this but I have thought about it a lot and I'm sure'.

'Even so, it's good to know what is available if you need some help later', my words sounded lame. 'I will pick you up, you shouldn't drive after the anaesthetic', sounding more matter of fact than I intended. 'If you change your mind, about wanting to talk, I'm here', I tried again.

'Thanks. I should be getting back to work', she pushed her chair back quickly, flustered, but as she reached the door she stopped, 'Really thank you, I appreciate this I'm just not very good at showing it'. I hoped my tight smile conveyed compassion rather than pity as she gave a quick wave of her hand.

I thought I could hear her talking to Rob in the drive, saying she had popped in to say hello but had to get back to work now. Needing time to drag sense from the mire of bewilderment I felt myself drowning in, I closed the bedroom door and started to change.

Poor Paige. I wondered if she knew that her pain was only starting, that she would think about this decision for the rest of her life. She was so brave sitting there in the kitchen but Wednesday would be one of the hardest days of her life. I let my mind go back to that drizzly morning nearly forty years ago when I'd had to walk past an old couple, singing hymns, calling to me to invite god into my heart.

The pulse on the side of my forehead was throbbing but I could hear the front door closing.

'Sorry I missed your call, I went to the pool to do a few laps', Rob was wearing shorts and a t-shirt in spite of the cold and his hair was dripping wet patches down his back. 'I will just have a quick shower', he gave me a peck on the cheek and continued on to the bathroom. Either I was inscrutable or he hadn't even looked at me. 'How was Paige?' he yelled over the steaming water but I pretended not to hear and went back to the kitchen.

The clock on the oven told me it was only three o'clock but the morning was a lifetime ago. In that life, no fissures had been struck into my reputation or aches of the past resurrected.

'How was work?' Rob asked, rifling through the fridge, hungry after his swim as I turned from contemplating the sink.

'Kate wants me to take a few days leave while this thing is sorted out. Morphine has been stolen from the ward on several occasions and I am one of the people under scrutiny'. I let my voice trail away.

Rob continued making a sandwich, his voice calm, ' Seems like a good idea. No need to be there in the thick of things'.

'Rob did you hear what I said? I am a suspect. Me, after twenty years on that ward. How can you be so blasé'. I felt my face flush and folded the building rage into my chest.

'Don't you think you are over-reacting. You haven't done anything wrong and the culprit will be found'.

My brain was ready to burst with heat. I had hoped for support, thought I would welcome his cool rationality but now it felt like he was dismissing the seriousness of the situation. Couldn't he at least be incensed on my behalf? The belated hug was hardly compensation.

'I didn't mean to discount your worry. Tell me everything that happened. Have you talked to the police yet or only Kate?'

I clenched my teeth while I filled a glass of water, preparing myself to relive the morning. By the time I reached the bit about the police questioning me about my mental state Rob was frowning.

'Was he suggesting that you weren't supervising your team properly? That you were negligent in some way?'

'At the very least...or that I took the drugs either for myself or someone else. He implied I might have wanted to ease Marjorie's suffering'.

'But that's ridiculous. You didn't even visit Marjorie, let alone give her drugs'.

'That is what I told him. He did not press me on it but I had a feeling that he only half believed me. To be honest I am more worried that my management may have been compromised. I should have picked up any discrepancies especially if I was on those shifts. There's no excuse'.

'But you can't supervise every narcotic injection on every shift, that isn't your job. Do you know who else the police are talking to?'

'I have been wracking my brains all the way home, trying to work out who the other two people could be. The only person I'm pretty sure has been on most of my shifts is Brian. He is a clinical nurse consultant and usually my deputy. He has been working more lately, saving for a big holiday with his new partner'.

'Isn't he the one who broke up with his wife a few months ago?'

'Exactly and the new woman is apparently gorgeous, ten years younger and a jockey of all things. Very successful, quite the A-lister by all accounts'.

'Could put him under pressure to keep up, not easy on a nurse's salary', Rob surmised.

'Yes, although to be honest Brian doesn't care about what people think and besides, he comes from a wealthy family himself. I doubt nursing is his only source of income'.

'Curious but I am still not seeing how you can blame yourself or think that anyone else will. It's not pleasant I grant you but not catastrophic either'.

'You think. Yes, I suppose you are right', I was mollified, prepared to try his approach—good intentions that would be put to the test in the middle of the night. For now I took Rob's advice and called Kate to tell her I would take the rest of the week as annual leave, reiterating if there was anything she or the police needed from me I was happy to be contacted. I knew people would talk but hopefully the case would be concluded quickly because the sooner the gossip was stemmed the better.

As I hung up, our dog, Lucca was dropped home from the kennel he'd stayed at while we were away. His happy face and mad dash around the house were a tonic, the perfect excuse for a walk and a chance to unleash my own thoughts. Strangely I found myself silently reciting a prayer from childhood that I had thought long forgotten, a remnant from when I had still believed in the mercy of a higher power. Part of me was repelled by the stupidity and the other grateful for an insurance policy. Was I praying for Paige or for myself? I was not certain.

Chapter 4

The crisp air had Lucca pulling me down the hill towards his favourite park, determined to make up for all those days I had deserted him. I absently noticed that he would need a bath, filthy after playing in the mud with other dogs. Such mundane thoughts were welcome after a tumultuous day. Lucca had been named for the ancient Tuscan town where Rob and I had walked Renaissance city walls, listening to Puccini and Boccherini on our headphones on the first days of our honeymoon. When I told Pippa we were buying a puppy she had sent me a congratulations card that featured a very dirty dog and the tagline, *Everyone needs a little chaos in their lives*. Her message implied that Lucca was our child substitute and I remember being annoyed at the suggestion at the time although now I wondered if she had been right. Either way, Lucca was as demanding of attention as any toddler and after half an hour of hypnotic ball throwing, I was glad to head towards home.

I called Cleo, breathless walking up the hill but feeling less anxious than an hour before. I told her about the interview with the police and taking leave for a few days. Like Rob, she thought it a good idea, unlike Rob she was up in arms that I could be a suspect. As she rang off, she said in passing that I should call Paige, ask her professional opinion. Not a bad idea I realized but the timing was not exactly ideal.

Kate had not been forthcoming with any new information in our conversation earlier. I could call Brian, see if he had been interviewed or knew anything more. His shift would be over for the day and I hated being out of the loop. Standing outside our front gate, something told me that Rob would not think this call a good idea. I dialed Brian's number.

'Hi, it's Nell. How are you? I wanted to check in after today, what with all the drama'.

'I gather there is a police investigation about some drugs. Everyone's talking about it but no one knows anything very concrete'.

'Did the police interview you or any of the staff?'

'Not me, a couple of agency staff I think and then just the bosses, like you. Are you okay? Kate said you are having a few days off'.

'Yes, nothing serious, some family things', I prevaricated.

'Well if there is anything you need let me know', he sounded cheerful and surprisingly uninterested in the police case. Maybe I was getting this all out of proportion.

I had worked with Brian for a couple of years and I respected his work. He could be laid back, cynical occasionally but that was a survival tactic in our job. He was always the first to pitch in when things were busy and managed chaos was a way of life in the Emergency. If he thought there was no big story to work-shop that was a good thing. So why this doubt? He could have been instructed not to discuss the case, even not to talk to me. Now my imagination was leading me back to that dark place.

After dinner, I was on the computer and more out of bore-dom than anything I googled Brian's new girlfriend. Jockey, model, TV presenter—there were a lot of postings, even her own Wikipedia entry. A piece halfway down the screen caught my eye, *Roxanne Hughes in serious fall*. I did not remember Brian mentioning anything about a fall, he probably assumed everyone knew given it was all over the papers, going by this report. Roxanne had taken a fall during trackwork and broken her clavicle and fractured her leg. Surgery and rehab would keep her out of racing for three months according to the article. Next I googled Brian. Nothing. Hah, nurses were not as interesting as jockeys.

On a roll I decided to check out the website for the clinic that Paige had mentioned. There was an impressive amount of information and links to support groups, even the written blurb oozed compassion and acceptance. Paige had obviously chosen well but I couldn't pretend I was looking forward to the visit.

That night lying in bed, I raked over the day. Initially preoccupied with the investigation at work, it was memories from nearly forty years ago that claimed me. Sad eyes that came to me at night usually when I was stressed and anxious. Some people dreamt of the French exam they had forgotten to study for or the plane they were running to catch. For me it was a wet winter's morning.

The grey sky had suited my mood that day. I had not bothered with an umbrella, the light drizzle running down my face and neck welcome after the storm clouds that had obliterated clear thought for days. From the outside, the building had the anonymity of an accountant's office except for the elderly couple with their placards and songs. Inside the paint peeled off in large clumps, it had once been white but now was stained with nicotine and time. There was a damp mouldy smell, neglect or disintegration. I tried to remember the conversations I must have had that morning but they were lost. All I saw were haunted eyes, gaunt young faces swamped in fear or terrifyingly blank. Some came with their boyfriend or mother, others like me were alone. The reception room was unnaturally quiet, people whispered if they talked at all, there was a low haze of cigarette smoke (no problem smoking in a public area back then) and music from the radio in the adjoining nurses room that spilled over from time to time. Someone turned up the volume when Tina Turner came on singing *What's Love Got to Do With It?*.

*

Neither of us had spoken for twenty minutes and while I pretended needing to concentrate on the wet road and crazy traffic it was Paige's quiet, taut body that occupied my thoughts. In all the years I had known her, she had been self-assured, certain in almost everything. When Marjorie was ill, she had leant on her eldest daughter more than anyone and Paige had never faltered. Today an imposter was sitting in her place.

I must have startled when Paige started speaking because she gave a laughing apology as she said, 'You can speak to me you know, I'm okay about this. I wish I didn't have to make this decision but I do. I'm comfortable it's the right one'.

'Was the counsellor helpful?' I asked.

'So, so. Yes, definitely about the process, less so about my decision making. She implied I was being too rational, not letting my emotions in. I told her that's just how I am: cold and hard'.

'Oh Paige, I saw you with your Mum. You were caring and considerate, you grieved, you fiercely fought for her wishes when there was talk of hospitalization. I'm sure you have been as emotionally involved in this decision'.

'Of course but I don't necessarily need to display it to total strangers'.

I nodded and taking this confidence as a sign I launched into the topic that had been worrying me ever since Paige had told me her news, 'Your Dad told me that Caroline and Cristiane are starting to investigate surrogacy. I wondered if you ...' Even from the corner of my eye I could see Paige's head jerk a defiant no.

'No, I don't want that'.

No doubt there. 'I shouldn't have said anything, sorry'. In normal circumstances I would have left it there, been glad of the return to silence but this morning I was propelled by an urgency to answer all the questions that beleaguered my saturated brain. 'Look, do you mind if I ask you about something that's been nagging at me since your mother was diagnosed?' I bit down on my thumb, belated second thoughts, too late to stop now. 'I feel like you and Caroline blame me for Marjorie's illness, for causing her so much stress it made her sick', I waited feeling acid form in my stomach. Had I invited an explosion?

Instead Paige looked at me as if I was mad, 'What on earth are you talking about? We've all been stressed and I know that I have been nasty at times but no one blames you. Do you think we don't know how happy you've made Dad? I loved Mum to bits but goodness she could be hard to live with'.

'Oh really, I was sure that neither of you had forgiven me for breaking up your family. You were so angry when you first found out. And...and, well, you've never seemed to like me'.

'Shit, that was ten years ago. We have both grown up a lot since then. Nell to be honest we don't know you very well even after all this time. I was really nervous about asking you to come with me today; thought you would judge me...'

'Oh'. I felt lost more than relieved. How had I misread everything for so long, it seemed impossible. 'No, I would never judge you, I'm here to support you however you need'.

As we pulled into the carpark, Paige gathered her things quickly. 'I will ask the nurse to call half an hour before I'm ready'. And then she was at the entrance, straight-backed, no backward glance. The rapport of the last few minutes snapped as she faced her morning.

I wandered the shops for as long as I could stand the aimlessness of it and then found a small coffee shop to wait out the morning. To fill the time I started an email to Pippa, two finger typing on my phone. News about our weekend away, some ideas for what we might do when she visited, good wishes from Cleo. There was no need to include the weightier matters responsible for the dull headache I'd had for the past few days.

The coffee shop was quiet and no one came to take my cup away. I wished I had brought a book to read as I found myself thinking back over the police interview and previous weeks at work. There had been a rotation of new doctors recently but by mid-year even the interns were competent. We'd had trouble sourcing agency staff from time to time and I had heard a lot more international accents over the last year but again, nothing to suggest any problems. Everyone was working more shifts than they wanted, more overtime. As far as I knew there had been no patient complaints save for the usual ones about long waiting times or people jumping the queue.

For the first time in days I admitted to myself that there were events from years ago that the police would find interesting that I may be better to disclose voluntarily. Better to be on the front foot and all that. My thoughts were interrupted by the vibration of the phone, Paige was ready to be picked up, I could text her when I arrived. It was only a little over two hours since I had left, obviously everything had gone smoothly.

Looking at her sitting in the discharge area, you would never know that her morning had been anything other than ordinary. She was scrolling down her phone, tapping one foot gently against the carpeted floor. She glanced quickly to the door as I pulled it open, 'You were fast, I've only just come out here'.

'How do you feel?'

'I'm okay, let's go. This waiting room is depressing'.

It was true the room was cold and bland. 'I hardly noticed, too well conditioned to public hospitals. Do you have to sign out or anything?' I expected there would be some last minute paperwork or a final check that she was feeling alright.

'No all done, the nurse said I could leave once you arrived.

Paige's mood had lifted noticeably since this morning, the relief of it all being over no doubt. She stood quickly and brushed me away as I moved to support her or hold some of her things. 'Truly, I'm fine. Please don't fuss'.

'Do you need me to stop at the Pharmacy for anything, pain-killers, pads, I'm not sure what they recommend these days'.

'I already have everything at home. I'd like to rest for a while and I have a work call I need to take later this evening so the sooner you can drop me the better'.

We arrived at Paige's apartment half an hour later and I pulled into the no standing zone at the front of the building. 'You get out here and I will find a park and bring your stuff in', I said.

She was already opening the car door and holding her bag and papers against her chest. 'No need, I can manage from here. Thanks so much for your help today, it means a lot'.

I sat in the car, worrying that she would be alright as she disappeared into the apartment block. Shrugging my shoulders I had restarted the car, disappointed to realise that I was simply her chauffeur after all. I was rehearsing a story for Rob should he ask about my shopping trip, when I saw Paige coming back towards me. I frowned and opened the passenger side window. 'See you for dinner tomorrow night, looking forward to the curry. I might be a bit after seven but will try for earlier'.

And she was gone again. Not sure if I was more worried for her apparent lack of emotion or simply in awe of her strength, I jumped as the phone beeped but stopped myself looking at the message. I seemed to be constantly on edge at the moment.

At the only set of lights before home I could see the message was from Kate—so difficult to contain the curious dread but I was determined to wait until I reached home. When I finally read it, it simply asked me to call. I dialed her number as I exited the car, not wanting to prolong not knowing, hardly noticing Lucca welcome me with enthusiastic sprints back and forth across the garden.

'Kate, hi it's me. I got your message just now as I was driving'.

'Thanks for calling back so quickly. Could you come into my office this afternoon? The police will be here again and there are a couple of things they want to clear up. When I spoke to them, I had the impression they are ready to tie this up'.

'Sure, yes of course. I can come now', I could hear a tremor in my voice and coughed to disguise it.

'Great, no rush. The police are due here in an hour and they always seem to run late'.

Abandoning all plans for lunch or making a start on the curry for tomorrow, I sat quietly for a moment determined to collect my thoughts before I went in. There really was no reason to be concerned, I knew I was innocent and yet the tug of anxiety was back in full force. I had no idea who the police had been talking to or what they'd found. I hadn't even heard the ward gossip as a heads up. For the first time since this thing started, I wished I had a lawyer with me, a cool head because I wasn't sure I could trust myself.

The parking at the hospital was impossible at that time of day and I drove around the carpark, dithering about whether to go back out to the street. The indecision cost me twenty minutes and two missed parking spots but it also acted as a wake up call. I needed to get it together before I went inside—a few deep breaths and a forced smile at the sunshine, paltry therapy for the apprehension in my gut.

'Nell, good to see you', Kate was more upbeat than I had anticipated.

'Hi, sorry I'm later than I thought. The parking was hopeless'.

'Afternoons are the pits. The police only arrived five minutes ago. They're ready for you', she nodded towards a room at the end of the corridor.

Walking slowly, deliberately I recalled Paige's straight back from the morning and pulled back my shoulders.

'Nell, thanks for coming in again', it was the same detective, alone this time. 'I have a couple of questions that I need to clear up with you', the same even tone, giving nothing away.

'Of course,' I swallowed hard, holding the sides of the seat so tightly my hands began to ache.

'First of all, we looked back over your medical history and we can see you had spinal surgery a while back, care to tell me about that'.

'It was a long time ago, must be twelve years; definitely before I met Rob my husband. I'd had back trouble for years but it had become worse. I was needing to take strong pain killers, even Valium to help with the spasms but it was so bad that I was having trouble doing a full shift at work. The orthopedic surgeon recommended a spinal fusion. It's still not perfect but I have full function and the pain is only rarely a problem now'.

'Do you still take pain killers and other medications for the pain?'

I didn't like where this was going and decided to face it head on. 'Not anymore. That was one of the reasons I decided on surgery. I was needing to take more and more painkillers to get relief and after a doctor at a medical centre refused to write me a script one weekend, I realized I had a problem. He made me feel like a drug addict but it worked. I stopped there and then, never took another painkiller, threw away the Valium and made the appointment with the surgeon'.

I stopped, out of breath. I hadn't mentioned the sleepless nights that followed or the even more severe pain that had meant I needed to take sick leave before the surgery was scheduled.

'What do you do for the pain now', the detectives eyes were on mine, watching carefully.

'Swim, Pilates sometimes but since the surgery it's been okay'. Not sure it was a good idea I ground down on my back teeth and added, 'I never want to find myself constantly checking my handbag for medication before I go out. I never want to be dependent like that again'. There it was said.

'I see, well that sounds like a good idea with your history', he paused, threading and unthreading his fingers.

'Thank you for clearing that up. It's consistent with what we can see from your recent medical history and work performance. There is one other matter I wanted to ask you about', he paused again, taking his time, letting my anxiety resurface after that tiny moment of relief.

'Your colleague Brian has worked a lot of evening shifts lately. Do you know why?', the change of direction threw me.

'Well, he said he is saving for a big overseas trip'. I was going to say more about working with Brian for years and him being a great nurse but the detective cut across me.

'Yes, that is what he told us too. Have you met his partner? She's quite the celebrity, isn't she?'

'I haven't met her and Brian doesn't talk about her much at work. He's a very caring and competent colleague. I always enjoy working with him', my voice trailed off.

'Hmm and did you know that not only narcotics but other medications have probably been stolen from the ward. Seems there has been a spike in requests for blood pressure medications and some hormones'.

I shook my head trying to make sense of his questions but he was already standing and holding out his hand. 'Thank you for coming in again Nell, we appreciate the cooperation'.

My legs were unsteady as I walked back towards Kate's office. She called from her desk for me to come in and I have rarely been so grateful for a seat.

'Shit that was weird', the words were out before I realized.

'It has been a difficult few days, some of the hardest I've had in this job', Kate's honesty helped me calm my own thoughts. 'I'm not sure how much they told you', she cocked her head slightly.

'Nothing really, asked about my medical history and then some random questions about Brian. That was all'.

'There were some questions about motive. They are going to charge him this afternoon', Kate confided.

'Brian? I can't believe it', I thought back to my conversation with him. He'd seemed so casual, not in the least concerned.

'I spoke with him a few days ago, he seemed very laid back about the whole thing'.

'Well there may be more going on than we realise with his new partner. It seems she had a big accident and needed narcotic analgesics to get back to the track as quickly as possible. The police believe Brian was supplementing her supply, we even think he gave some patients saline instead of the morphine he drew up for them. There were quite a few cases of people needing much more frequent morphine doses than normal when Fiona looked really closely at all the records'.

I closed my mouth, 'And what about the other medications the detective asked about?' I asked starting to understand.

'For doping, I guess. His girlfriend's brother has been charged in the past with doping horses. That's the likely connection apparently'.

I shook my head, more stunned than relieved. How could I have not noticed anything? A close colleague, seeing him almost every day, I should have twigged to this. I rubbed one foot against the other shin, 'You must think me incompetent. I should have picked this up'.

'Oh Nell, really. If someone wants to cover up what they are doing they can be very clever. Brian was devious. He made sure we all trusted him to keep scrutiny to a minimum and then he played us'.

'I guess', I was unconvinced it was that simple. I knew him, he wasn't inherently evil. But his choices? Well he had made some really bad ones if all this was true. My gut told me we had failed him even if reason said otherwise.

Walking back to the car, I was grateful that I'd had to park so far away. I needed some fresh air and to stretch my legs. I rubbed the back of my neck trying to ease the tension that lingered there. Brian could already be in custody, hung out to dry.

Not wanting to go home right away I drove to the beach. The air was cooling down quickly as evening approached but I took off my shoes and walked along the sand. My mind wandered, hardly noticing the last of the surfers going out for a late afternoon ride or the runners on the soft sand building up their calf muscles. The sound of the waves was a salve and the wind blew through the fog that sat stubbornly obscuring clear thoughts. It smoothed the last of the creases across my forehead and slowly dislodged the dread that had gripped me until now.

Chapter 5

Rob was at the front door, wearing an ancient jumper and jeans, his hair tousled after changing out of his work clothes. He had Lucca on the leash in one hand and an umbrella in the other. 'Wow that must have been some shopping trip! You've been gone all day', he joked pleased to see me.

I shook my head, smiling, 'It has been a long day but lucky for the credit card not all of it was shopping. Wait a minute 'til I change and I will come with you'.

As we walked, I told Rob about the interview and then the conversation with Kate. He wrapped his arm around me when I reached the part about my own brush with painkillers. I'd never mentioned it before and his silent acceptance meant a lot. When I told him that I felt I had let Brian and everyone down by not picking up the problem early on, he dropped his arm and turned me to him. His mouth was stern and his eyes bore into mine, 'Nell for heaven's sake, stop blaming yourself. Be kind to yourself for once'.

'You're right but old habits die hard as they say. Let's go home, I have a curry to make and my enforced leave is over so I better start on it tonight'.

Curry was my specialty for family dinner and it felt good to be planning to bring the three of us together after a roller coaster week. I first learnt to make it when I flatted with two Indian girls from Fiji soon after I started nursing. They were school friends who came from a small village and somehow

had a scholarship to study nursing in Australia. Their specialties were lamb curry, dhal, fresh tomato chutney and roti, the
Indian flat bread. I was an appreciative student and now they
were my specialties too.

Thursday was remarkable for how normal it was. Everyone
at work seemed pleased to see me back and other than a few
whispered comments about Brian's absence it was as though
nothing untoward had happened. Of course, the fact that we
were run off our feet helped. A big accident on the highway
involving a truck and several cars sent ambulances blaring
in from early morning and from there on there was no respite—overdoses, confused nursing home patients, chest pain,
screaming babies and then as the afternoon started, school
sporting injuries, people with coughs and colds who should be
seeing their general practitioner.

It was only as I was leaving for the day that I saw Kate and
even then, she only nodded hello and kept walking. I marveled
at her ability to move onto whatever new bushfire she was
hurrying toward. There had been a time when I had ambitions
to do her job but I was beginning to see the toll that it would
have on me emotionally. Instead of remaining objective and
reframing the problem I threw myself straight in, desperate to
fix whatever had gone awry. It's what I loved about my current
job and what I worried would eventually wear me out.

Evening was closing in as Lucca met me with his usual
tarantella, telling me all the while what a terrible Mum I was
for leaving him so long. Poor boy but I knew he had probably
been asleep all day and that with a treat or two all would be
forgiven.

The curries were made so I prepared the chutney and the
dough for the roti before going upstairs for a quick shower. I
expected Rob soon and Paige shouldn't be far behind. It felt
good to wash away the grime of the day and let the scorch of

water burn away the weariness. A car pulled up at the front, Paige had beat Rob after all.

'Paige. Hi, how are you?' I tried not to put too much emphasis in the wrong place but her grimace told me I only partially succeeded.

'Crazy day—new clients who don't know what they want and are too angry to think straight'.

'Your Dad's still not home, hopefully on his way. Oh, that's him now', car lights shone into the house as he drove up the driveway. I wanted to ask if she was okay after the procedure but for once held back.

'Would you like something to drink? Some wine?'

'Just water, I have more work to finish when I get home'.

'You work too hard', Rob gave Paige a hug and then kissed me.

'You're the one just getting home', a relaxed smile lit her face.

They sat in a huddle on the sofa while I sipped wine and rolled roti. It was good to see them catching up like old times.

Paige wasn't very hungry but luckily Rob devoured her portion as well—still feeling the effects of the anaesthetic I guessed. Rob was telling her about our weekend away as I went to see if we had any ice cream. 'The house was great and Cleo and Marco kept us entertained all weekend. They are a funny pair, both larger than life and yet so different. I'm always surprised they got together', he laughed.

Paige nodded, smiling, letting him describe the beach and the bush walks we'd taken. There were no judgements, Rob was revelling in her attention and acceptance. I left them for longer than I needed, happy to see the healing.

We were clearing up after dinner, Paige had left to finish her work and Rob was whistling under his breath, 'Great that Paige could stay so long especially when she had work', he said. His phone beeped a new message saving him from filling the dishwasher. He came back a few minutes later with a broad smile, 'Caro wants to Facetime tomorrow evening. I told her about six o'clock, I think that's ten in the morning her time'. I nodded, happy for him that he and the girls were getting back to normal.

Even though she had told us before she left about their plans for a baby, we were both shocked next day when Caroline told us she and Cristiane were going to Quebec. Cristiane's brother had agreed to be a sperm donor and Caroline was hoping to become pregnant as soon as possible. The IVF clinic was lined up to ensure all went smoothly, they were confident of a quick result. Rob was over the moon at the prospect of being a grandfather and deeply happy that 'his little girl would not miss out on motherhood'. My reaction was more ambivalent and I tried to distill my feelings later that night as I lay sleepless trying not to disturb Rob.

Top of mind was wondering how Paige would take the news so soon after her own experience. It was cruel timing and yet I could understand Caroline and Cristiane wanting to move on with their lives. A new little life was the spark the family needed right now, a new start for everyone. 'Provided Paige doesn't feel left behind', countered the other voice in my head. At thirty five she still had time to find a partner and have children but the pressure would have started to build if my own experience was anything to go by.

I tried to imagine Caroline as a first time mother. She would be good at setting routines and creating order, as much as the baby allowed at least. Her work would be on hold at first but most likely her career would not suffer too much in the long run. She and Cristiane could share performance days, touring would be difficult for a few years but home concerts in Paris would work for both of them. I had been impressed by Cristiane when I met her a few months ago—compassionate but no bleeding heart, too pragmatic for sentimentality, someone who does, not says. Two mothers would be the ultimate gift for a young child and maybe, temporarily, the ultimate cross for a teenager especially if they have a girl. I smiled in the dark, imaging a little replica of Cristiane, not knowing if she and her brother looked alike.

Rob was already referring to himself as Grandad but Grandma was the old woman in the shapeless floral dress and black shoes large enough to accommodate bunions, who had lived in the old weatherboard house up the hill. She occasionally looked after me when I was little but she died when I was still young so my memories of her were mixed up with stories Mum had told me. I do remember a big verandah at the front of her house, the perfume of just-pruned geraniums and a hot water metre that took coins for when we wanted hot water for a bath. The backroom had louvred windows made of a dimpled glass that provided some privacy but let the rain in. I can clearly see that there was a potty under the bed at night because the toilet was in the backyard, fifty yards from the house. Sometimes when I was looking after an older patient, a whiff of sour old age and lavender would bring back that time.

Nanna had been another matter. She was my mother's Mum and she spoiled us kids every chance she had. Her house smelt of ginger and cinnamon, a testament to the freshly baked cakes and biscuits that Stephen and I wolfed down in vast quantities after school. We'd had a pact with Nanna, we would not dob her into Mum for giving us cake and she would make more the following week. I learnt to bake watching her whisk eggs and make magic with flour. In my memory she is always smiling, her eyes crinkled so hard I used to wonder how she could see properly. Even when she was being stern, and she definitely could be, her voice was mild and that smile did not entirely disappear. The only downside was having to get up at seven o'clock every Sunday morning so that we could go to

Mass with her but she made up even for that by letting us buy a bag of mixed lollies on the way home.

It would be so different for us as grandparents. We would visit and technology would let us be in touch often but I wasn't Caroline's Mum and so it was hard to grasp what being a grandmother to her child would be like. The honest voice from earlier reasserted itself, acknowledging the nervousness I felt being thrust into this new role. I was hardly equipped to be the wise, experienced elder—I would need to carve out another role which seemed unlikely when I couldn't even visualize what it should be. At least my nursing training might prove useful during pregnancy or in times of illness, beyond that I had nothing.

A soft bark from Lucca who was lying in his bed at the foot of ours could have been a rebuke but more likely he was dreaming of chasing pigeons in the park. 'Shh go back to sleep', I whispered, careful not to wake Rob although that would be a first. The dog raised his head in a kind of acknowledgment and snuggled back into his comfortable crescent. Sweet sleep was finally creeping in when a beep startled me. A nice surprise— my niece Trudy would be in Sydney on the weekend and was asking to stay. She was growing up so quickly, it would be great to see her.

*

Saturday arrived quickly and I was glad of a lazy start to the weekend. Even Rob was happy to potter around the house, catching up on all the chores that had been neglected of late. Half an hour before her train was due, I headed out to collect Trudy. I hoped we would be able to entertain her for the weekend although my brother had assured me, she spent most of her days on her phone when he called to confirm that it was okay for her to stay.

He was right I realized later as I enticed her to the backyard.

'Can you help me with these?' Rob was taking the sheets from the line. I nodded and picked up one end of the sheet to perform our weekly ritual. When we had first moved in together, Rob had teased me about my fastidiousness but now he was more particular than me about how the sheets were folded.

'Actually, Trudy why don't you do this with me', I turned to where she was crouched over the dog's ball.

'Why are you doing that?' she had asked flatly, dropping her end as I pulled the sheet tight. 'Wouldn't it be easier to roll it up and shove it in the cupboard? It's only going on the bed'. I tried to explain the process: stand well apart to stretch out the wrinkles, fold it like a map, bring the ends together in halves The simple beauty of the neatly folded result that always gave me a little shot of pleasure obviously eluded her.

'It's the way I was taught to do it when I was a girl', my only defense. 'Think of it as a gift passed down our maternal line for generations'. Now I had really lost her and with an eye roll she wandered over to Lucca in search of a more entertaining alternative.

'Is there anything as disdainful as the patronising look of a sixteen year old', I laughed with Rob as we came back inside leaving Trudy playing ball with Lucca. 'I'll text Stephen and let him know she arrived safely. It's the first time they have let her travel to Sydney by herself', I went to find my phone. Stephen was my younger brother and Trudy was his youngest, born ten years after the boys. The only girl, she had been feted and spoilt more than should have been good for her but she was turning into a sassy and smart young woman.

Stephen and I had been close growing up but distance and responsibilities had meant we saw less of each other these days. His wife Melody had brought strength and stability to my dreamer of a brother and we had grown close sharing stories of his absent professor antics, made all the more amusing because he was an academic. Melody was a high school teacher and had her feet firmly on the ground that so often became ethereal under Stephen's poorly considered notions.

Stephen had followed up the initial text to explain the reason for Trudy's visit was to buy an outfit for the end of term school dance. I was the designated shopping assistant—cooler than her mother or at least I had been until this morning.

'Lunch is ready', Rob called out. I had picked up sushi on the way to the train and Rob had brought out the chopsticks and Japanese plates we bought in Tokyo a few years before. Trudy was so impressed that we weren't using the standard takeaway chopsticks that I decided it was best not to tell her just how much purpose-made tableware we owned. The fish knives would surely do her head in.

As we ate, I asked Trudy about her dance. 'What sort of dress do you have in mind?' I said hoping it wouldn't be anything too risqué.

'Here's some pictures', she pushed her phone towards me. I had never heard of most of the shops, teenagers had their own genre, but was relieved to see cute A-line dresses, all very age appropriate and not too bare.

'Do you have a budget?' I crossed my fingers that Stephen and Melody had been sensible.

'Mum said up to $100 and definitely no more than $150'. Generous but not too crazy.

Having decided to start in the city, my feet were hot and red after two hours of traipsing through shops full of fast fashion. Even Trudy's initial eagerness to look at every possibility had waned. Her shoulders were slouched and step heavy as we backtracked to the first shop we had visited.

'You liked that lacy purple dress, remember. Let's have another look at it now that you have other things to compare it with'.

'I suppose'.

Her enthusiasm was killing me. 'It was a good price so you would have enough left over for shoes as well', I hoped the added incentive might swing the deal.

'That's true', her brighter tone suggested there was hope . Only then did the prospect of more hours trudging around the city hit me. I must have verbalised my dismay because Trudy turned to me quickly, concern on her face, 'Are you okay? Did you hurt yourself'.

'No, no, all good', I reassured, pasting back a smile and filtering through the rack of dresses to find the lavender one.

'Here, try it on again and I will ask them if they have any shoes that go. What size are you?'

She emerged from the cubicle a few minutes later tottering on the high heeled sandals that the shop assistant had suggested as a good match. Her short blonde bob and long legs made her look like a newborn foal—beautiful, innocent and oh so clumsy.

'The dress looks great. Do you like it?' I said thinking there was no way she would survive a night in those shoes.

'The dress, yes, but these strappy sandals are so not me'. Trudy ducked back into the change room and when she reappeared, she was wearing her Doc Martens. 'What do you think?'

'Fabulous, cute but with an edge', I crossed my fingers we were close to wrapping up this outing. The shop assistant had gone to hunt down more shoes but Trudy was dressed, the dress under her arm, heading to the counter to pay. I liked her decisiveness even if it had taken a few hours to get there.

'Could you put it in a garment bag', I intervened as the shop assistant started to fold the dress. I was guessing that Trudy would enjoy the touch of drama for a special purchase.

I intended to drive home via the gelato shop but Trudy's head had dropped to one side and a soft burr told me she was asleep before we exited the carpark. Switching plans, I ran in and picked up takeaway for dessert. I was careful to close the car door softly but need not have worried, this girl could sleep through an earthquake.

Traffic was slow and my mind wandered. While secretly pleased that Trudy had wanted to go shopping with me, I had also been slightly anxious, worried I wouldn't know what to say to a teenager. None of my friends or family ever asked me to help with their kids. I winced at the recollection of my friend Annabelle who had laughed, 'Oh Nell, you don't have a clue do you?' when I had offered to babysit her two toddlers. That was a long time ago when I was single and therefore obviously irresponsible, as a married colleague had implied at the time. This woman had been reading *Bridget Jones' Diary* and her comment was along the lines of 'well you can afford to be selfish and self-centred when you don't have kids'. All tarred with the same brush, as my Mum would have said.

Trudy snuffled and shifted position as we arrived home. I shook her shoulder gently, 'We're home'.

'Oh, did I go to sleep?' she gave an enormous yawn and stretched her arms, elbows bent to accommodate the confines of the car.

'Any luck?' Rob looked pleased to see us and Trudy held up the garment bag by way of reply.

'You look beat' he said as Trudy went to try on the new outfit and I slumped onto a kitchen chair.

'I swear we looked at a hundred dresses although to be fair, she only tried on half a dozen. And she's happy with this one, that's all that's important. My feet will recover, eventually', I gave a rueful smile that relaxed with gratitude as Rob placed a glass of white wine in front of me.

'Well earned, take it easy for a while before dinner', he said.

'Ta, da', Rob provided the vocals as Trudy twirled, showing off her pretty purchase with pride. 'Aunty Nell thank you so much for today. This dress is perfect. I would never have found it without your help and now I will have something different to all the other girls'. The hug was as unexpected as it was clammy, with the deep sincerity of adolescence.

That night before bed, Trudy came to find me, phone in hand. 'I thought you might like this', her smirk giving her away. The image was the meme of a ghost and read, *I've just realized that ghosts are people who died trying to fold a fitted sheet.* A warm swell of recognition caught in my throat as I recalled the playfulness of my favourite uncle and my own silly jokes; a genetic thread that knit us.

'You know how you said maternal line before? You mean my grandmother?'

'Yes, and my grandmother and hers. It's sad that you never knew your grandmother, she was an amazing woman and she would have been so proud of you'.

'Why, I haven't done anything special'.

'She'd have loved your independence and confidence. In her younger days she was the brightest person in the room. She was creative and funny and had the best dress sense. You look a lot like her, has your dad told you that?'

'Yeah, when he gets out the old photo album he always says that I look just like his Mum, even his grandmother!'

'Ah, you'd have liked Nanna. She was feisty as well but also kind and happy whenever she looked after us kids. We loved going to her house'.

'Most of the kids have two sets of grandparents but I only have Gramps and he lives far away so we don't see him much. Besides, Mum and his new wife don't get on—it gets awkward after a few days'.

'Maybe you could have a holiday up there sometime. It's beautiful in Cairns and there's so much to do. Lots of adventure stuff'.

'Yeah, maybe but Mum says they need to invite us'.

Odd I thought but didn't say anything more. You shouldn't need an invitation to visit your grandfather. Still every family has its own way of doing things. 'Let's have a hot chocolate before bed,' I said. I need something cosy to help me get to sleep'.

Chapter 6

Sunday afternoon I dropped Trudy at the train station having treated her to brunch at Manly. The weekend had disappeared and I'd barely had a minute to think, let alone do any of the tasks that would make next week run smoothly. It could have been Trudy's carefree adolescence rubbing off on me but more likely the happy prospect of an uneventful week ahead that was making me slack. Not dwelling on the reasons I decided on the spur of the moment to see if Cleo was free to extend the relaxed weekend feeling.

Two questions had been playing tag in my head in the early hours of the morning for days now: what to say to Paige once she heard Caroline's news and what to do about work. I had no intention of breaking Paige's confidence and even if I was subtle Cleo would smell a secret and there would be no end to the questions. Walking up her front path I resigned myself to having to work through that one alone.

Cleo opened the door before I had a chance to ring the bell. 'Nell, darling, so great you could pop over. Perfect timing too, Marco is pouring us a glass of chardonnay in the kitchen but I thought we'd sit out here in the sun if you are warm enough'.

'Yes, this weather is gorgeous. Early spring I hope. Trudy and I spent the morning near the beach soaking up some of it before I put her on the train'.

'Oh nice. How old is she now? Twelve or thirteen?'

'Ha, no a very grown up sixteen. It was good having her to visit, a chance to see her maturing without her parents around. I was pretty impressed to be honest, she's a lovely young woman'.

'I know. It's cool seeing them make that transition especially when you don't have to live through the daily angst of it. I remember when Bella was about the same age, could have been a year or so older, she started to really engage in politics and world events and her views were incredibly mature and well informed. It was a glimpse of the powerhouse she has become'.

'Nell, welcome', Marco's voice was booming over the three brimming glasses and bowl of nuts he carried without juggling.

'If I tried to carry all of that it would land on the floor', I laughed as he set everything down on the old metal table that would have been at home in a French country garden with its peeled green paint and traces of rust.

'Here's to us and to friendship', he raised his glass making deliberate eye contact with both of us. 'How is old Rob? Did you leave him at home'.

'He is mowing the lawn, seems it was absolutely critical that he do it today while the weather is good'.

'Ah well, we all have priorities. Mowing I'm glad to say is not one of mine', Marco leaned against the balustrade looking out over his own yard. I suddenly realized why something had seemed wrong when I arrived a few minutes before. No Rex, his time must have come.

'How was it with Rex in the end?' I asked.

'We told you we planned to do it at home, I think. Well we did but we had to ask Pete to come over and give the injection. Neither of us felt like we could do it'.

'At least he was at home and you know he didn't suffer'.

'It all happened very quickly. Pete gave the injection, the old boy shuddered and then after a few seconds he went limp.

He wasn't Rex anymore, strange how clear it was that he had gone'. Marco was still looking out over his yard but there were tears in his eyes, and the sadness made his face seem to droop in an unusual way.

'How is everything at work now, Nell? Since the investigation, I mean. I presume it has all settled back to normal', Cleo changed the subject after a moment.

'Yes, it's like it never happened except Brian isn't there of course. I haven't heard how he is doing but I feel for him'.

'Has the case already been heard?'

'Not entirely sure, I was told he was pleading guilty but I haven't heard anything official. These things can drag on for ages so who knows when it will all be finished'.

'Do they still do those incident investigations at the hospital. I remember they used to do this root-cause analysis thing, ghastly when you have been through some difficult situation and have to relive it'.

'They do and I am not looking forward to it either. I understand that it's necessary and that it's all about improvement yada yada but it's hard not to feel you are in the spotlight'.

'Exactly, I remember one awful case we had. A baby died unexpectedly and the family were naturally looking for answers. One of the worst times of my working life'.

'Well our internal investigation starts next week. The team is a good one so I'm trusting it will be a constructive experience. Things have moved on quite a lot. These days there is less blame, more attention to the system'.

'Hmm, hope so'.

'Anyway, once it's over I am hoping I can clear my head properly. I have been finding it hard to find any pleasure in work for weeks now'.

'You should take a break, give yourself some time to recharge'.

'I've been thinking the same thing actually. Pippa arrives in a few weeks and I could take some leave while she is here, I have heaps owing. I was wondering what you think about the three of us going away together for a few days. Like old times', I hesitated not wanting to exclude Marco.

'That's a fantastic idea', he immediately chimed in. 'You girls should definitely have a bit of fun while Pippa is here', he beamed encouragement at Cleo.

'Do you think so?', her lack of enthusiasm was uncharacteristic. 'We should wait until after Wednesday before I commit'.

Marco pointed in my direction with his chin and raised his eyebrows, 'We can tell Nell. I know I said I didn't want to talk about it with anyone but Nell saw me at the hospital the first time I saw the specialist'.

'You didn't say', she looked from Marco to me and I felt crimson spreading up my neck.

'I finally summoned up the courage to tell Cleo', Marco explained, 'and the doctor hasn't been testing me for carpal tunnel. I'm seeing a neurologist because it looks like I may have some neurological problem. That's why I have been dropping things and having trouble with my hands. Mind you part of the problem is my eyes, I need new glasses'.

'I see, have they given you any idea what they are expecting to find?'

'Not really but the specialist said the next phase was ruling out some of the nastier possibilities so that we can concentrate on the more likely causes'.

'Well that sounds positive', I said my mind involuntarily beginning to list some of those nastier possibilities. I knew Cleo would already have done the same many times over and even Marco would have been busy Googling. 'Try not to worry too much', it was a meagre offering but Cleo gave a small smile of thanks.

'If you are free, we could have coffee Wednesday. Knowing how these things work we will be sitting around for hours waiting for tests'.

'I can always make time. Text me and I can meet you at a coffee shop. The hospital coffee hasn't improved since you worked there so I suggest we go up the road to one of the little Italian places'.

'It's a date', Marco said going inside to retrieve the wine bottle.

'Do you think it's serious?' I kept my voice low.

'Hard to know but there have been a few things, not just the clumsiness. Remember I said to you when we were away for the weekend that he'd been forgetful and more tired and lethargic than normal'.

I was about to reach for her hand when she held up both hands as though to stop the flow of worry, 'We have to stay positive'.

'Of course and forget my suggestion about going away. Now isn't the best time'.

'No actually, Marco is right. Whatever we find out on Wednesday we can't let it rule our lives. Let's plan for a four day break somewhere warm and gorgeous. You and Pippa can surprise me'.

'Hah, so long as we don't disappoint you', I did squeeze her hand then as we both watched Marco reappear and begin to refill our glasses. 'Just a tiny bit for me, I have to drive remember'.

'The cops have been brutal around here lately, random breath testing all over the place even the back streets. Best be careful', Cleo agreed.

The sun was low in the sky when I left to drive home and I saw Marco come behind Cleo to hold her close to him. Rob would admonish me to not catastrophize their situation when I arrived home but in the meantime, I let my mind run, free of the curbs of reason and good sense. A sinister shadow settled over my mood and I felt flat and irritable. I was worried for my friends but I was not ready to face another tragedy either.

Rob smiled broadly as I came into the kitchen and it took all my willpower not to snap when he haplessly asked, 'Nice afternoon?'. He was still hot and sweaty in his mowing outfit, shorts, gaiters and paint- splattered, ratty t-shirt.

'Go and have your shower and I'll tell you all about it', I stalled for time.

'Paige dropped by while you were out', he called disappearing into the dark of the hall, 'She talked with Caro this morning and wanted to celebrate the news, I think. I told her to come for dinner tomorrow'.

I was reheating some soup when Rob reappeared. 'Nice visit with Cleo?' he asked.

'Marco is seeing a neurologist', I blurted. 'You remember how he was dropping things the other weekend, well it could be something serious. Anyway he has a lot of tests on Wednesday to rule stuff out'.

'What sort of stuff?' Rob frowned.

'They weren't specific but I am assuming brain tumor, multiple sclerosis, nothing good that's for sure'.

'God, they must be worried'.

'On the surface they seemed to be taking it remarkably calmly. It felt like Marco is in denial, hoping positive thoughts will yield positive results'.

'Well, no point in worrying about things you can't change I suppose and they are both optimists?'

'I guess but Cleo is pretty worried. She didn't say much but I could tell she is staying strong for Marco'.

'He's lucky to have her. Have they told his kids yet?'

'No, they only told me because I saw Marco at the hospital at his last appointment. When I asked him about it previously, he said it was for something minor but now that he has confided in Cleo he is more open'.

'I'll stay mum until I know officially and, in any case, there isn't much to know until they have the test results'.

'Exactly', I agreed, relieved that Rob as usual could be relied on to be discreet.

Sleep came quickly after the busy weekend but at three o'clock I was wide awake. Meditation did not help, my mind was galloping and refused to be harnessed. The to-do list was written and the radio offered only talk back that was too depressing to countenance. Marco's news had rocked me. I wanted to believe he was too young for his symptoms to be caused by anything serious but Marjorie had only been a couple of years older.

How had she felt when she got her diagnosis? Fearful and angry was the impression I'd had from Rob. I tried to imagine how I would react but drew an emotional blank. Always easier to imagine what I would do than how I would feel. I wondered what I would regret: not having made peace with Marjorie, my relationship with the girls, always playing it safe, avoiding conflict. Of all those things, one was entirely in my control. I promised myself to have those honest conversations that would be uncomfortable but that were important for me.

Chapter 7

Mondays were messy in Emergency, the clean up after a busy weekend of too much booze, drugs and high living. Typically we were underwater by ten o'clock, all those people who didn't want to come to hospital on the weekend slamming into the cases from the night before, people on stretchers in the corridors and ambulances out the front waiting. I had filled in my leave application online the previous night knowing I would barely have time to go to the toilet much less anything less urgent.

I was wishing I'd had the foresight to ask Rob to pick up some meat for dinner as I changed out of my uniform close to six o'clock. A patient who had initially presented with a headache early in the day had become progressively distressed and eventually disorientated. I was the only senior nurse available to help with the lumbar puncture and so my day had been a long one.

Back in civvies I felt better and headed to the supermarket. Impatiently I ran an amber light that must have been closer to red. 'Damn!', the camera flash would mean loss of more points on my licence not to mention a decent fine. I took a couple of deep breaths to slow myself down, trying to focus on the two or three things I needed from the shops. Paige would be at our place in less than thirty minutes and I was desperate for a quick shower before I started on dinner.

My hair was still wrapped in a towel when Paige's car door slammed signalling to Lucca that a noisy welcome was called for. Rob was not home—this is becoming a habit, my first thought, quickly followed by the acknowledgement that he must have had a busy day as well. I ran a comb through my wet hair and dabbed on some make-up as Paige let herself in. 'I'll just be a minute', I called down the stairs. There's a bottle of wine in the fridge, help yourself'. I fiddled some more with my hair and make-up aware I was procrastinating, hoping Rob would arrive home before I had to go down.

'Hi Paige, how are you?', I asked coming into the kitchen a few minutes later, having duly berated myself.

'Good, busy as ever, but feeling better now', I assumed she was obliquely referring to recovery after the procedure.

I started to open the wine and took some cheese from the fridge for later. 'It was a crazy day at the hospital as well. I was late getting away so dinner will be a while. Is pasta okay? I have some pesto in the freezer that I made last week'.

'Sounds great', she shook her head as I went to pour her a glass of wine, 'Not for me, I've decided to have a dry month...to prove to myself I can'.

'Oh, good for you. Do you mind if I don't join you tonight? I've been looking forward to this since I arrived home'.

'Caro called to tell me their news, I'm so excited for them. She said if all goes to plan, she could be pregnant in three or four weeks time'.

'Your Dad was over the moon too, so excited to have a grandchild', I cringed as I heard the words leave my mouth. 'Oh sorry Paige, that was insensitive'.

'Of course he is excited, we all are. It's marvellous news and please don't feel you need to walk on eggshells around me', her smile seemed genuinely relaxed. I wondered at her ability to not place herself in the centre of this news—you had to admire that strength of character and yet admiration was not my honest reaction.

'Paige, can I ask you honestly how you are feeling after last Wednesday? I've been concerned but at the same time I don't want to pry'.

'I am adjusting to my decision, if you don't mind, I'm not ready to talk about it yet, maybe in a couple of weeks. I'm not shutting you out Nell, I just need time and I promise I'm doing well'.

I nodded, mollified.

'Caro said, they are hoping for a girl. She could be born as soon as July next year. Have you thought about what you want her to call you?', Paige could have been deflecting but she was uncharacteristically effusive.

'Not really. Also I don't want to assume, you know, it's up to Caroline and Cristiane really'.

Paige looked puzzled, 'Assume what?'.

'Well, you know, if they want me to be a grandmother or …', I wasn't sure where I was going with this thought.

'Of course they will, two Mums and I think Cristiane's parents both have new partners so lots of grandparents. What do French people say for grandma? Or Quebecoise?', she brushed aside my uncertainty.

'Paige, sweety, good to see you', Rob gave her a hug before coming over to kiss me hello. 'Sorry, long day, I hoped to be home an hour ago', he apologized.

'We've just been talking about Caro's news', Paige was multitasking looking at her phone. 'Here, I've just googled it, Mamie is one of the names for a grandmother in Quebec. Mamie Nell sounds good'.

'What about for me?' Rob asked.

'Just looking, it's Papi and for me it would be matante but that sounds awfully formal don't you think?'.

Paige and Rob continued with their banter while I finished making the salad. Thank goodness I had been suitably unambitious with the menu tonight, I thought noticing it was already after seven thirty. It had been a long day for everyone.

'No cheese for me', Paige said as Rob cleared away our plates a little later, 'I couldn't eat another bite after that delicious pasta'.

'But it's your favourite, that stinky soft cheese from near Dijon, remember we had it that time we had a family holiday in Burgundy? You must have been about fourteen and you loved all the new flavours and experiences', Rob insisted.

'It was the best holiday and yes, normally I would find room for a small piece but tonight you have defeated me', she held both her hands on her stomach. 'I think that holiday was when Caro decided that one day she would live in France; we both fell in love with the place'.

'Easy to do', Rob said cutting a substantial slice of cheese for himself and spread it over the not very good baguette that I'd found at the supermarket. 'Perfect end to a beautiful meal, thanks Nell'.

I smiled, pondering how many shared experiences Rob and his daughters must have had that I would never fully appreciate. It could feel lonely if I dwelt on it too much, better to plan for future times together, that was my special opportunity.

After Paige left, Rob and I sat companionably reading but I was finding it difficult to concentrate on my book. The plot was sinuous and my attention span was abysmal tonight. I had been surprised by how Paige had included me in the family news, for the first time I was within the circle, not an added extra. Over ten years was a long time to wait but I was beginning to realise that I was the cause of the cold war. I had built up so many protective layers they couldn't get to know me properly and all our communication had been through Rob and frequently about Marjorie. Hardly healthy.

Caroline was so much more mature and courageous than I was even now. Sure of her relationship and prepared to jump through the hoops necessary to have a baby on her own terms, she was clear-sighted about motherhood and their plans to navigate it their own way.

'Rob', I interrupted his reading, 'I know you are super excited about Caroline and Cristiane getting pregnant but do you have any qualms about the baby not having a father'. Part of me saw how suburban and middleclass my question sounded but I'd promised myself to have honest conversations from now on.

'It's something we talked about when she was here last. We were sitting beside Marjorie's bed waiting for her to wake when Caro asked me, what I thought'. He took a long moment, 'You know in my field I have seen all sorts of families and the standard mum, dad and two kids is not always a perfect unit. Same sex couples can raise well adjusted children as well as anyone and they can have the same problems too'.

'I suppose I am in awe of them. I'm not sure I would be strong enough to take a less than traditional path', I was trying to be honest about my own lack of aptitude for motherhood but couldn't bring myself to be any more explicit. Rob had never asked me why I hadn't had children, his acceptance both reassured me and reinforced my view that I would have messed it up.

'I hope Paige finds the right person or the right time to have a family', Rob said. 'A career is all very well but she deserves more'.

'Have you ever asked her? About wanting to have children I mean?'

'Ha, only once and she bit my head off. You know how she can be if she doesn't want to talk about something'.

This conversation was starting to be uncomfortable, so easy to say too much. 'Can I ask you something else entirely unrelated. Do you think I'm too old to retrain? Do something different?'

'Why, I thought you loved your job', Rob was shaking his head like I'd suggested a really dumb idea.

'I do, at least I did but I've started thinking I need a change'.

Rob wrinkled his nose and his mouth twisted, 'What's brought this on? Is it because of the police thing? You know that will all blow over'.

Determined not to be put off, I went on. 'That's part of it but I've been unsettled for a while, not connecting with patients the way I used to, not as available to the younger staff. I don't want to end up a cranky old dinosaur'.

'What would you do? It's not straightforward changing jobs at our age. Do you really want to be the least experienced person on the team when you are getting on towards sixty?'

'You did it six year ago', I persisted.

'That was different, a sideways move. Yes, I had to learn new skills but I knew all the basics and I had the contacts'. I had hoped Rob would help me form a sharper idea of a new path instead he was throwing obstacles in the way. Not like him to be negative, he must truly believe it was a bad idea.

I let it drop and Rob picked up his book, my shoulders slumped half-heartedly accepting his good sense.

Wednesday morning I had an early meeting and then a morning tea for a staff specialist who was retiring after almost forty years in the Department. Moira was one of the most popular senior doctors and the buzz of congratulations and questions about future plans were punctuated with frequent laughter.

Someone clanked a glass and Moira was ushered forward to stand beside the boss who made a short speech. These occasions were never particularly formal but this was a milestone and Moira unfolded a sheet of paper to respond. After the usual thanks and a couple of funny anecdotes she ended by saying,

'Working in this Department has made me frantic, exhausted, irritable but ultimately proud to make a small difference in the lives of people when they need urgent care. Being able to do this with all of you has made the bad times bearable and the occasional wins a true celebration. It has been a privilege'.

A low murmur, much clapping and nodding of heads, a few tears—people built for action, we still knew truth when we heard it. The lift in my mood was short-lived as the ping from my phone showed a message from Cleo. I delayed opening it for a moment, not ready to put on the smiling reassuring face I knew I was going to need: *sorry will take raincheck on coffee still waiting to go in for tests talk soon C xo*

Off the hook. I should have busied myself with waiting patients but instead I turned to the computer to enter new data from the shift. These days I spent more time in front of a computer than with patients. We all did.

Late afternoon, Kate appeared at the nurses' station and asked if I had a minute. All the previous worries clutched at my gut while I tried to look accommodating and unconcerned.

'I have a favour to ask', Kate was quick to dispel any misapprehension.

'Of course', my heart was still hurtling but I managed a smile inviting Kate to continue.

'Three new grads have put their hands up for the mentorship program—you probably saw my email last week calling for expressions of interest', her voice had the slightest of inflections. 'Monique Petrie asked if you would be her mentor. She said she had worked some shifts with you,' that inflection again, stronger now.

'Yes, she's a good young nurse. Heaps to learn but good instincts. I've never been a mentor though, not sure I would be the best person'.

'There will be support from HR and from me. I think you'll be terrific. Would you at least think about it?'

Kate had manoeuvred me into a corner, 'Sure, I'll let you know Friday. Is that okay?' After the debacle with Brian and the way he had been treated I doubted I was in the right head space to be a mentor.

'Perfect, thanks Nell. Hope you'll give it a go, you will love it'.

I was pulling out of the car park close to five o'clock when Cleo phoned, 'Can you talk, sorry about earlier but you know what Outpatients is like'.

'I'm driving but you're on speaker'.

'I can call back when you're home', Cleo's voice was strained.

'No, now is fine. How did you go?', I pulled over to the curb.

'So many tests and the waiting, it's exhausting. He's had an MRI and they did some sort of electrical activity tests of his nerves and muscles. The blood test results will take a few days so we have another appointment next Wednesday'. Fatigue made Cleo sound flat.

'Did the specialist give you an idea of what she expects to find?'

'We hardly saw her, said once she has the results, we will have a better picture. Nell, I'm scared, one of the technicians said something about motor neuron disease'.

Silence. What to say? We both knew it was possible.

'Oh Cleo, let's hope not. I've been Googling as you must have and the symptoms don't exactly fit. And if it was something else like a tumour they wouldn't be waiting until next week to see you either'.

'Maybe but I have a bad feeling. Everyone was treating us as if we were terribly fragile today, very careful not to make us worried'.

'How is Marco taking it?', I asked.

'Remarkably okay so far but I've sent him to bed now. He was so tired when we got home that he was seeing double. Luckily, we had asked Theo to look after the restaurant tonight'.

'I can imagine, it's been a big day'. Another silence. I tried not to jump in but after a moment asked, 'Have you told the kids yet?'

'There's no point until we know more. They would have a hundred questions and there aren't any answers. After next week'. Cleo paused again, this staccato pattern so unlike her.

'Would you rather I don't say anything more to Rob as well?', I wondered if she might be hesitating to ask for my discretion.

'If that's okay', she sounded relieved.

'Of course and if you need to talk with someone, either of you, I'm five minutes away'.

'Thanks Nell, we may take you up on that. Talk soon'.

After the call I sat thinking about Cleo and Marco. It didn't sound good. I could understand why they were not ready to talk about it yet, especially with Marco's kids. A good amount of Italian melodrama ran among them.

Joe was the eldest, opinionated and charming, he had finally quit his job as an audio-engineer in the world of indie music to concentrate on podcasts and audiobooks. An ultimatum from his wife and now the impending birth of their child had set him on the prosaic but more lucrative path. Theo and Bella, on the other hand always seemed to have a new grand plan. At the moment Theo was between jobs, his work at a Hunter Valley winery had ended and he had applied to do a sommelier's course. Bella was an actress who dabbled in writing children's stories when work was scarce which was most of the time.

My mind drifted to Paige and Caroline, they had had to weather some tough times. I did not wish the same on Marco's family. As I restarted the car, I remembered how Rob had been careful to keep me in the loop at each stage of Marjorie's illness. He was good at that. But I would say nothing more about Marco not only because I had promised Cleo but because to give voice to my fears would make them come true. Suspicious nonsense—perhaps but I dare not put it to the test.

Chapter 8

My phone beeped, 'Argh, someone is at it early for a Saturday', I grumbled but on the off chance it could be work I flicked up the screen. I could hear Rob downstairs unpacking the dishwasher before he headed out for a morning run: *Hi Nell, I know its short notice but I wondered if you have time for a coffee this morning. Cleo has to work and I could use some company. 9am at Frank's Deli?? Marco* 😊

What could I say? Of course I would go. There was time to give Lucca a quick walk and still make it to the café, one way to make the most of my weekend.

Marco was sitting inside with the newspaper spread out beside an empty cup when I arrived. 'Sorry I didn't wait to order, needed a quick shot of caffeine this morning', he said as I sat down. 'What will you have, I was about to go and order a refill?'

I gave him my order and sat back to look around the café. It wasn't a place I came to often but I had been once years ago with Paige, that was during my *trying to be an older friend stage*. The drone of voices was hard to hear above the racket of the coffee grinder that seemed to be employed full time. People bustled in for takeaway and regulars settled down at tables to slow down their morning. The woman behind the counter knew everyone by name as well as their coffee order, greeting locals with a well worn, 'Your usual love?' Easy to see why it was so busy.

'Thanks', I accepted a cappuccino from Marco and waved away his offer of a pastry. 'I need to lose some weight, I had better stick with coffee'.

Marco made a face, 'It's Saturday, you can afford to be decadent' but he didn't force the issue.

'How are you feeling?' it seemed disingenuous not to ask the obvious.

'No worse, the muscle weakness only bothers me when I'm tired. I almost wish I hadn't started this medical circus; I could just learn to live with whatever it is'.

'True but then if it's something easily dealt with wouldn't it be better to know?'

'No one is thinking that I have something that is easy to fix', Marco met my gaze squarely, no pretence now. 'The doctors won't say anything until they have all the test results but everyone goes silent when I come into a room. I figure they are stalling for time'.

'You could be misinterpreting them, neurologists are famous for being sticklers for detail, armchair intellectuals', although I doubted the stereotype was accurate these days.

'The thing is', Marco took a sip of his coffee and looked into the middle distance, 'Whatever label they end up putting on me, I don't want to become a burden for Cleo'. Holding up his hand to halt my interjection, he went on, 'I'm not naïve, worst case scenario is ugly, you know as well as I do'.

I nodded slightly not wanting to give weight to negative thoughts while knowing he was right.

'Anyway, I'm not asking you for anything except to be there for Cleo'.

'Cleo is my best friend. I'll do whatever she needs'.

'Yeah, but don't wait for her to ask and don't let those kids of mine make her feel guilty. She is going to need to look after herself for once'.

I was taken aback by his fervour and let the sentence hang. This conversation was becoming more uncomfortable than I had reckoned on, 'Okay but we can cross those bridges if and when they eventuate'. I walked around to his side of the table to give him a hug.

Marco was still looking morose but his eyes flicked to the outside tables in recognition, 'Isn't that Paige?'

I turned but there was no sign of her, 'Could have been, she comes here sometimes. Must not have seen us'.

The distraction had allowed Marco to reset and he apologised for dumping all his negativity, 'like a lead balloon', as he said with the hint of a smile, albeit a self-deprecating one. His desire to protect Cleo was noble and yet surely ill-founded. Whatever news they got next week, they were going to need to be a team and that meant sharing the good and the bad. I decided now was not the time for counsel, especially not from me, I was hardly an expert.

Rob was home when I got back, 'Out for a walk?' he asked.

'Yes and a quick coffee down the road. How was your run?' my answer was broadly honest.

Late afternoon, I was sitting darning a favourite jumper that I wore in the garden on cool days when my brother Stephen called. He wanted to tell me about Trudy's dance and how fantastic she had looked in the new dress. Melody came on as well, thanking me again for helping out and promising to send through pictures. Trudy it seemed was still at an after party, hopefully a more innocent one than I remember from my years as a student nurse. Stephen hastened to add, it was an all girls' party and while I could still envisage a host of mischief, I decided not to remark on it.

'Anyway, the other reason I called was to ask you and Rob down the weekend after next. The weather is warming up and we haven't seen you for ages', Stephen said.

'That would be lovely, I'll check with Rob and let you know. Even if we come for a day trip'.

'Check what with Rob', he asked coming into the kitchen where I was sitting in the afternoon sunshine.

'Stephen and Melody have asked us down, week after next.

'Great idea, tell them yes'.

'Did you hear that?' I asked Stephen, assuming Rob's baritone had carried clearly.

'I'll text some ideas but come Saturday and stay overnight, then we can have a nice cosy dinner together, like old times'.

Their lives were so uncomplicated, it would be relaxing to immerse ourselves in their routine for a couple of days. Stephen had always had a sixth sense for when I needed time out but I wondered if Trudy had said something as well. Or as Rob said they could be starting to feel lonely as Trudy became more independent and the boys got on with their own lives.

Rob squinted at my handiwork as I rang off, 'What's with the darning? Getting into the grandma role early?' he gave a cheeky grin.

'It's an old faithful and you would be surprised how many times I've pulled out this darning needle over the past few years'. I intended my tone to be an admonishment but Rob's interest had been fleeting and he whistled as he switched on the football.

*

I rounded the corner into the nurses' station to find Cleo and Marco waiting. It was close to one thirty on Wednesday afternoon and I had been hoping for a ten minute break, ideally a quick coffee and lunch. The morning had been taken up with meetings and I need to oversee the management of a couple of more complex patients before the shift ended.

'Nell, do you have some time now? Or we can wait'. No greeting, brains inundated, faces taut, they looked spent.

My stress levels escalated, caught between the claims of my patients and those of my friends. Trying to think clearly, I suggested I meet them at the end of my shift, 'I can drop over to your place', I offered. Their apologetic acceptance made me feel like an even worse friend.

The rhythm of work usually made time pass quickly but not that afternoon. I was going through the motions: seeing patients, chasing down specialists, sending people off for more tests. I was on automatic, reacting to whatever was in front of me, trying not to think beyond that. A senior doctor asked me to find some test results for a patient and although he'd said it was urgent, I found myself walking another patient down to X-ray first. As I was hurrying back, he yelled from the end of the corridor, 'For Pete's sake where are those results, we have an emergency here'. I propelled myself into gear but not before I heard him say, 'What the hell is wrong with Nell lately? It's like she's checked out'.

I would apologise tomorrow, explain I'd had some bad news and was distracted. He wasn't my favourite doctor but he was influential and it would do me no good if he decided I was losing it. I didn't contemplate what he had said seriously but reasoned that he was stressed as well. We did not have a close rapport that would have lent a compassionate intent to his words.

The doorbell was not working and only after I'd knocked twice did Cleo open the door. Her face was red and her hair had been raked into an atypical tangle. She drew me inside in a big hug, 'Thanks for coming'. It was after five and the faded evening light hung in their kitchen like a pall.

'Sorry, I'm so late, busy afternoon'. It was true but I had found extra tasks to delay me when I could have made my excuses and headed off. I wanted to show my commitment at work I told myself after the earlier interaction but I knew that was not even half the truth.

'No problem, sorry it's darker in here than I'd realized', Cleo turned on the lights.

'Where's Marco?' I asked.

'He's not up for talking about things today, gone for a walk', Cleo waved her hand implying he wouldn't be back for a while.

'Should I come back another day?'

'No, no. He asked me to tell you. We're so grateful for your support'.

I nodded, hoping my silence would give her space to find the words she needed. Instead she walked over to a small desk in the corner of the kitchen that was set up with a computer.

'I made some notes', she laughed 'Following my own advice, that's what I always tell patients to do'.

'Well the good news is that he doesn't have motor neuron disease, thank god. We were both so convinced that's what it was, we forgot to ask sensible questions about the actual diagnosis'.

This was excruciating, 'And did they tell you'.

'He has Myasthenia Gravis, the muscle tests apparently pointed to it and they confirmed it with a blood test'.

'How serious is it?' I felt like I should know but other than what I'd learnt as a student on the neurology ward I didn't know much about it. We'd had a patient years ago in Emergency in a myasthenia crisis which had been terrifying but the doctors had said at the time that it was a very rare complication.

'The neurologist has given him a prescription for some tablets that should relieve the muscle weakness although she warned they wear off after a few hours so he'll need to take them regularly'.

I waited, assuming there was more.

'If the medication doesn't work there are other options that I've been reading about on the internet. The doctor said the prognosis is good, most people with the condition live a normal life and, in her words, "die with the disease not of it". They will probably suggest he had a thymectomy in a couple of months but otherwise he should be okay'.

'What about work, the bistro?'

'That is going to be a problem. He will be tired and one of the best treatments is rest according to the doctor. We haven't talked about it but I know it's on his mind. Marco lives for that place but the time has come ... ', her voice trailed away.

'It's a lot to take in', the idea of a long term condition at our age seemed premature. Living with illness was not in the plan—too soon and too sudden, like a random hex.

'We will have to adapt, life won't be exactly the same but it can still be good', Cleo lifted her chin and smiled. 'Who knows, the slower pace could be a godsend, make us smell the roses and all that'.

I raised my eyebrows involuntarily, barely aware I'd done so.

'I know, I know being Pollyanna isn't going to solve any-thing, there are some rough times ahead but it will be okay. I need to stay positive for Marco, he's in a dark place at the moment, asking *why me?* and angry with the universe'.

'And Marco is so lucky to have your positivity'. I didn't add, 'he is going to need it', stopping myself in time to say instead, 'You're a great team, you can bend this thing to fit your lives if anyone can'.

'Thanks Nell, just telling you has helped. We have decided to tell the kids on the weekend, Marco is asking everyone over on Saturday afternoon. Wish us luck', Cleo crossed her fingers as her folded hands rested in her lap.

I had told Rob I had an in-service this evening. These white lies about my whereabouts were becoming a pattern I thought uncomfortably. Fortunately he didn't ask any questions and when he went to bed early, I started searching for information on Myasthenia Gravis online.

Everything was consistent with what Cleo had said. There were some immunosuppressant medications that could be helpful and some new expensive medicines that had been used in very severe disease. According to the patient foundation's website, there were going to be some pretty major changes in their lifestyle—more rest, less stress, no big parties, less alcohol. I had no idea the fatigue could be so debilitating and Marco had mentioned double-vision, he would possibly have to give up driving. I knew Cleo must had read all of this when I saw her today. How had she covered her devastation so well?

Cleo called the following week to tell me about their Saturday. She said it was exhausting, especially for Marco. Joe had asked angry questions, as if trying to prove the diagnosis must be wrong, that there was a loophole that would mean everything would return to normal soon. Bella had cried and wailed, as usual the queen of melodrama but eventually she had realized her father needed support not tears and had become uncharacteristically practical. She'd even suggested they install some labour saving gadgets and think about getting a cleaner. Theo had been the most surprising. He had immediately understood the gravity of what they were being told. He said, he understood that decisions would need to be made about the bistro and that in the meantime he could continue to run it. He even offered to move home for a while if they needed it.

The good news was, the medicine had helped and provided he had plenty of rest, Marco was feeling better than he had for months. When I asked Cleo how she was doing, she told me instead that they had had the occupational therapy people in to assess the house and see if there needed to be some hand grips in the bathroom. I had read that hot showers could make the muscle weakness worse so this was a sensible precaution. Although as Cleo said , 'they are all so butt ugly, why can't someone design a stylish version'. When I suggested she had identified a gap on the market she was quiet for a moment but did not respond.

I was uncomfortable asking about the planned weekend break with Pippa but Cleo saved me from having to raise it, asking if I had made any bookings yet.

'No, I thought you would want to reconsider now that you know what you and Marco are dealing with. We can do it another time'.

'Actually, I want to keep with the plan. Apologies in advance if I'm sad but it will be good for me to have a couple of days away from Marco. Good for him as well. He's been more reliant on me than I think is healthy since we got the diagnosis, like he has lost his nerve'.

I was about to ring off when Cleo interrupted, 'Oh, I almost forgot to thank you for talking with Marco the other morning. He said it helped him clear his thoughts'.

'Anytime', I said, not ready for her suggestion that I invite him for coffee on Friday morning if I was free. She had an appointment at the hairdresser and he would appreciate the company.

Friday was my rostered day off and so Marco's suggestion of a ten o'clock rendezvous was easy to accommodate. Like last time, he wasted no time on preliminary chat before launching into what was top of mind.

'You know I was ready to have motor neuron disease, had even planned how I would organize to access the drugs I would need to end it when the time came and now I have this blasted thing instead'.

'You must be the first person ever to be disappointed not to have motor neuron', I shook my head, trying to stifle a huff of irony.

'Yeah, I know, ungrateful bastard. But you know me, except for Cleo and the kids, I have never signed up to anything for the long term. And this thing is for life'.

I was tempted to reassure him that it could be mild, well managed with medication but held my tongue for once.

'Cleo says I will find my own new order, that I won't feel off-balance for ever. But I have to tell you, right now that is hard to imagine'.

I nodded and reached for his hand, sympathy welling up in my eyes. I hadn't fully grasped how he must be feeling until now.

'When I read the leaflets from the doctor and started searching online, it was like I would have to have a personality transplant. Rest, stay calm, stay quiet, no parties, no fun...,' his voice trailed off but his face was set hard.

'So awful'.

'Awful! It's dehumanizing. I feel like I am losing myself', he unconsciously stroked my hand—seeking the comfort of physical contact, I thought.

'It's enough to make you scream?' I suggested.

'Exactly! Or take to the bottle which I'm not allowed to do either!'.

'Can you talk to someone else who has myasthenia?' I asked.

'There are some videos online and a patient group that has gruesome sounding meetings but... maybe. Not sure I'm up for it yet though'.

'It's early days, you don't need to do anything. And Cleo said you already feel better on the meds'.

'Yeah, suppose so', he sounded unconvinced and his gaze was strangely intimate. 'Talking to you helps a lot, Nell. I've always thought we had a special connection'.

I could feel heat climbing up my neck but surely I had misread that last comment. Where was my mind these days? I shook my head to erase the unbidden thoughts and changed the subject.

I tried to distract us both with other news but we kept finding our way back to his diagnosis and the changes it wrought. 'Even my bloody bathroom is being redesigned, nothing is spared!', he grumbled as we were getting up to leave.

'Oh look', I said brightly, 'There's Paige at that table in the back'. I almost hadn't seen her behind the computer screen that had all her attention.

'Hi Paige. Marco and I have just been having coffee. Didn't see you there?'

'Hi. I often work from here for an hour or so in the mornings. I saw you earlier but I didn't want to interrupt', she sounded brittle, defensive. Clearly, I had encroached on her private space and it was not welcome.

On the drive home I was preoccupied with Marco's response to his diagnosis. He was understandably angry but his resistance to even name the condition made me think he was hoping willpower would be a match for the unwelcome truth. His low mood had been infectious after less than an hour. How was Cleo coping with it every day? No wonder she wanted a weekend away. Grief, raw anger, depression—Marco seemed to be in the grip of all three and I worried my platitudes may have done more harm than good. I was the last person with life experience that could be helpful. With sudden clarity, I called Marco on the handsfree phone.

'Marco, look, I've been thinking about what you said. I may be out of line but I wonder if you need to see a psychologist?'

Nothing, silence.

'You have so much to work through and sometimes an objective ear can be helpful', I could hear my voice rising, an entreaty for him to understand I was only trying to help.

'Yeah, thanks Nell. I'll see how I go', and he hung up.

Shit, I stuffed that. Now he would stop talking to me as well and Cleo would bear the full brunt. I should have discussed the best way to broach it with Cleo or even Rob but as usual I barged in with two left feet.

Chapter 9

The afternoon was sunny and I took the long route through the park, enjoying the ducks and geese from a distance so that Lucca did not try to chase them. He was generally an obedient dog but the smell of water birds was deep in his DNA and he was unable to control himself. The afternoon light should have been transfixing, it lent a soft golden-pink glow to everything, but I was still dealing with my conversation with Marco from earlier in the day. I regretted the hasty follow up phone call. It had been clumsy and patronizing. A texted apology might not be ideal but it was unlikely he would want to speak with me at the moment.

There was a bench in a sunny spot, near the rose garden and I perched on its edge to read the message I had missed from earlier before thinking about what I would write to Marco. Probably Rob, I thought as I fumbled in the tote bag I always carried with Lucca and my heart sank seeing, instead, that it was from Cleo: *Hi Nell, thanks so much for chatting with Marco today. He seems motivated for the first time in ages. Even agreed to see a counsellor. You're a magician. Xx*

I read the message again. I must have misunderstood, missed the irony. But no, she sounded genuinely pleased. Well that was a miracle of good luck, I thought and relief flooded my shoulders which had been clenched around my neck for hours. The headache that had ensued would take longer to resolve but the brisk walk home helped as did my lighter mood.

Hopefully Rob would not be too late tonight. We both deserved something special for dinner and the steak I had bought earlier would be perfect. In the meantime, I needed to bake that sponge I had promised Stephen for tomorrow. It was an old recipe from my grandmother's *Coronation Cookery Book* which had been produced by the Country Women's Association in the early fifties—a ginger fluff sponge that I had been making since I was eight years old. The old rotary egg-beater had seen better days but I still preferred it to its electric cousin for this task, beating until my arm could bear no more and the eggs were perfect peaks. I always thought of Mum as I folded in the flour, using her special method to prevent the mix from collapsing. A workout and a meditation to produce an airy confection that my mother and hers would have been proud of.

My face was flushed from the oven and my apron covered in flour when I heard Rob arriving home. I smiled, pleased he was on time.

'Hi sweetheart. Good day?', I asked, walking from the kitchen to find him at the front door.

'Alright, what about you? You had the day off, right?' he sounded tense, it must have been a tough one.

'I had coffee with Marco this morning and then ...'.

Rob's voice was sharp, 'Paige told me. She said it's the second time she has seen the two of you together lately, that both times you have been so caught up in each other that you haven't noticed her'.

'Yes, we met last week as well. I was planning to tell you all about it this evening'. Why did I feel defensive. I was being a friend, nothing more.

Rob appeared not to have heard me because he went on, 'And the weekend at the beach, you and he ...', his face was twisted like he had a stubborn cramp.

'Rob!', I held up my hands to stop him. 'You remember, I told you Marco was seeing a specialist? Well, I've been acting as a kind of sounding board while he and Cleo come to terms with his diagnosis'. His mouth was tight but he was listening. 'I'm sorry I couldn't say anything until now. They wanted to tell their kids first'. I hesitated, half expecting a response but he waited in silence.

'Marco has been diagnosed with Myasthenia Gravis. I don't know how much you know about it ...', my upward inflection invited an answer, still nothing. 'It's a disease of the muscles, causing weakness, fatigue, problems with vision, a whole range of symptoms that have to be managed over the long term'.

'Is there a cure?', he asked finally.

'No, not yet. It can be managed but the reality of having to make big lifestyle changes is beginning to hit both Marco and Cleo'.

'I'm going up for a shower. You can tell me the rest in a minute', and he was gone.

What sort of reaction was that? An apology for jumping to conclusions was the least I expected. I could feel heat build as I let the unfairness fuel the self-righteous anger I was entitled to feel. It was still simmering when Rob reappeared half an hour later and I was tempted to comment on the longer than usual shower but refrained, not wanting to escalate the bad feeling.

'How long have you known what's wrong with Marco?' Rob asked, in a skeptical tone.

'A week or so. They told their kids a few days ago but they are both pretty shell-shocked'.

'He was okay when we were away for the weekend. All seems very sudden'.

'He has had symptoms for a while. I told you—the clumsiness, blurred vision, lethargy. Lately it has been worse. They were worried it was motor neuron disease so this is a lot better than they feared'. Why was I feeling like I had to defend the truth of the diagnosis.

'Hmph. Well hope he's alright. He's not the sort of bloke who'll take kindly to having a long term condition'.

'Exactly, it's going to be tough and I hope we can be good friends, be there for them'. Rob didn't reply and so I went on, 'Why didn't Paige call me and besides I spoke with her this morning?'.

'She was worried. She didn't want me to be hurt'.

'Hardly helpful though', the words were out too quickly.

'It's not usual for you and Marco to be meeting up for coffee all the time. She had my best interests at heart', he stood up for his daughter and I knew better than to say more but the chill pervaded the rest of the evening and I immersed myself in a novel as soon as dinner was over.

We had agreed to leave for Wollongong first thing Saturday morning and it would have been easy to blame the early hour for our monosyllabic exchanges. Ultimately, it was Rob who was the mature one. 'Look, Nell. I shouldn't have assumed you and Marco were... you know. But you have to admit you are moody all the time lately. I've been asking myself why you are so unhappy and if I'm being honest I also feel excluded from the friendship; this secret being withheld the way it was'.

I searched for a way to defuse the tension, 'Sorry I've been grumpy, it's mostly work and then having to keep this awful secret has been uncomfortable. I don't like not telling you everything'. The tiniest twinge of guilt pricked my conscious but at least we seemed to have cleared the air for now.

The ten o'clock news broadcast came on the radio as we arrived at Stephen and Melody's place. Precisely on time, that was us. I gathered some of our luggage from the back seat while Rob dawdled, listening to the news and sorting out Lucca in the back seat.

'Isn't that the partner of your colleague, Brian?', he asked.

I shook my head, 'I wasn't listening. Why what was it about?'

'Roxanne Hughes, that's her, isn't it? She and her brother have been suspended by racing stewards and there's a police investigation. Something about race fixing'.

'Oh, wow, must be the fall out from Brian's case'. I would catch up on the news later because Stephen and Melody were on their front verandah, calling hello.

The morning passed with an agreeable mix of sibling banter, walking on the beach and catching up on family gossip. Melody showed me the pictures from Trudy's dance and the glow on her face told me what a proud Mum she had been. It was the last weekend of school holidays and she had obviously spent a good part of her week preparing for our visit. It was unusual to have someone fussing over us and made a nice change although neither Rob nor I were good at just sitting and relaxing.

Trudy arrived home early afternoon from her new part-time job at a local dry cleaners. She was starving and after quick hugs we didn't see her again for a while. Rob was having a tour of the garden with Stephen, a thinly veiled excuse to debate the likely winner of Sunday's grand final games and Melody had gone to lie down with a migraine.

It was so warm in their sunroom that I had almost dozed off over my book when Trudy reappeared.

'Where is everyone?'

'In the garden. Your Mum is having a rest, another migraine, poor thing. She said they have been worse lately'.

Trudy nodded, 'She had a day off work before the end of term for like the first time ever. She's such a workaholic'.

I smiled thinking that Trudy's idea of a workaholic was pretty much anyone in full-time work. I had probably been the same at that age, so long ago, impossible to remember how that felt. 'Tell me all about the dance. Your Mum showed me the photos, you looked fabulous, so grown up'.

'Thanks, yeah it was fun. My friends all met before and we went together. Mandy's Dad is a limo driver so he took us in his stretch limo. So cool!'

'How lucky! Hope you drove around town first to enjoy the full experience'.

'Yeah, he drove us down to the beach and along the esplanade and you know all these people were looking trying to see who it was'. After a minute she carried on, 'You would have died—the DJ was insane, so loud. I danced until I had to take my boots off, I was so hot'.

'Ha-ha, lucky you didn't buy those sandals, you'd have been a cripple. Any nice boys?', I knew I was pumping for information but someone had to ask.

Trudy looked sheepish, 'No, the same boys from school. Most of them are pretty gross. My friends and I all danced together'. She inhaled slowly and then casually dropped, 'I kissed a girl at the after party'.

'Oh, and was that nice?'

'It was okay. I'm not sure how it's supposed to feel but then she told me she already has a girlfriend'.

'Oh, I'm sorry'.

'Anyway, I think I am pansexual'.

I was impressed that my voice came out so evenly, 'That's interesting. Sorry to be so hopeless but is that the same as being bisexual?' I was only peripherally aware of the profusion of terms that young people were using to describe their sexuality.

'Sort of, it means you are attracted to the person because you like them whatever their sex. I'm more interested in them being kind and funny'.

'That makes sense', I said thinking that dating in Trudy's era was likely to be a whole lot more complicated than I had known. I gathered from the turn of her shoulders that the subject was closed. I wanted to ask if she had discussed it with her parents but instead, I opted for the banal, 'So long as you are happy'.

We were both absorbed in our own thoughts, Trudy was probably reliving the evening and I was thinking back to school dances and formals. The disappointment of being asked by a boy who was nice but not the one I had the crush on. The bottle of sweet Moselle my friends and I had shared in the park on our way. Mopping up my best friend, Annie, the next day after she'd had sex for the first time and was already regretting it'.

'I bet some of the boys smuggled in some booze?' no harm in asking.

A flush crept up her neck, 'Maybe. Some of the kids are almost eighteen'.

'What about you girls? I remember sharing wine with my friends at a school dance'.

'True?' impossible to believe her old aunt had been young once. After a moment she admitted, 'Mandy did bring a small bottle of vodka and we poured it into our cans of Red Bull and drank it in the limo'.

Enough of the inquisition, 'Shall we have some afternoon tea? I made my famous sponge and I can hear your father and Rob coming back inside'.

'Yum, I love that cake. I'll help you make coffee. Dad's got a new machine that's pretty cool'.

Afternoon tea merged into evening drinks and we were all pleased to see Melody reappear looking refreshed, the fog of pain having passed.

'You missed out on ginger fluff sponge', Stephen teased her, obviously relieved to see her back to normal.

'Oh no, what you didn't leave me a piece?'.

'Not a skerrick', his smug grin would have been annoying if it were not for his boyish delight.

Melody put her arm around him. 'Hmm this tummy is certainly showing the evidence of a very fine afternoon tea.

Nothing like those old recipes, thanks for bringing it, Nell. You've given him back a moment of his childhood', she laughed.

'You could teach me to make that cake', Trudy had been in the other room on her phone but hearing her mother she came to join us.

'What a great idea, you're on', I said, chuffed to be asked to pass on something I valued from my own mother. It was heart-warming to see a glimpse of her younger self as well after the grown up chat we'd had earlier.

Melody had brushed away Stephen's offer to pour her a glass of wine and had gone instead to the kitchen to start dinner. He and I settled back to have a second glass while Rob followed Melody into the kitchen, ostensibly to help but perhaps also to give us some time alone.

'Never thought I would hear Trudy ask for a cooking lesson! Nice one, Nell'.

'She's a great girl. You must be very proud'.

'Yeah well, not sure how much that has to do with me but she is pretty spectacular. I didn't like to ask Rob but how are his girls since Marjorie died?'

'It was a hard time but they both seem to be doing okay. Caroline and her partner told us they are exploring surrogacy to have a baby. Probably with Cristiane's brother in Canada'.

'Wow, that's amazing. Will that make you a Nanna?' Stephen winked.

'Up to them really – hope so but I'll play it by ear'.

'Rob was telling me outside about that business at the hospital', he changed the subject, presumably not wanting a deep and meaningful on my relationship with the girls.

'Yeah', I drew out. 'Hasn't been the easiest time. Did he tell you that I was one of the early suspects. It was hugely stressful and then when it was over, nothing, you know. No apology, no offer of a friendly ear from my supervisor. And the poor guy who has been charged, I know he did the wrong thing but I also feel like we've let him down,' I finally took a breath.

'Was he someone you knew well?'

'We'd worked together for years. He's always been a good nurse so it was pretty shocking. He must have been under huge duress—just not like him to leave patients in pain by swapping out their painkillers'.

'Rob said you've been stressed about work lately?' he let the question hang.

'Not only work, our friend Marco has been diagnosed with a horrible neurological condition and I've been supporting Cleo as best I can. It's a lot of things', I said, not sure I had the energy for further analysis, a bitter taste displacing the wine I had gulped down.

'Seriously though, you do seem flat, not your usual self. Even this morning on the beach, I wondered if you were enjoying yourself at all, you were so quiet. I missed seeing that sunny smile you normally have when you're near the ocean'.

I didn't respond, surprised I had not noticed that lack of joy before. He was right as usual and as much as I hated to admit it. It seemed a long time since I'd truly taken delight in everyday things.

'I have been toying with the idea of a late career change', I tried out the thought that Rob had pooh poohed.

'What would you do?'

'That's the problem. I don't know and as Rob said changing direction at my age could be disastrous. No one wants a novice fifty seven year old'.

'Well universities are always looking for tutors with clinical experience'.

I rolled my eyes, 'Me? Teaching undergrads?' That would definitely underline what an old fossil I am, I thought.

'You'd be great. I've seen you with Trudy, you develop rap-port super fast'. My expression must have stopped him, 'Okay, okay, something else then?'

'Hmm. What will you and Melody do once Trudy leaves the nest? Not so far off'.

'We were talking about it only the other day actually. Went to see our financial advisor and so had us thinking about how much longer we'll have to work. Bottom line, we aren't retiring any time soon'.

'And you love your job'. I added for him.

'Yeah, I do. I hope Trudy finds something that she really enjoys although they say this generation will have five careers so plenty of chances'.

'Does she know what she wants to do?'

'Forensic pathologist or actress—not so realistic'.

'Plenty of time for that and remember Mum used to per-form radio plays in her young days, almost an actress'. At her age, there had been posters of the band *Split Enz* on my bedroom wall, my haircut was an attempt at emulating Farah Fawcett and I wanted to be a meteorologist. Not being an especially capable maths or science student the latter must have amused, possibly bewildered, my parents and teachers. I don't recall them being as relaxed about early career choices as Stephen was.

Chapter 10

Next morning, Trudy and I were in the kitchen for the promised sponge-making lesson. I had relented and let her use an
electric eggbeater but otherwise was insisting she learn all the
tips and tricks handed down to me.

'Let's see. Those egg whites look perfect. Mum always said
that you can overbeat them. Not sure if it's true'.

Trudy was sifting in the flour when she said without looking
away from the bowl, 'Aunty Nell, can I ask you something? It's
sort of personal'.

'Of course sweetheart'.

'I've been thinking of going on the pill. You know, in case I
want to...you know'.

'I see, is there anyone at the moment?' I kept my voice
gentle and didn't make eye contact, trying to reconcile this
with yesterday's revelation about the girl at the after party.

'No but my two best friends are already taking it and I'm
curious what it would be like with a boy'.

'What about the girl you told me about, from the party?', I
was becoming confused.

'Like I said, she is already with someone else and she asked
me not to tell anyone about the kiss, like she wanted to pretend it didn't happen'.

'Well', I paused for a moment. 'If I were you, I would talk
with your Mum and if she is okay with it I would ask your
family doctor what she thinks'.

Finally she looked up, her eyes beseeching, 'Could you maybe mention it to Mum for me?'

'I could but you know I think she would prefer to hear it from you', I felt as mean as those manipulative teenage eyes intended.

'You have no idea what she's like. Besides she'll say she has to ask Dad and then he'll ask if I'm having sex already and I'll have to explain about liking girls'.

'They might surprise you and anyway it's important to be honest with them. Have you told them that you think you are pansexual?', I asked, relieved that she still seemed to be inexperienced. She and her friends clearly thought about their sexuality in terms that would never have occurred to me at that stage or even now if I was being honest.

She bit her lip, 'I can't. Can you imagine the questions? It would be a nightmare. Please can't you just mention the pill to Mum?'

'Okay, I will say something but then you have to talk with them yourself. It is a very grown up step to start on the pill', I stopped myself from adding the obvious corollary and hoped Melody wouldn't think I was overstepping the mark.

Trudy was quiet for a moment, 'No, it's okay you're right I will talk to Mum', she shifted her weight from one foot to the other before blurting 'Aunty Nell, what was your first time like?'

I took a minute to respond, long enough that Trudy started to say that she shouldn't have asked. 'No, it's okay. My first time was with a boy that I met at a party and I was almost twenty, lots older than you, and unfortunately it wasn't great. The best times have been when I am really relaxed with some- one. You know I like them and trust them, that's when sex is great'.

Trudy was quiet again and I wondered if there were more questions or confidences to be shared but her next question was about how to make the butter cream icing for the sponge so it seemed the topic was closed for now.

The drive home took longer than usual, thanks to both the Sunday traffic and the dull throb in my temple. Head back and mouth agape, Rob wouldn't wake until home. Seeing Stephen and the family had done me good, their calm certainty a reminder of what normal felt like. I smiled at the memory of Trudy, covered in flour, licking the cake bowl minutes after she'd told me she wanted to start taking contraception. Sixteen—wonderfully paradoxical.

All those years ago I had been finishing fourth form as we had called it, socially awkward, not as mature as some the girls with serious boyfriends and job plans. Mum and I were always clashing and Stephen simply revolted me. He picked and rubbed at all the most inappropriate parts of his anatomy, drenched the entire bathroom even when he only brushed his teeth, and the unholy stench that came from his room was worse than a Mumbai slum. Dad and Nanna were two of the few people to escape my arrogant ire. What a pain I must have been, I chuckled quietly seeing the young Nell, yelling at Mum, saying that she had no idea how embarrassing it was being her daughter. Who knows what she had done to deserve such outrage? The buried memory of dismissively rejecting a summer dress she had bought me made me grimace.

Nanna had been an interesting woman, tough and unrelentingly loyal to her brood of four girls. Pa had come back from the war a different person, or that's what Mum said. I only remember him sitting in their dark lounge room, curtains drawn, chain smoking during the day, drinking whisky at night. He died when I was seven or eight. Nanna's parents had a big sheep property on the western plains and she was sent to boarding school in Sydney from the time she was twelve. It was through those connections, the brother of her best friend, that she had met Pa. A year or so before the war they moved to a country town, back in the days when every town had a thriving newspaper. Pa was going to run the local newspaper, Nanna would care for the family: two kids under five and pregnant with the third.

Pa came from a newspaper family and the plan was that he would cut his teeth on a country rag and after a time move back to Sydney to help run the small suburban mastheads they owned but war intervened. He joined up as a military journalist early on, something Nanna was angry about all her life. He would have been exempted based on age and family responsibilities but he had insisted on going, seduced by the glamour of reporting on something important. No family support, no forethought, left alone with small children, she had had to quickly rustle up home help and find two young women who could write a bit to help with the paper.

When I was growing up, I loved her stories of how she had 'done a man's job', while helping out at the local hospital and bringing up three and eventually four girls. Jill was a late-in-life baby born after Pa's return. Mum must have been almost five then and she talked about printing ink on her hands and clothes and the trouble she would get into almost every night at bath time. Her voice had had a fond warmth whenever she recalled the smell of the printing press, the rush to have the daily edition ready, the sound of the paper boys early in the morning coming to collect their parcels for delivery.

Nanna was a staunch Catholic and she was the one who insisted that Stephen and I should be sent to Catholic schools. The nuns could be pretty severe and I used to try to imagine what their life must be like. The idea of living in a house full of women was my worst nightmare, especially as they told us they had taken a vow of poverty. I used to pray every night that I wouldn't have a vocation for the convent which apparently was an irresistible force if you had it. The irony of that prayer never dawned on me. My life was so different, hard to draw a line from Nanna to me. And Trudy would live in yet another world, possibly more like that of Nanna if the way politics and climate change were going was any indication. It wasn't only the encroaching dusk that was casting darkness, my mood was sinking as well as we approached home.

I needed to take myself in hand, this moodiness was not helping anyone. Rob snorted, waking himself, 'Almost home?' he yawned.

'Ten minutes. You had a good sleep'.

'Hmm hope I don't pay for it tonight. The sun through the window and wine for lunch, bad combination'.

'Your phone beeped a while back', I said.

He dug into his pocket and twisted uncomfortably to reach it. 'Paige, she wants to pop in tomorrow. That's alright, isn't it?'

My smile was only slightly strained, 'Of course, ask her to stay for dinner'.

She replied a few minutes later, 'Says she'll come for a drink, not dinner. Probably has other plans'.

When we arrived home a few minutes later, Rob immediately headed upstairs to unpack and start the washing. Normally I would have been right behind him, ensuring everything was back in order after a weekend away but tonight there was something I needed to do first.

All weekend I had been going back and forth on whether I should contact Brian. I closed the kitchen door and dialed his number, still not sure if my sense of injustice was badly misplaced.

'Brian. Hi, it's Nell, from work'. There was silence 'I just wanted to see how you are doing', I stopped not sure of how to go on.

'Nell, this is a surprise', his voice was cautious.

'I know it's a bit out of the blue but I've been concerned about you'. He didn't answer immediately and I stumbled on, 'I heard the news about your partner on the news and to be honest I've been feeling guilty that you weren't better supported by the hospital or me. I was supposed to be your manager...'

'Nell', his words were slow and deliberate, 'I did something wrong. I may have been under pressure but I made my choices. Don't waste your worry on me'.

'They say at work that your case will go to court soon. I was thinking if you needed a character witness or something I could help'.

'That's very kind. I'll tell my lawyer but I doubt he will take you up on it. They would start asking you questions about what a good nurse would do and I'll look even more loathsome'.

'Ah, yes I see, well if there is anything', I was regretting this call.

'Thanks for calling Nell. I appreciate the thought', he hung up abruptly.

Shit. How stupid could I be? And how self-centred? I seemed to have lost all perspective, not to mention common sense. A nerve in my eye started to twitch and nausea welled up. I was still sitting at the kitchen table when Rob came down with a basket of washing to hang.

'Everything all right. You look positively green'.

'I just did something really stupid, I called Brian'.

'Brian from work?', he sounded incredulous.

'I know, don't lecture me. It was irresponsible and unkind. Only thinking of myself. I feel so bad'.

'Don't know about unkind but not a good idea. I'd have thought after the last time you called him ...', he didn't finish and his mouth twisted into something between reassurance and distaste. 'Well it's done now, nothing to be gained by brooding on it. Go and have a shower and clear your head'.

Rob's solution for all anguish was a stream of hot water and as I stood letting the shower cascade over me, I could see but little merit in that belief. I was more relaxed but nagging thoughts were not far away.

Chapter 11

Monday I called in to work to say I was sick. A mental health day, I reasoned. I had intended to spend the day reading, walking Lucca, gardening—things that brought me back to myself —so that by early evening I would be ready for company. Instead, I sat down at the computer, still in my pyjamas, and started to write.

The presenter at a leadership course I'd done years before had recommended reflection and writing as a way to manage one's state of mind, to stay positive and engaged with the job. Three thousand words later I saved the file as *The Burnt Out Nurse*, surprised that the morning and most of the afternoon had passed before tight shoulder muscles forced me to stand and stretch.

The flow of words had been more effective at expunging bad thoughts than the shower of the previous evening although, in that moment, if you had asked me what I had written I would have had trouble recalling much. When I looked back over it a few days later I would delete large swathes of text but for now it was done and I really needed to shower and dress before Paige arrived.

It was not like her to visit early in the week, she usually had too much work on, but it had been a while since we had seen her and surely, she wanted to apologise for jumping to conclusions about Marco and me. I was ready to be magnanimous. As

Rob said she had only had his welfare at heart or so I had to trust if we were going to have a better relationship.

As promised, Rob was home early. 'How was your day? Feeling better?', he asked. He had offered to stay home with me that morning, worried because neither of us ever took a day off work. 'You are looking more like your old self', there was relief in his voice and something else, a soft generosity. It felt like absolution.

'Much better, thanks for your text earlier. I only found it now, my phone was on silent'.

'Let me make you a pot of tea', Rob had his back to me already filling the kettle. 'Paige is on her way so she can join us'. Tea and sympathy I thought, Rob's kindness more eloquent than the words I had been waiting on.

' Sounds good', I was fiddling with my phone. 'Just setting the alarm for tomorrow. Pippa's plane gets in just after six so if I leave here at quarter to, I should be there in time to meet her'.

'Early start for you, I had forgotten it was tomorrow'.

'Hmm, I'll drop her at her hotel and head to work. Kate knows I could be slightly late and she isn't worried. That sounds like Paige now'.

Paige's broad smile replaced the normal jerked words of greeting and self-conscious hug I had learnt to expect of her. I had never seen her looking so relaxed, almost blissful. She must be in love was my immediate thought.

'Paige honey how are you' Rob was delighted to see her looking happier than either of us could remember.

'Good Dad, crazy day but I'm here now' she exhaled audibly. 'Ah, tea, I could die for a cup'

' You and Nell sit down and I'll pour. Is there cake?' he asked and I smiled quietly at the predictability of his question. Good that somethings never changed.

' Should be some banana bread left', I said as I hugged Paige.

Once Rob had stopped fussing about tea and cake, Paige put her cup down and made deliberate eye contact with Rob, ' I have some news' she began.

I was right, she must have a new boyfriend or maybe a promotion.

' Good news', I never thought I would hear Paige enthuse but there was no other word for it.

' I'm pregnant, almost ten weeks. She is due in April'.

'Oh Paige that's fantastic news', Rob was holding her in a bear hug. I was catatonic.

My brain had stalled, desperately trying to recalibrate. That Wednesday. I'd been so worried for her; she'd seemed to appreciate the support. It had all been a lie.

I tried to force a smile but worried it was closer to a sneer , 'Congratulations that's wonderful news'.

Paige looked at me fully for the first time that evening with what could have been either a request or a demand in her gaze, ' Yes, I know it's a shock but I'm so happy. I had started to wonder if I would ever have children'.

' Maybe I shouldn't ask this, but is the father involved' I was trying to provoke her and Rob's cringe told me I should stop, now.

' We aren't together and no he won't be involved. I will tell him about the baby but he won't have a role in her life'.

'That's a big call', I couldn't stop myself. The ache in my heart demanded I hurt her as well.

' Nell!' Rob looked mortified but Paige was unperturbed, 'Yes and it is my call'.

'You said she—it's a girl then?', Rob was quick to move back to more positive subjects.

'Too early to know but I've been saying "her". Better than "it" which is what the obstetrician says'.

'Ten weeks you say, so you are due when?', Rob was counting off months on his fingers.

'Early April. The doctor says she can make a better estimate after the next ultrasound. It's a couple of weeks away and I was hoping you two would come with me'.

I wasn't listening anymore, my mind back at the Wednesday morning three weeks earlier. My eyes couldn't focus on the kitchen or Rob and Paige; all I could see was the carpark of the clinic as we had driven up in the rain. The sound of the water squelching under the tyres drowned out their voices.

'Nell!', Rob was trying to get my attention, his clenched jaw and intense gaze evidence of the annoyance he was feeling.

'It's all right Dad', Paige interrupted, 'There's a good reason Nell is confused', her voice had lost some of its glow.

The kitchen was silent, even the appliances seemed to lean forward, impatient. She stood up and walked to the far window, her face half turned away from us before she began to speak. Slowly at first and then with increasing insistence she told of how she had started an affair with a senior work colleague soon after Marjorie's death. It hadn't gone on for long. He was married and considered a 'player' by most of the women in the firm; she had needed to let off steam.

'I was only about six weeks along when I realised I was pregnant and my immediate decision was that I would terminate the pregnancy', she winced as she saw the pain in the tight squeeze of Rob's eyes. 'I just couldn't imagine myself, with my career, looking after a baby. I asked Nell to come with me to the clinic as my support person—I swore her to secrecy', she pre-empted the next question we both expected from Rob. 'As far as Nell knew I had the termination but once I was in the clinic I started having second thoughts. The nurses sent me home to think about it some more and made another appointment with a councillor for me. In the end I decided to have the baby. My reasons for not having her were all about fear and when I heard Caro talk excitedly about surrogacy and IVF I felt ashamed of my need for certainty'.

The silence returned but now compassion floated gently beside it. Rob hugged his daughter, tears in his eyes whether of sympathy or pride I couldn't be sure. I was holding my head in my hands trying to digest all that I'd heard when Paige turned to face me fully, 'Nell, I don't know if you remember but you asked me if I would consider adoption, possibly even to Caro and Cristiane. It's weird but that question gave me the perspective I'd lacked until then, let me flip out of the vortex of panic I had created'.

I nodded my understanding, not trusting my voice, knowing I was the least likely person to be able to accomplish what she was crediting me with. Rob was asking her about what would happen with work, if she had any names picked out, when we could tell family and friends. The laughter had returned to Paige's voice as she joked about whether Beryl or Mildred would be preferable names if it was a girl.

I patted Lucca absently, paying enough attention to respond to direct questions but not enough to contribute to the repartee. I knew Rob had noticed my disconnection but he let me be. Paige was showing him an app for the list of foods she needed to avoid in pregnancy, presumably as future reference for family dinners. He was asking her to send a diary invite for the ultrasound so he could schedule time off work.

The faint ticking sound of the kitchen clock echoed in my head, counting down until Paige would leave. I must have sighed loudly because both Rob and Paige looked up at me sharply.

'Are you okay?', Rob frowned. 'Nell hasn't been well today', he explained to his daughter. More fussing, promises to see each other in a couple of days, kisses and congratulation, then Paige was walking to her car with Rob.

That evening Rob was particularly solicitous, making dinner while I pretended to read in the front room. I was truly happy for Paige and yet I knew I needed to work through my reactions and talk honestly with Rob. For years I had promised myself I would eventually tell him the one story that I had never shared with anyone. Draining the glass of red wine he had placed next to me I decided that it should be tonight.

'Rob, can you come in here a minute? There's something I need to tell you'.

Rob appeared in the doorway, aproned, holding a tea towel, 'Two minutes, just need to turn off the oven'.

When he returned I positioned myself opposite so that I could watch his face. 'Paige's news tonight is amazing, just wonderful, but it's set off something for me', my voice was thin. Rob's eyes widened and he leant forward but he did not say anything.

'Taking Paige to the clinic was pretty difficult and then finding out tonight she changed her mind has raised all these emotions—stuff I buried a long time ago'.

I could see myself, a scared nineteen year old who made a hard decision, the right one but not one without repercussions. I heard a famous humanitarian say once, *'I have not made sacrifices, I have made choices and with all choices there are consequences'*. I had only been half aware of those consequences at the time.

It was necessary to tell the whole story, from the beginning although I doubted I would be truly able to describe my state of mind. Slowly I started to tell Rob about that time.

I started at the beginning, a B&S at my friend's Susie's property near Narrabri. We all dressed up, there was a band and a lot of alcohol. Susie was a friend from nursing, two years older than me and very worldly. A group of us had driven the six hours north for a weekend of celebrations. I remember it was the beginning of summer and already warm as we drove with no air conditioning, the windows down and music blaring. We all had a bit to drink at the party, some of the guys were entirely out of it by ten o'clock but we were staying the night so no need to worry about driving. And to be honest, back then we may not have worried too much anyway. About two or three in the morning I went to find a swag from the pile in the rumpus room. A lot of people were sleeping outside, mostly on their utes but I'd scored a spot on the floor inside.

Neil was one of Susie's friends and I hadn't met him before. We had talked during the evening, had a dance, nothing much. I was almost asleep when I felt someone burrowing into my back and Neil's voice telling me I was beautiful. I was embarrassingly a virgin and there was no way my first time was going to be in a room full of people. He kept persisting, I kept resisting and eventually he passed out, having had more than his fair share of beer.

The next day Neil and his mate offered to give me a lift home which Cleo and Pippa ribbed me about. Susie did say quietly, 'Are you sure?' but telling myself, 'You only live once', I had agreed. We arrived at my flat late Sunday night, all tired and happy to be home. He said he would call in a few days but the moment must have passed, I didn't hear from him and after a month I stopped expecting to. Then late one night I was dressed for bed, watching a mindless television mystery when there was a knock at the door. Cleo and Pippa were both on night shift and not expected home, besides they should have their key. I looked through the peephole taking care to walk quietly as I assumed it was the neighbours upstairs who were always complaining about how much noise we made. Walking too loudly, emptying the dishwasher or (for heaven's sake) flushing the toilet and showering when we arrived home after a double shift in the early hours of the morning were endless causes of vexation for them.

A jolt of anticipation shot through with embarrassment, he had come after all. He waved cheekily at the peephole, somehow knowing I was there. I wished I was still wearing my jeans and jumper, wished I could pretend not to be home and I opened the door anyway.

'Neil, this is a surprise' I said, taking a step back as a waft of alcohol followed him into the room. I had forgotten how tall and lanky he was and his red curly hair was longer than when I'd seen him weeks before. We made small talk; he teased me about the quilted dressing gown I had pulled over my pyjamas when I'd heard the door. His kisses distracted from that humiliation only to lead to greater ones.

That night should have been the end of it but I was deluded enough to think that if we kept seeing each other things would get better. At the beginning there were regular dates, the movies, picnics, all the normal stuff, but after a few months those petered out to be replaced by last minute invitations to visit his flat. I was embarrassed by my lack of experience, yet I also knew intuitively that my friends wouldn't like him very much. He was more sophisticated and sure of himself, his family wealthy landowners and business people, completely different to anyone I knew. I didn't know many of his friends although I did meet his family—a Sunday barbeque at their place on the leafy north shore. His parents were kind but his sister clearly thought I was the most boring person she had ever met. After that he often made snide comments that signalled what I assumed was his embarrassment at my goucheness. There were lies as well and angry swearing whenever I pressed him about seeing each other in a more normal way.

I had been so desperate to have a boyfriend that I overlooked his bad behaviour for months but finally I admitted to myself that I was being used and that the relationship was one of convenience at best. I longed for something more meaningful and that meant I had to like and respect him but with his flimsy moral compass I knew that would never happen.

I had a holiday to Melbourne coming up, my first flight, my first time travelling alone and that seemed like the perfect time to break it off. It was going to be my first big travel adventure, instead, after only two days, I started to suspect I was pregnant and a test from the chemist confirmed the bad news. I knew I couldn't have the baby, I was too young, I had no money, my parents were dead and I would struggle to finish my nursing training. For almost two days I stayed in my city hotel room, sick to the stomach, in a fever of panic as I tried to decide what to do.

I can see that hotel room with its grey walls, olive chenille bedspread, yellowed blinds. I had told myself that I just needed somewhere to sleep when I was booking a budget hotel and now I was suffocating. Finally, I asked reception for a telephone book, intending to look up 'Abortion Clinic'. There was no entry so I tried 'Termination' but all I found was termite services. At last I had luck with 'Family Planning'.

I wrote down the address, looked up a street directory and walked the five kilometres to one called Women's Care Clinic. I talked to a counsellor, had some tests and they made an appointment for me two days later. I walked for hours over the next day and a half, not arriving at the hotel until well after dark in the hope I would fall asleep immediately. On the morning of the appointment I checked out of the budget hotel and moved to better one I had seen near the clinic. It would max out my credit card but the counsellor had said I shouldn't travel for a few days and the thought of one more night in that grey box was more than I could bear.

I don't remember much about being at the clinic—other frightened faces, soothing words, changing into a hospital gown, waking up with someone asking me how I felt. I had been on the other side of surgical procedures but that did not prepare me for how I would feel. The next day I lay on the crisp white sheets of my new hotel bed feeling exhausted but otherwise remarkably normal. I had expected writhing cramping pain, maybe hoped for it, but even the bleeding was not especially bad. That night I sat at a table for one in the hotel dining room, telling myself I was doing well, that I was dealing with this.

Back in Sydney, I moved on quickly, determined not to be defined by the relationship with Neil and the abortion. I even remember laughing to myself that I had made a lucky escape, Neil and Nell could never have been a couple. I threw myself into my work, excelled in the exams that followed soon after but some of my carefree youth had gone forever and that made me sad.

Rob had listened quietly while I was reliving those days in Melbourne but now he asked, 'How do you feel about that decision now?'

'It was the right decision. I was not ready to be a mother and I did not want to have a baby with Neil. But ...'I hesitated. 'I do regret that I did not have another chance at motherhood and,' this part was harder to say. 'Sometimes I see her face in my dreams. Of course I never knew if it would have been a boy or a girl but in my dreams she is always a sad-faced girl with tight blonde curls and green eyes'.

Rob sat watching me. Was he collecting his thoughts or feeling repulsed? 'I had no idea, no wonder you were strange about Paige's change of heart. Why haven't you told me before?' he sounded wounded.

'I could say shame but that wouldn't be true. The truth is I buried those days so that I would not have to keep reliving them, so that I could stop myself from second-guessing. I knew my decision was for the best but I was afraid to give my doubts oxygen'.

Rob nodded and reached for my hand, 'You were brave to deal with all of that by yourself. Do you wish we had tried for a baby? I never asked you when we were first married', his voice was calm but his eyes were searching my face.

'Not really. I was already over forty and you had the girls. That was enough'.

Rob did not say a lot more but he held me tightly all night as if trying to right the loneliness of earlier times.

Chapter 12

After dropping Pippa off at her hotel, I quickly called Cleo to confirm our arrangements for next week. Marco answered her phone, 'Hi, Cleo is driving', he said.

'How are you? I was calling to let her know about our booking next week but I can message.

'Yeah, that's best. I'm pretty good; the medication is making a big difference and I'm not as tired'.

'That's good to hear. You definitely sound better in yourself'.

'The psychologist has given me some tips that help and I am reading this book about staying in the moment. The two things that keep coming up are about being grateful for the small things and assuming that other people are generally well-intentioned. Sounds obvious I suppose but I feel a lot more positive'.

More of a deep and meaningful than I had anticipated when I dialed Cleo's number but good to know Marco was in a better place. I really needed to be at work and reluctantly cut the call shorter than he would have liked. Just one more day, I told myself as I walked into the Emergency which was already full of patients, one of them loudly asking when he was going to see a doctor and another pacing while in conversation with an invisible friend.

The day dragged and watching the clock every ten minutes didn't help. My last patient was an elderly woman, confused, transferred from the nursing home with a suspected infection.

She was calling out loudly and thrashing about, apparently re-living some sort of nightmare. My soothing words were not calming her and when I tried to put a drip in her arm, she slapped my face. I knew she had no idea what she was doing but the adrenaline still kicked in and I felt a rush of blood to my cheek which was still stinging. She had landed a solid hit. It was a relief at four o'clock to finish handover and know I could forget about it all for the next week. Kate stopped me as I was collecting my bag to leave, 'Did you give anymore thought to that conversation about you mentoring one of the younger nurses?' I had forgotten all about it.

'To be honest Kate now is not the best time for me to take that on'. How did I explain that my negativity was infectious, that I was tired all the time, that I was more annoyed by needy patients than compassionate these days? Nursing was a wonderful career but I had lost the job satisfaction I used to feel.

'Oh, sorry to hear that. I think you'd be terrific but maybe in a few months time when we do the next round', I nodded without any intention of changing my mind.

As I drove home, I thought about Marco's words from the morning. There was so much to be grateful for and I owed Rob a big thank you for the steadfast way he had dealt with my dramas, not to mention his forgiveness for the secrets I had kept from him. I used to be more fun, I needed to reclaim the playfulness that had eluded me lately. And the other thing Marco had said—most people are well-intentioned. I had lost sight of that especially when it came to Paige. I seemed to assume the worst which made no sense after the conversation we'd had before the incident about Marco. She was clearly trying to build our relationship and the least I could do was to meet her half way rather than imagining sabotage everywhere. No one was waking up in the morning wondering how they could spoil my day. It was only the chip on my own shoulder doing that. I knew there were remnants of the hurt from when

Mum shut Stephen and me out of her grief that I had never faced up to. I didn't have the courage to follow through on that just then but I knew I had to come back to it sometime.

Tomorrow I would do the shopping and other preparations for our few days away but tonight I planned some 'me' time. Rob had a Board meeting and dinner, so a mushroom omelet in front of the television, a long hot bath and reading were on the agenda. Yet, like on Monday, having planned total relaxation I found myself in front of the computer, albeit with a glass of wine this time. Two hours later I read through the piece I had started then:

> *There aren't many jobs where you really find out what you are made of and nursing is a career that stretches you to your limits. For years it has grown my confidence and self-esteem but lately it has been tough. Being a nurse is an important part of my identity and that is a problem.*
>
> *When I first started in Emergency I enjoyed the daunting days and the feeling of having nothing left after a job well done. Now I always feel tired and I find myself zoning out. Recently I ignored a request from one of the specialists because although I heard it I did not register the information. Instead, I prioritised a task that kept me busy although it wasn't urgent. It was like I heard him talking but failed to understand what he was saying.*
>
> *Work is definitely busier than it used to be; like everywhere else we are short staffed and there isn't the same camaraderie with agency staff. I can't remember the last time our team went out for a drink or a meal. Plus the amount*

of data we are expected to record has quadru-
pled. I spend less and less time with patients
—it not only means the job is less satisfying but
it can lead to short cuts that put people at risk.

At home there is a simmering anger, a
resentment that has nothing to do with my
partner or family but that I take out on them.
When you are a nurse everyone tells you their
stories—family, friends, strangers at the pub.
And it's not just medical stories, its relation-
ships, life events, the lot. Normally, I am the
first person to provide a listening ear but it's
another drain now.

This week our daughter came home with
some wonderful news, she is pregnant. Instead
of joy, I felt anxiety some of which relates to
my own past. But it wasn't only that. How will
I cope with being a grandmother when every-
thing else is getting on top of me? It will be one
more thing I'm expected to be good at, some-
thing I have no experience of and I fear letting
everyone down.

It was a rough draft, a list of the stuff I was mulling over
but perhaps I could turn it into the start of a blog, something
that other nurses would relate to and want to contribute their
stories to. I could even interview some people. I was certain
there would be plenty of material, war stories that we tended
not to share. Worth thinking about sometime I thought, relieved and more energized after putting the words on paper. I
hoped it would help me get out of my own head because 'here,
there be dragons'. I could almost laugh at myself again.

I quickly made dinner, keen to put at least two things
right. Reflection was all very well but... willing positive energy

I tapped in Paige's number. She answered on the first ring, hopefully I hadn't woken her.

'Hi Nell, is everything okay?', she sounded more worried than surprised.

'Everything is great, sorry it's a bit late. I didn't mean to worry you. More importantly how are you? No morning sickness or anything?'

'No I've been lucky that way thank goodness. A bit tired but nothing too bad'.

'When you told us the news yesterday, I was pretty shocked and I wanted to tell you how happy I am for you. It's the most wonderful news, you'll make a great Mum and you know your dad and I will do anything we can to help'.

'Thanks Nell, that means a lot and I should have been honest that day at the clinic after I changed my mind. It's just I wasn't completely sure I wouldn't change it back'.

'I understand but...', my nails dug into my palm, 'there is something else. You see when I was in my late teens, I was pregnant and I decided not to have the baby. It was the right thing to do at the time but you can see how your news stirred up some old emotions'.

'Oh Nell, I'm so sorry', Paige gave a quiet gasp and then paused as though trying to catch her breath. I had been too blunt, almost harsh, rushing the words out before I could second guess myself.

'It's okay, it was a long time ago. I'm telling you because you said the other day you feel that you hardly know me. And you were right, I have kept a lot of myself from you and Caroline. I'd like to try to change that', I stopped wondering if I had misjudged this and should have started with more banal insights.

'Me too', there was a gentleness in Paige's voice. 'And Nell, I'm sorry about that business with Marco. I had no right to tell Dad without talking to you first. I wish I could blame baby-brain but part of me wanted to hurt you ...', her voice trailed off as though uncertain of what to say next.

I was equally at a loss—an uncomfortable silence, a choke in my throat. Finally, I managed, 'Wow that was not what I expected you to say'.

Paige interrupted me, 'Can we start fresh, do you think?'

I must have said yes because we rang off soon after. Almost immediately I received a text message: *Thank you for trusting me xo*

Still feeling disorientated, I set about my second mission, a treat for Rob. I booked tickets for the rugby test next weekend, followed by dinner at a steak restaurant nearby. As I was confirming my credit card details I had a moment of inspiration. I would suggest that he take Paige, as he had when the girls were young. Marjorie had never been a fan and Paige had become his regular rugby companion until I had started going with him instead. It was a small step towards repairing the bridges we had been so careless of.

Lying back on the couch with Lucca's head in my lap, I slowly stroked his head. Paige and her dad were so close, I really needed to make our relationship work this time. My mind wandered back to memories of my own father. He'd been my favourite person in the world and then one night he was gone—a car accident when he was driving home late, a truck had crossed to his side of the road. They said it would have been instantaneous, like that made it alright.

I had been seventeen, Stephen fourteen, neither of us were prepared to lose him. Even less prepared to lose Mum but she faded after the accident, closed like a sunflower without the sun. After she died we found half empty bottles of Librium in her drawers and handbag as well as an unhealthy supply of vodka. We learnt from her doctor that she'd started taking tranquilisers when Dad died to help her sleep but that over time she had relied on them to get through the day. That must have been when I took over the cooking for the family and Stephen became chief gardener. We used to talk about our memories of Dad, usually when Mum was out—the time he took us to the zoo, his terrible swimming technique, the belly laugh that made you giggle too, the time he made pasta and didn't drain off the water before adding the sauce, his enormous hugs.

Two years later, Mum finally disappeared completely. A recurrence of breast cancer that she thought she had beaten thirteen years before. Those few days before she died, we sat by her bed as she drifted in and out of consciousness, telling each other stories. We laughed about the time we had gone on a family picnic to the local swimming pool with all our cousins. Jenny who was only three had fallen in the deep end and Mum had jumped in clothes and all to save her. Dad knew Mum couldn't swim well so he jumped in after her to save both of them amidst much shouting and spluttering. Then there was the time we were driving home along a country road late at night, all tired after a long day with friends when a horse came galloping down the road, right in front of our car. That was the same day I had been car sick after having a Passiona spider for lunch. Stephen confided that when he was nine he had confessed to the priest that he had committed adultery. Intrigued the old priest had said that wasn't likely but what had he done and Stephen explained that he had been touching himself. We both laughed at that childish innocence and ability to misunderstand the adult world.

Mum had been vibrant, when we were young, always in reds and yellows. She smelt of lemons and her broad Australian accent became even stronger when she was excited. We recalled those times rather than the staid, beige years after Dad died.

Stephen went to live with our aunt for a couple of years until he started university. I was already living in a terrace house with Cleo and Pippa. Thank goodness for their support

—only later did I realise how stressed I was during that time. Grief and anxiety vied for dominance and it would have been a lonely time without their compassion. Stephen's response to losing our parents was to make creating his own family a priority and I adopted them as my surrogate family for a long time, especially as first Pippa and then Cleo married.

Funny, I had never thought about it before—my world had been rocked and in came Neil with his sophistication and the promise of first love. No wonder I had wanted to believe in our relationship in spite of all the evidence. I had lost touch with Susie soon after the infamous B&S ball and had not heard from Neil since we broke up. On an impulse, I typed his name into a search engine.

Neil Hollows. Former CEO of the RiverTide Insurance Company, Board Director of several arts organisations, an honorary doctorate from a regional university.

He had done well for himself, scrolling down I saw he even had his own Wikipedia page. Third wife was a former model and they had four kids; two older boys with previous partners; lived on the south coast; part-owner of a winery. His email was provided on a social media site. Did I dare?

> -----Original Message-----
> *From: Nell Saunders*
> *To: Neil Hollows*
> *Subject: Memories of 1981*
> > *Dear Neil,*
> > *I wonder if you remember me. We went out briefly so many years ago it feels like it happened to different people or it would do if was not still carrying baggage from back then. For a long time, I felt ashamed about our relationship and how badly you treated me but at the same time I wanted to believe you liked me. Now I realise that*

both my shame and expectations were misplaced, the former at least belonging entirely to you. No need to panic, I don't plan to tell your children or your current wife, I won't talk to a friendly journalist, won't make accusations on social media or anywhere else. I am doing this for me and if you feel remorse so much the better. There is one thing I should tell you. After we broke up I found out that I was pregnant but I did not go through with it. Perhaps you deserved to know but truly, I don't believe you deserved anything.

Nell

Save as Draft.

Chapter 13

Our reunions were uncommon these days and Cleo had suggested a health spa about two hours from Sydney, in spite of originally saying that I should choose. She was taking Pippa in her car but on Saturday morning, while I was doing some shopping to ensure Rob would have everything, I had decided to take the train.

I read the paragraph about a dystopian city a third time, telling myself I should persevere with the story that had failed to grip me so far. It was easy to be distracted by the charred eucalypts and snatches of ocean that we sped towards each time the train emerged from a tunnel. Equally fascinating to watch the young couple opposite who were discussing what they were going to tell the girl's mother. Their heads close together, occasionally the girl's voice rose in anger but the man said little. His eyes were sad, reproachful, like Lucca's when he knows we are going out without him. They left the train in Mittagong to be replaced with an older man who was halfway through a salami sandwich that had been carefully wrapped in waxed paper before he left home. I went back to my book, hoping the descriptions of overheated pavements and burnt flesh would take my mind off the pungent smell opposite.

Cleo and Pippa must have thought it odd when I said I would take the train but neither of them pressed me. It would give them a chance to catch up on all of Cleo and Marco's drama I reasoned, at the same time wondering if that was what

I had been avoiding. Giving up on the novel, I reopened the notebook I had been writing in earlier: thoughts about what I wanted from life, pros and cons of changing jobs, reflections on what would make me feel better in the short term. I tore out the pages and crumpled them into a tight ball that I threw into the bottom of my handbag. The word game on my phone proved to be even less of a distraction: *Routine, Route, Rout, Rut*. Thankfully the muffled announcement to say the next stop would be Bowral came soon after.

The girls were on the platform, offering waves, hugs and bag carrying services before my feet hit the ground. I absorbed that excited energy, giving myself over to the pleasure of being together again after so long.

'The spa is divine', Cleo yelled above the noise of the train. 'We dropped our bags before we came to get you'.

She was right, it was beautiful here. I tried still my thoughts and follow my breath but my gaze found distractions out the window and my mind was a cluttered mess. I closed my eyes again as the teacher had instructed to savour the slow inhalation, determined to push away invading worries that Cleo was too bright and bubbly to be real. She had talked non-stop after they collected me from the train and only when we immersed ourselves in the pool for a few laps before lunch was there silence. The meditation was led by a woman with long grey hair that had been pulled into a low knot and as she chanted in Hindi the melodic rhythms finally claimed my tense muscles if not my mind. We were sitting in the front room of the old homestead that acted as a base for the spa and the afternoon sun warmed those of us close to the window. Soon after we arrived there had been a tour of the facilities with instructions about quiet rooms and timetables for yoga and meditation classes. The old house had a colonial charm but it was the small rainforest at the bottom of the property that beckoned to be explored at the first opportunity. Apparently, that would be tonight, to see the fireflies after dinner.

Pippa had gone for a walk rather than meditation and Cleo and I met her for a drink before dinner. 'I was worried this might be an alcohol-free zone', Cleo laughed as we ordered gin and tonics.

'And I was thinking they would make us detox from caffeine but I saw some people having cappuccinos at lunch. Not as hard core as some places, thank goodness', Pippa agreed.

'How was the wedding?' I asked.

'It was a pre-wedding dinner as it turns out, not the main reception. Cassie didn't want to cause a scene with her dad ...'

'Not surprising I suppose. Were you disappointed?'

'Of course but as you say, not a surprise really. The original invitation seemed to be for the wedding so not sure if this was always the intention or if Gary insisted on the change. Anyway, doesn't matter. The important thing is I was able to celebrate with her and Jarrod, her new husband'.

'I would have been pretty put out if had been me', Cleo said, 'Especially coming all this way'.

'Yes, I should be but it's what I've come to expect since the divorce. I was never sure if it was guilt or plain meanness but Gary seemed to want to pretend we had never been a family'.

'But the girls are grown ups... and it's been what? Thirteen years?' I sounded more indignant than I intended.

'Since I've been in France I've only seen them three times and twice was when I came home for a visit. At the beginning Gary didn't encourage them to see me but later it was their choice', she shrugged in resignation.

How could she be so sanguine, even after all this time? Pippa had remade her life but she had raised those two girls, it must hurt. Cleo was studying her drink and I thought she had tuned out but when she looked up, I could see there were tears in her eyes.

'Marco and I have been talking about making a will since his diagnosis. He's worried the kids will put pressure on me for money or not be there for me'.

'But you are so close', I started but Pippa interrupted.

'He's right you need to think this through now so that you aren't left in a vulnerable spot'. Her voice was matter of fact but there was a hardness around her mouth.

'I know it's sensible and this is a stupid thing to say but I feel like it will jinx us', she shook her head at her own lack of common sense.

'You told me in the car, that Marco's illness won't affect how long he lives', Pippa looked puzzled but didn't push her point. Cleo gave a thin smile without elaborating. Her silence, in such contrast to the hyperbole of the morning was less brittle, more accepting.

Finally she added, 'Marco is going to be more dependent on everyone, including the kids and by extension so will I. That's not something I look forward to'. She raised her voice slightly and rushed the next words to forestall either interruption or lack of resolve. 'We are thinking of down-sizing to an apartment so that we can give them all a part of their inheritance now and hopefully take the pressure off me in the future'.

'But, you love your house. Wouldn't it be better to wait a while and see how things go?'

'We absolutely love it but it's going to get too much for Marco soon and I want us to be as independent as possible. The worst thing would be leaving a move so late we can't do it entirely on our terms. And... well, I've seen how the kids responded to Marco's diagnosis. Joe, especially has been having a lot more to say about what we should and shouldn't do'.

The mood was sombre as we each headed to our rooms for a few minutes before dinner. Cleo's comments shocked me— she had always been so positive about her role in the lives of Marco's children and their relationship. I had seen Paige and

Caroline when they were grieving and they had been harsh, sometimes unfair, but finally they were more open than ever before. I had started to believe we had turned the corner but now I wondered if I was deluding myself.

Thankfully, everyone was determined to move onto happier subjects when we sat down for dinner. Pippa was vegan but Cleo complained about the lack of meat options although in the end even she admitted it had all been delicious. I saved my news until we were eating the very high fibre dessert.

'Paige called in to see us this week and she has the best news. I'm not really supposed to tell you yet but she's pregnant'.

'Oh wow, amazing. I thought you said Caroline was trying', Cleo said.

'I did. She is. And Paige wasn't but you know sometimes things don't go to plan'.

'I didn't know she was with someone. Is the father on the scene?' asked Pippa, practical as ever.

'No, she didn't tell us much except that he won't be part of the baby's life or at least not a big part'.

'Good luck with that' Cleo was skeptical. I guess she had seen all sorts of scenarios play out when she worked in maternity. 'We'll be grandmothers together', she added after a moment. 'When's she due?'

'End of April or early May. What about Joe and his wife?'

'December'.

'What are you two old grannies going to be called?', Pippa's playfulness spurred on by our disconcerted expressions.

'We'll be Nonno and Nonna', Cleo said.

'We haven't talked about it but a while ago Paige was looking up Canadian options for me, if Caroline and Cristiane get pregnant. She said I could be Mamie. We'll see'.

It was already dark as we headed down to the copse of rainforest and the damp ground was uneven with tree roots. Competing smells of decay and regeneration rose from the undergrowth and hung in the air as heavily as the vines that looped from trees. We had been warned not to walk as far as the small pond at the middle of the patch of forest for fear of stumbling into it. Yellow and green flashes of light filled the space around us, males desperate to attract a female with their frenzied courting dance. Life is short for these tiny creatures, no time to waste. Someone startled when a possum scampered up a nearby tree but mostly there was silence. Cleo caught hold of my hand and squeezed it and her other hand held Pippa's— pure magic.

We walked behind the main group on the way back to the homestead, sharing the easy quiet of a lifetime friendship. How glorious not to have the think before you speak for fear of being misunderstood. We had all been so young when we first met and with that came an openness and willingness to trust that would eventually be tempered by life events. The threads of our lives were woven together in a way that later relationships had stretched but never broken. I remembered the time our three families were visiting at the same time and we organized a picnic for them to meet. I had warned Cleo that my aunt and brother probably wouldn't eat her parents' Greek food and she'd immediately laughed loudly, 'Don't worry, they won't eat her salads and devilled eggs either'. Pippa's Dad on the other hand had been very keen on the homemade retsina that Cleo's father insisted everyone try and he went home more than a little tipsy, much to the annoyance of Pippa's very correct mother. We were inventing ourselves in those days, becoming more like each other and less like our families, or so we thought.

Pippa's mind must have run along similar lines because when we were back inside, having an herbal tea, she gave me a hug from behind before taking her seat. 'Remember that time, Cleo told us we were all invited to her cousin's wedding?'

'Oh god, it was so embarrassing'.

'No one knew we were coming, they made up places for us at the last minute and Cleo was so busy charming all her rellies that we hardly saw her all night'. We both looked at our friend in mock accusation.

'But you had a great time in the end, admit it. All those Greek boys! You danced all night. And the food! Remember— it was a proper feast'.

'It was the first time I tasted lobster', I said. Pippa and I grinned, so many of Cleo's good ideas had left us mortified but somehow they mostly turned out well.

'What about the time we went skiing?' Cleo said, determined to get some of her own back. 'That was your idea, Nell!'

'God, I have never been so sore. We spent more time falling down than we did actually skiing'.

'And that ski instructor! He said I had legs like a billiard table!'

'At least you two could share the driving home', Pippa said. 'My muscles were so stiff I couldn't push the clutch down on that terrible old Torana you had'.

'That Torana took us on a lot of adventures', Cleo defended her first car. 'I seem to remember you begging to borrow it for a weekend at Caves Beach with that young doctor you were keen on. What was his name?'

'Eugene Thomas, he was gorgeous', she said. 'But so boring, he only listened to classical music and when we were sun-bathing at the beach, he took out a medical journal to read. I couldn't believe it'.

'He is a very successful urologist, I see him occasionally at work', I said. 'The gossip is that he's onto his third marriage and the latest is a junior doctor. Smart, gorgeous, A-lister— you know how it goes'.

'Let's have a nightcap in the bar', Cleo suggested.

'I was going to start on my new knitting project before bed but that's a much better idea', I agreed.

'Knitting, you're kidding?' Cleo spurted out a laugh.

'I hear it's very on-trend actually', I pretended to defend myself. 'I decided to make something for Paige's baby. Hope I haven't forgotten how to do it, it has been a very long time'.

'You know, a combined yarn shop and tea salon opened up in my street not so long ago and it's always packed', Pippa supported me. 'And it's young women and men who are knitting, not the oldies'.

'If you say so', Cleo couldn't resist raising her eyebrows ever so slightly. 'What is this masterpiece going to be? The full blown christening gown?', her amusement had not abated.

'I'm starting simple with a baby blanket. If I get into it, I have a pattern for a cute jacket and leggings that I might make'.

'We really need that drink now, Mamie. Let's go', Pippa winked at Cleo as she led the way.

Chapter 14

Mornings at the health spa were full: yoga and a swim before breakfast, then meditation and a massage. Pippa and Cleo had already gone for their massages and I was sitting in the reading room, finally trying to make headway with my knitting. The basics slowly came back to me and the modern pattern was more descriptive than I recalled my mother's old ones being. It was like old recipe books, an assumed knowledge necessary to successfully reproduce the desired item. I thought of my grandmother, painstakingly explaining terms like 'cast off' and 'slip one purlways' and wished my memory of the detail was better. The codified secrets of lost arts that were known to few followed the family line until it broke and they disappeared into the cauldron of time.

My reverie was interrupted by two women who were sitting in the other corner, talking louder than necessary about their various treatments and I irritably realized I'd drop a stitch. This knitting needed more attention than the meditation session earlier.

'This afternoon I'm having the colonic lavage', the older of the two was saying.

'That's so cool. The coffee or the herbal one?', her friend was fully supportive. I was queasy.

'I did the juice detox, last time and it was phenomenal. I lost five kilos. Some people lose twice that with the lavage.'

Fearing she was about to go into further detail, I packed up my wool and needles, wondering at people's ideas of suitable conversation topics and trying not to think too deeply about what I had heard. On the verandah, a wicker chair that had seen better days was positioned to snare the sun but the resident cat had already taken possession and I doubted my negotiation skills were up to convincing him to move. I walked on into the garden, inhaling the perfume from the first flush of roses which was mixed with the remnants of wattle and jasmine. The morning air was clear, cooler than I would normally prefer but today I enjoyed the sharp sting on my arms and legs.

In the bar last night, Pippa had been telling us about her exhibition. Her life in Paris as a translator for a big publisher had always sounded exotic enough but painting was her new passion. I tried to imagine her world, a place I loved but which I understood superficially as an occasional tourist. Harder still to see her in the art world and yet she was bravely navigating its sinuous paths and apparently making a name for herself.

When she'd moved to Paris, all those years ago she had been running away after she and Gary split up, as well as, following her dream to work as a translator of literary novels. Doing the work she loved in her favourite city had saved her from the bitterness and depression that had threatened soon after the break up. Last night she'd said she was grateful for those dark days because they had given her courage to make big changes. She wondered if Gary knew her better than she knew herself back then—consciously or not maybe he knew that they were not enough for each other.

Generous of her, I'd thought, but I was beginning to wonder if she might have something. Gary had always seemed surprised that he had been lucky enough to marry Pippa. It is possible it was that insecurity that had taken him down the route of infidelity. Or maybe he was just a player, as I'd always suspected and it had simply been a matter of time.

Either way, Pippa's ability to see Gary in the best possible light after all the turmoil he caused her had moved me. Not for the first time my own tendency to hold grudges and make snap judgements about the motivations of others left me feeling contrite. My feelings, however, were not so much about me misjudging people but about my own inability to accept that most of them were likely to be neutrally disposed towards me at worst.

Last night Pippa described herself as an emerging artist, in the act of re-inventing herself again. She was still working part-time for the publisher but spending at least half her time painting in a small studio at the back of her cottage in Sarlat. The arrangement with her employer was that she worked three months on and three off so that she could focus exclusively on the task at hand. Although she admitted, more and more of her down time was taken up by thinking about her next series of paintings.

The exhibition in Salat had been a success, thanks to the support she'd had from the local gallery owner. She described him in detail: tall and thin, a beanpole with a long thin nose, who hastened balding by shaving his head. His heritage was Italian and Polish but his parents had immigrated to France in search of work before he was born. She was looking across the room as though she could see him as she told us about how he'd taken her under his wing, introduced her to potential collectors, coached her to do media interviews and encouraged her to keep painting no matter what.

Cleo was quicker than me to suspect that they were already a couple, pouncing with feline precision on the significance of that dreamy look we'd both observed a few times since we arrived yesterday. Pippa had brushed us aside but the flush on her neck suggested she was more than a little smitten.

As far as I knew she hadn't had any serious relationships since Gary. I presumed there would have been occasional men but she'd never mentioned anyone and we hadn't seen her with anyone on any of our visits. All of us were getting older and the likelihood of new friendships, let alone new relationships fell away sharply. Companionship was worth a lot, I reflected. Sure there were irritations and disappointments but having Rob in my life gave me a confidence I had never had before. Having a secure base, a safe place that I could rely on meant I could be more daring but old habits were like ruts in the road, they needed to be fixed at the source of the problem, not covered over.

A while later, Cleo and Pippa passed me, their unfocussed gaze and languid gate raised my expectations that the massage would be especially good. And it would have been if I could have turned my brain off.

There had been a message on my phone when I got back to my room last night from Brian. He told me he had been released with a suspended sentence and that he would have to do a period of community service. The Nursing and Midwifery Council had also disqualified him from practice for at least two years. He said he was grateful that the penalty had not been more severe and thanked me for my support.

I tried for the umpteenth time to predict how events might have played out if I had noticed his problem earlier, if I had asked him about his new relationship, if I had taken more notice of how patients were being cared for. I had a chance to prevent the loss of his career and the suffering of all involved. People like me weren't held accountable because we omitted to do something but poor Brian would be because he had committed the offense. There was blame on both sides of that equation.

I recalled a conversation I'd had with my supervisor when I was a young nurse. She had warned me to be careful of my colleagues, she'd called it horizontal violence. What she meant was that nurses tend to blame each other, to gang up against individuals and make work intolerable. I had never seen my-self as a nurse who did that but my neglect of Brian was as damaging as any harassment could have been.

The masseuse pummeled my shoulders, mercilessly correct-ing tight chords and knots which was a welcome alternative to the mental self-flagellation I had been wallowing in. What if I took a leaf out of Pippa's book and decided to reinvent myself? I wasn't sure I had any idea of what that would look like. Writ-ing the blog last week had been cathartic but hardly something serious. I was a nurse through and through, who was I kidding? I shook my head so noticeably that the masseuse stopped her torture for a moment to check I was okay.

Hours later when the three of us were sitting reading after dinner, I looked up appreciating this quiet time and was surprised as my view blurred with tears. Less nostalgic than the previous evening but more sentimental. Neither of them noticed, lost in stories of other times and places. Cleo was reading some sort of historical romance judging by the cover. I imagined Pippa's selection would be something more erudite but there was no way of telling as she read on her phone. Cleo looked up, arching her eyebrows when she saw I had lost concentration.

'You look sad', she said.

'No, just sentimental. I must be getting old', my smile was strained but genuine.

'I know. I don't feel this relaxed with anyone else, even Marco', she shook her head. 'Don't tell him I said that'.

Pippa put her phone aside, 'What's made you two so soppy?'

Cleo laughed but I found myself wanting to confide in them.

'You know how I told you that work has been difficult, I've been thinking I need a change. Trouble is I don't know what I would do instead'. I bit on my thumb nail, neither of them rushed to offer advice. Pippa frowned but it was Cleo who spoke first.

'My only advice is not to rush. There are many days when I'm bored out of my brain taking bloods and I wish I hadn't given up midwifery'.

'But you said you love the flexibility and being able leave everything behind the minute your shift ends'.

'That's true but it doesn't make the job fulfilling. I wonder if there were other options that would have given me the best of both worlds but I was in such a hurry to have more time with Marcus that I jumped at the first opportunity'.

'So you think I'll regret leaving?'

'I didn't say that'.

Pippa agreed, 'You know what they say, try some things out while you are still in the old job before you commit'.

I nodded slowly, 'I know that would be sensible but if I don't make a change soon, I'm afraid either I never will or that it will be a forced one because I've lost the plot'.

'Well, at least take some leave so that you have time to think through what you really want. Cleo is right, it's easy to jump out of the fire into something worse'.

'That's a good idea. Maybe I will feel better when I'm not so tired', I said but my voice lacked conviction. My brow crumpled and as if reading my mind Pippa explained her caution.

'You probably think I'm being a hypocrite but it took me years to start to shift from translation to painting even part-time. For ages I fitted it in when I could, dabbling and hoping for a break. Recently I realized I had to take the next step or I would never know if I am any good but I still wasn't ready to burn all my bridges'.

Thankfully, Cleo interjected in a brighter tone of enthusiasm, 'Let's stop being so sensible. What is Nell born to do?'

'Besides nursing you mean', I tried to visualize options but all I saw was fog.

'You know that old line: let it go; let it be; let it come. Maybe you need to take a big jump and then wait and see'.

'Cleo!', my voice was exasperated. 'Five minutes ago you said not to rush and now you're pushing me off the cliff'.

She smiled mischievously, 'You know me, never one to shy away from ambiguity and contradictions'.

Pippa suggested that I think about roles where my nursing experience would be an asset and that were less clinical but I was only half listening. I stupidly longed for the unbridled enthusiasm for new adventures that would have pervaded our conversation thirty years ago. Unrealistic, a folly of time, we had done and become so much more than a cheer squad in the intervening years. I was the only one who could work through the convolutions of what I could or should do next—time to grasp the nettle.

Chapter 15

Three months vanished in the scramble of Christmas and household tasks that had waited years and could have continued to wait. It had taken a few weeks to detox from the adrenalin of Emergency but I still had not kicked the habit of avoiding the hard stuff when there was something else that I could react to immediately. When Paige asked for my help setting up the nursery I bought new paint brushes and rushed over. When Marco called for a chat over coffee, I was available within the hour. When Rob needed me to run a few errands because my time was freer than his, I was making a list before he finished speaking. Still I had no plan for me.

There were bright spots too: going with Paige for her regular ultrasounds and seeing the little girl (Paige had been right about the sex) who we had nicknamed Jelly Bean. Seeing that tiny human grow made me smile so hard my face ached. And, then the news from France, Caroline was pregnant with twins. We talked to them at least every week and Rob and I celebrated each little milestone as though it was our own.

I had been proud of myself that morning when I had made the decision, lucidly, determined to create the space I needed for reinvention. Check out from the spa had been at eleven o'clock and I was early, waiting for Cleo and Pippa to join me at reception. On an impulse I had filled out the request for long service leave on my phone. Kate would not have been happy but I was fairly sure she had no choice but to approve it. The thought of going back to work even for a few weeks had been weighing heavily on my mood and I felt instant relief, air finally reaching all the way down into my lungs.

A tight chest and the acid of anxiety had played havoc in the dark pre-dawn. For hours I mentally workshopped future scenarios, seeing obstacles everywhere. Steadily fear convinced me that changing jobs could be a gigantic mistake. The lack of enthusiasm from my friends and Rob, was a warning to go carefully. Normally I would have heeded those voices yet I had found myself propelled towards the void, feeling anything but brave.

Alone in reception, phone in hand, I was back in control yet still entirely lost. I might have wanted to walk away from the reactive chaos of my job, to find a new path, but that did not mean I had had a personality transplant. I had been looking forward to seeing Rob that evening, having missed his level headed antidote to my emotion. Cleo's hyperbole had given me a false sense of my own rationality and Pippa's slow and steady good sense had grated with my impulsivity. Rob would eventually challenge me but he would also support me; that safe base dared me to take the risks I could not normally contemplate.

On the train, I had read without concentration, constantly rechecking my messages for a response from Kate. I'd tried to convince myself that waiting a few weeks or months to start leave wouldn't be such a bad thing. It would give me time to make some firmer plans. I had not believed a word of it.

As the national park gave away to cars and high rise congestion my phone pinged: *Hi Nell, Got your request for leave. I will process today and you'll hear officially in a day or so but shouldn't be a problem. Can't say I'm thrilled but will support it. Backfilling will be tricky in the current climate. Is everything okay—not like you to not ask me this in person??? Kate*

Relief and guilt in equal proportion. I knew I should have talked to her but I was worried that I would cave when she reminded me, as I had no doubt she would, that we were already short staffed. Now I hated to think about what she would say if I told her I had all but squandered the time so far.

Well not entirely squandered it; I had eventually convinced a nursing magazine to publish my opinion piece on burnout. The response had been heart-warming but also depressing, so many other nurses with stories of fatigue that bores into the human spirit. There had been a few trolls as well who told me to 'get over it princess' and reminded me I was lucky to have first world problems to wallow in. An unexpected outcome of the piece was that several old colleagues had got in touch to reconnect.

I worked with Sophie when we were young nurses; she was with a drug company now but she reminded me of our first days in Emergency together. Then there was Cathy and Tessa who I supervised when they were students almost ten years ago. Peta had resigned after discovering she had breast cancer at fifty and it was great to hear she was doing well all this time later. There were messages too from people who seemed to know me but who I had forgotten or barely recalled. Gillian's tone was especially familiar, reminiscing about shared boyfriends but I could not place her and I thought she must have mixed me up with someone else.

The light was dull and I needed to return my full attention to the road which was becoming winding and steep. Rob was at a conference for two days and I was taking the chance to visit Stephen and family. Trudy had been begging me to come ever since Christmas when we missed seeing them because they'd gone to Melody's family. Dusk came early with an impending storm darkening the sky over the escarpment and a queer yellow-orange light suffusing the air.

Best to go slowly I thought, in spite of the car behind me being impatiently close. I braked into a tight bend as a blur of grey fur filled the road. Swerving, rubber screeching, skidding gravel, before the acrid smell of carbon and sulphur that made me think of my father complaining when Mum 'rode the clutch' as he called it.

Someone was banging the side of the car but they were upside down. My head hurt and it was difficult to breathe. I undid my seat belt and tried to open the door. Shifting my weight to push it harder I swore loudly as a sharp pain shot up my leg. The door finally opened and a man was holding my arm and telling me to sit on the ground. The sound of sirens drowned out whatever else he said and the pain in my leg was all I could think about.

I tried to make sense of what had happened—a kangaroo, the car sliding, then nothing until I woke up to the banging. My car was on its side in a narrow ditch beside the road which then gave way to a long drop. A young woman wearing navy overalls was kneeling beside me asking if I was alright. I pointed to my right leg but my breath caught as I tried to speak. Lying on the stretcher brought some relief but it hurt to breathe.

'Concussion, broken ribs, a shattered ankle. You never do anything by halves', Stephen's voice was jovial but his eyes were watching me closely. The room was cold, clean, white— for a moment I thought I was at work but this was another hospital. The smell and the constant rattle of metal trolleys being wheeled along linoleum floors were unmistakable.

'Am I going into theatre now?' I asked.

Stephen smiled wryly, 'You are in recovery, they operated on your ankle when you came in'. I reached down to feel the hard outside of a cast on my foot and leg.

'Have you called Rob? And how did they know to call you?' my forehead creased with confusion.

'Rob's on his way and they called me because you gave them my number. The concussion and the anaesthetic must have made you forget'.

'Hmm', I was very tired. 'Tell me when Rob is here'.

The sun hit the window at an angle making the beam of dust particles visible down to the floor. Hospital bed, television in the usual awkward position on the far wall, a tray with water and some sort of red jelly covered in plastic wrap, just out of reach, reminded me where I was. The pain in my leg had gone but it still hurt to breathe. Stephen had said I had broken ribs. I tried to recall if I had seen Rob last night, perhaps I was already asleep when he came.

A nurse came in soon after, 'Awake already. I have some pain medication for you that should ease the discomfort around your ribs. How does the ankle feel?'

So cheery, her shift must be almost done. 'I'd rather wait a while and take the painkillers later', the pain was bearable while I was lying down.

'Are you sure?' she shrugged and gave her attention to the chart she was holding. I wondered how I had scored a private room, even with insurance I knew I was lucky.

'Do you know when I will be able to go home?' I asked, wishing I was at my own hospital where I could have relied on some inside contacts for information.

The nurse gave a small smile but her eyes were disinterested, another shrug, 'The surgeon usually does his rounds early before he goes into theatre and again around six in the evening'. Not a satisfactory answer but the best to be had for now.

'Use the buzzer if you need anything. You'll need help to transfer to a wheelchair for your shower and if you need the toilet. No pressure on that ankle for now', I recognized the bossy tone that I prided myself on avoiding. The joys of being on the other side of the open-backed seersucker hospital gown.

Reaching for my phone which someone had thoughtfully put on a charger beside the bed, I saw there were a string of messages: Rob saying he would see me this morning; Cleo asking if I was okay; Paige and Trudy sending kisses and get well soon messages. I was contemplating whether the fluorescent scrambled eggs were edible when Rob put his head around the door.

'How are you sweetheart? It was late when I got here last night and you were sound asleep. The nurses said you had a good night'. I smiled wanly, letting myself relax into his concern—reinforcements at last. I remember when I was training, a crusty old matron telling me that being alone in hospital is the loneliest experience you can imagine. She had been spot on.

'Better for seeing you. Stephen was wonderful last night but it's not the same'.

'Do you remember what happened? Stephen said you hit a kangaroo'.

'I swerved to miss it, maybe I hit it, I'm not sure. It's a haze'.

Rob frowned, the worry creases around his eyes deeper than usual, 'Are you in a lot of pain? The nurse said you didn't take any medication this morning'.

'It isn't too awful. I'll take something before my shower but otherwise I'd rather not. The worse thing is this cast, it's so itchy and I'm not allowed to weight bear on this leg at all. Not for a couple of weeks at least. When the surgeon comes, I'll ask when I can change to a boot. In the meantime it's crutches or a wheelchair for me'.

'What about those scooter things. I remember Caro had one when she broke her leg at the end of high school'. I nodded, that could be a possibility.

The morning dragged; ear cocked every time footsteps approached both of us watched the door expectedly. Finally, around one o'clock a young woman, wearing a floral summer dress flat shoes and a stethoscope around her neck arrived to

check on me. She introduced herself as one of the team working with Mr Simpson, my surgeon. She looked fifteen and I
wondered how she was managing orthopaedic procedures with
her petite stature. The good news was that I could go home tonight once the occupational therapist or physio checked that I
could use crutches and after I had made a future appointment
to see Mr Simpson in the outpatient clinic. I should make an
appointment for the following week, Wednesdays were usually
best, she advised.

So, unexpectedly there I was having a week at Stephen's
while I recuperated and before I could see the surgeon. Rob
had gone back to Sydney for work and to look after Lucca and
so Melody took over the role of endless fussing interspersed
with remonstrations to rest.

The fourth night after I left hospital I was feeling like my
old self. I had gone to the coffee shop a few streets away, confi-
dently wielding crutches and a backpack against the morning
rush. It was a relief to sit and catch my breath while I waited
for the coffee that tasted especially good when it finally came.
Tomorrow I would see the surgeon and fingers crossed I could
go home Friday. Stephen had been late home from work and
Melody and Trudy had gone to the movies. It was the first
time they had left me for more than ten minutes; my foray
into the suburbs proof that I wasn't entirely helpless. I knew I
should phone Cleo, I had missed a call from her earlier, but the
temptation of lazy solitude was too strong and I snuggled into
the couch as much as the rigid plaster allowed.

The rattle of keys in the door made me jump, Stephen home.
I had been replaying what I could remember of the accident,
hoping more of the details would become clear but everything
between the car swerving and waking in recovery was murky. I
wasn't even sure that the scant glimpses of memory I had were
not recreations, constructed from what others had told me.
My early childhood memories were like that. Only when the

memories were shared with Stephen could I be sure of their veracity. No one shared the memory of the crash with me, not even the good samaritan who had stopped to help. I did remember there had been someone tailgating me before the accident but I wasn't sure they were still there when I rolled the car.

Stephen's face was drawn and grey when he joined me on the sofa, handing me a glass of red wine to keep him company. 'Long day', I smiled my sympathy.

'The worst. I had to tell three people that their contracts will not be renewed. They're all in their fifties and sixties—getting another job will be difficult and one of them was in tears telling me she can't afford to retire yet'.

'That's tough. Hopefully the redundancies help, at least financially'.

'That's just it. They were all on short term contracts that the university kept renewing. On paper, they aren't entitled to a redundancy but I've suggested they fight it. Morally and ethically the university should pay. It's a long shot'. His shoulders sagged and he took a long swallow of wine. 'How was your day? Melody said you went to the shops'.

'For coffee, yeah it was good to be out. My arms ache, should have been more diligent with those bicep exercises at the gym', I laughed.

'I didn't think you were into the gym'.

'Exactly. Swimming yes, weights definitely not but it would have been good training for a broken ankle'.

'I've been meaning to thank you for talking with Trudy when you were down last time. She told us she asked you about starting the pill and you said she should talk to us'.

'She thought you'd over-react, full on protective Dad. I'm glad she told you'. I wanted to ask if she mentioned anything about her sexuality but that was a separate confidence.

'It made me think back to when we were her age. The world seems so much more complicated these days'.

'Hmm, Trudy is more savvy than I was at her age. We'd been through more emotional upheaval but she has way more street smarts than I had'.

'Too much sometimes. Or is that the full-on-dad, again?', Stephen gave a lop-sided smile before becoming more serious, 'I've never properly thanked you for how you looked after me after Dad died. Mum disappeared into the shadows and you were the one who made sure everything stayed normal at home. You somehow managed to cook and wash our school clothes and tell me off for not doing my homework and still do your own schoolwork'.

I shrugged, 'We both did what we had to. I've been thinking about that time lately as well, wondering if that was when it became a habit to try to fix everyone else's problems'.

'The positive of course is that we are probably closer than we would have been. I've watched some of my friends grow away from their families as they start their own. We didn't have that luxury'.

'At least you made a family. I've only tinkered in other people's', I said trying to sound matter of fact but could not disguise a sour note of disappointment.

'Nell!' Stephen looked like he could shake me but I was determined to finish.

'I've never tried to understand the walls I hid behind until I met Rob but I've been trying to be more honest with myself in the past few weeks. Deep down I was afraid that I would be a bad mother, that I'd let my family down. Part of me is afraid I don't deserve to have a family'.

'Whoa, who is being full on now. Not to mention ridiculous. Maybe that concussion is still wearing off,' he gave a smile but his eyes stayed firmly on my face.

'I suppose I expected I would be like Mum and I couldn't bear that'.

'You are nothing like Mum and besides she was a great Mum for most of our lives. The last years weren't so good but not because she didn't love us'.

'I know, I know'. Poor Stephen he'd had a shitty day, he didn't need to hear my newly discovered truths. 'Sorry, shall we start dinner? I think they went to a five o'clock session so the movie must be about over'.

Stephen looked relieved if unconvinced by my change of tack. 'Yeah, Melody said they'd be home about seven thirty. I was going to cook steak on the barbeque. You okay with that?'

'Sounds good. I'd offer to help but I'm not sure I can perch on the kitchen stool and keep my balance', I chuckled to lighten the atmosphere which still felt strained.

Stephen nodded and disappeared into the kitchen. A while later when Melody and Trudy came home, we were both happy to let them tell us about the latest sci-fi movie that they'd seen.

'Aunty Nell, you used to tell me the best stories about Martians who lived next door when I was little. That must have been when I started to love sci-fi', Trudy was sitting on the arm of the sofa. 'I used to stare out the window for hours waiting to catch a glimpse of them but all I ever saw was old Miss Reed and it seemed unlikely she was a Martian'.

'Really, I don't remember. Sure it wasn't your Mum, she is the sci-fi fan'.

'No it was definitely you. You even told me that they wore bright orange suits so I would spot them easily. So when I saw SES workers in their high vis vests on our holidays that year, I thought I had found the Martians'.

'That's right. I remember you telling us that the guys, who were cleaning up after that big storm knocked down trees, were from outer space', Melody joined in laughing at the memory.

Chapter 16

The surgeon agreed to refer me to a colleague in Sydney and so I could finally go home. I would still need to keep the leg up for another few days but at least I wouldn't be under everyone's feet here. It would be good to get back to normal, even a sedentary version of normality.

Cleo came over the first afternoon after I got home. Her hair was frizzy in the summer humidity, her face flushed without makeup. She started speaking before she was fully inside, 'I've spent all morning cleaning out cupboards. You have no idea how much stuff we've accumulated, not to mention a whole lot of things that belong to the kids. I've asked them to come over and see what they want and we'll give the rest away'.

'Sorry, I was supposed to be helping you this week'.

'I know, you poor thing. How are you? You seem pretty good on those crutches now'.

'Getting there. How about you and Marco'.

'He's okay, more tired than he has been but that's understandable. This preparing to sell and move caper is getting to both of us'.

'I still don't understand why you don't stay in the house. Surely it would be easier in the short term'.

'No, we've decided', her voice was firm. 'And we have some news?'

'Have Joe and his wife had the baby?'

'Not yet, most likely the end of next week. No, we have decided that when we sell, we are going to buy a place on the south coast. We both love Milton but we are open to other small towns'.

'Wow, really! That will be a big change for you', I hoped I kept the doubt out of my voice.

'I know, crazy, right? But the idea of being in a smaller community is appealing and I need to be further away from the kids. Joe and Bella have been so bossy lately. We're both over it'.

'Worried, I guess. What about the restaurant? Is Theo going to run it permanently?'

'That's the other great news. Theo is engaged', she paused, 'To the maître d' that we appointed before Marco was diagnosed. She's fantastic, a perfect foil for Theo's exuberance. So yes, we are going to sell them the restaurant which is, of course, another source of contention with Joe. He keeps implying that Theo is the favourite and to be honest right now Theo is much better company than his big brother'.

'Things are moving fast for you guys'. I couldn't help comparing their decisiveness with my own procrastination, 'I wish I could be so certain about making my next move'.

'You will. When it's time, you'll know what to do', unlike Cleo to be so philosophical. The last few months I had noticed the change—she was stronger, less flamboyant, more determined. Like her cupboards, she had cleared out the pretensions that weren't useful anymore.

'So this time next week you'll be a grandmother. That's amazing'.

'We had our whooping cough vaccinations yesterday so that we can see the little one straight away. Yes, it will be interesting to see them as a new family, maybe it will soften Joe'.

'Last time I saw Marco, he said you two were thinking about a holiday in Mexico later this year but maybe babysitting duties will get in the way'.

'No, Mexico is off', she turned back to deal with the jug she had set to boil for tea. I wanted to ask more but the set of her shoulders said to tread carefully. We continued like that Cleo making tea, me, leg raised, offering direction from chair, avoiding what was presumably a hairy topic.

Eventually Cleo met my eye, 'I promised myself I wouldn't tell you but... well, Marco wanted to go to Mexico to see if he could buy one of those euthanasia kits. Apparently, you can get a kit with Nembutal in unmarked bottles that is pretty easy to bring back through customs'.

'Oh, I had no idea', how stupid had I been encouraging him that a holiday was just what they both needed.

'Yeah, well now he has joined this group online and it seems it's almost impossible to know if what you buy is the real thing. Same for online sales. There's even a fellow who sells kits so you can test if the contents are real or counterfeit'.

I was slow to respond, worried that my assumptions would be off the mark, 'And what do you think of this'.

'I was devastated when he told me. For the moment he has agreed not to actively pursue an early exit as he calls it but I doubt this is the last of it. He hates the changes he has had to make to his life. I'm hoping the change of scenery and country life will help him recalibrate'.

I hoped so too but like Cleo I knew that once Marco had an idea in his head, he would plough through whatever lay in his way. 'And you are sure he isn't depressed, that he is making these decisions when he is in a good place?'

'No, not really. He is still seeing the counsellor and he was prescribed an antidepressant a week ago. Maybe when that has had time to start working, we can have another conversation. At the moment, I'm making like an ostrich but I know I have to come up for air eventually', her rueful smile broke my heart and I held up my arms to hug her from my enforced position.

'I know it can't be easy for him but I'm stunned. I can't begin to imagine how you are feeling'.

'Stunned is one word for it, then there's furious, despondent, powerless to fix it. You know there has been a lot of media attention on the whole voluntary euthanasia thing and Marco has always been susceptible to suggestion', Cleo's voice trailed away as if she too was aware how reactionary that last statement had been. Whatever contrition she felt however was short-lived, 'He even made me watch a bloody movie about a woman who decides she wants to plan the time of her own death and the saintly husband who helps her'. The punctuating snort left no doubts about her intention to be supremely unsaintly in any such context.

'I assume he hasn't discussed any of this with the kids. You will definitely have allies there'.

'Exactly but not sure I want to be in that camp either. Anyway, it's on the backburner for now. Let's hope that his *Joie de vivre* hasn't deserted him permanently'.

'Marco is tough, he'll bounce back', I hoped my confident tone was convincing.

When Cleo had gone, I tried to sort through my feelings. I was sympathetic: for Marco's despair as much as for Cleo's anger. My short period of immobility was the smallest taste of what it was like to be restricted but I would be back to normal in a few weeks. Marco faced a future so different to everything he loved in his former life, it was like he had to redraft a perfectly good story, knowing he would end up with an inferior one. It would take the biggest mental shift to start believing that there was much to cheer about but voluntary euthanasia was a leap too far in the other direction. Fair enough for people with terminal illnesses to have that choice but whether it was my religious upbringing or nursing training, I couldn't reconcile Marco's situation with such an extreme option.

The enforced slow down of the past week had brought an unexpected peace. I would have predicted that I would be climbing the walls after a day or two but in fact every day it had become easier to accept that patience and time were all I had. For the first time since I commenced my leave, I really wasn't expecting anything of myself, neither activity nor decisions. Of course, I was keen to start exercising and rebuilding strength but not having any choice was oddly freeing. I began to wonder if all those years of being so deliberately in control had been misguided, held me back from experiences that would have fulfilled me in unimagined ways.

Deep in thought, I gave a small cry when the phone rang and vibrated on the table beside me. It was Kate: nothing urgent; some mail that had been addressed to work, should she send it to my home address; how was I doing, she'd heard about the accident; don't forget sick leave available even during long service leave; get well soon; must go, crazy day, must be a full moon. At the sound of her voice I felt my abdomen tighten and my brow cease, harking back to the stress I had become so used to. The information about sick leave abruptly settled the tension—of course, I had forgotten, I could claim sick leave and my total leave would extend accordingly. More time to make up my mind about work, about life.

That night I was in the midst of telling Rob about my conversation with Cleo, slightly guilty that my friend had implied it was not a topic to be shared but determined to have no more secrets. I was saved from going into details by Caroline and Cristiane's regular call to update us on the progress of the pregnancy.

'Caro, sweetie', Rob always half shouted on video calls, determined to be heard clearly from so far away.

Caroline modeled her bump and grinned broadly when we exclaimed at how well she looked. 'Still a long way to go. I've been enjoying the cold winter for the first time since we moved to Paris. We even had snow last week'.

'I've been telling her to mind the slippery streets especially in the mornings. It has been icy for the past week', Cristiane interjected.

Caroline had always been slim and even at 10 weeks she was beginning to show almost as much as Paige who was much further along. Twins I supposed, and the figure-hugging woollen dress that she wore accentuated it. She was delighting in every moment of her pregnancy—no morning sickness, energetic, rehearsing for concerts in the spring.

'We've decided to move to a bigger apartment before the birth. It will have to be in the suburbs but so long as we are on an RER line, we'll still be close to the city for work. Cristiane's Mum has offered to come and help us move when we find the right place'.

'I've been thinking we could come and see you too', Rob gave me a sideways glance, half question, half apology.

'That would be so great. When were you thinking?'

'We haven't really talked about a definite date but sometime before Nell finishes her long service leave'.

'And when I can walk again', I added, thinking that would be at least another couple of months away.

Rob looked sheepish as we rang off, 'Sorry to spring that idea without talking to you first. I've been thinking about it for a couple of days and, well, it just came out'.

'We can't let the Canadian grandparents have all the fun', I teased. 'It's definitely time for another visit to my favourite city. We'll just need to plan around this ankle and Paige, so maybe June or July after Jelly Bean is born. That would give Paige time to settle with the little one before we headed off' and I thought, for me to get some fitness back.

'But you'll be back to work by then'.

'Probably, depending on how this sick leave claim goes. I'll have two or three weeks of annual leave still owing—won't make me popular but it should be possible'. After last time, it seemed best not to broach the idea of not returning to the hospital at all until I had a firm plan. 'Speaking of which, Kate called today to say I had some mail at work. It's probably from one of the nursing organisations and not important but could you pop in on your way home and collect it?'

Rob agreed absently, already busy searching for cheap flights to Paris on his phone. 'If we book in the next couple of weeks there are good business class deals going via Malaysia. Let's look at it together on the weekend after we talk to Paige?' he was excited at the prospect of seeing Caroline after so long.

Maybe some time overseas would provide the circuit breaker I needed to make big changes but those middle aged, white women who 'found themselves' while restoring a decrepit Tuscan castle, travelling alone on the byways of France or in the arms of a swarthy lover in Istanbul, mocked me. Their stories never acknowledged ordinary lives that stayed ordinary even after horror years and Paris sojourns. Some would say the risk you take is proportionate to the changes you wright but that required more creativity or anguish than I foresaw as likely or desirable. The terror had to promise more than what it would replace; the stakes needed to be high. My life wasn't so very bad, was it?

A text message from Cleo interrupted my train of thought: *Baby girl born this evening, mother and babe both well, speedy labour, made it to hospital with an hour to spare. 3.3kg, 50cm, no name yet. C xx*

Chapter 17

Time moved slowly, rehab took forever, and at the same time it disappeared before I knew. I was fed up with the twice weekly physiotherapy visits, daily stretching and visits to the local hydrotherapy pool. My fellow regulars were all in their eighties and nineties: the bald wiry man with the patchy moustache; the shuffling Chinese lady who must have been taller in her youth; the chronically cranky woman who complained if anyone veered into her space; and the tall woman with the no-nonsense haircut who determinedly worked her left leg. I may have felt their age some days but all complaints died on my lips when I saw their commitment to getting as well as possible.

The tall woman introduced herself to me as Sonia one morning. She told me about the small stroke that had affected her left arm and leg. Her speech was barely affected, the slightest slur if you knew to listen for it, yet she was self-conscious that people would doubt her mental capacity. We were both in the change rooms, drying off and as she collected her things to leave she said she wouldn't see me for a couple of weeks because her son, Daniel, would be away in Melbourne. Catching the bus was a possibility but she was worried that she'd need help getting on and off.

'You know how they half pull into the bus zone? The step down can be pretty big if the bus isn't close to the curb'.

'Maybe I could give you a lift. Do you live far?' I had not noticed the well used laugh lines but as she smiled, I glimpsed the younger Sonia still there in spite of recent setbacks.

'Are you sure, that would be so kind...' she sat down again, searching her bag for a pen to write down the address. 'I hate being such a nuisance. Daniel has been such a help but I would give anything to have my independence back'.

'I will enjoy the company. Here I can put your address straight into my phone'. And so for the next two weeks I heard about Sonia's life: as a young doctor; years in Papua New Guinea doing aid work; meeting her first husband only to lose him in her early forties to cancer; marrying again but divorcing after two years; the son who was a high flying banker and still had time for his Mum. It was so easy to see only an old woman with some health problems, I was grateful I'd had a chance to know her a little. She'd had a rich life and I suspected wasn't done yet, squeezing out every last drop. My last session at the pool was in late March and I took a cake to celebrate with my co-rehabbers. I was genuinely sorry to say goodbye albeit relieved to move on to more normal activity—who would have thought that weight bearing exercise and regular walks would be such a treat. Getting around the house and driving had pro- vided some reprieve from total boredom but finally my body began to feel like its normal self. I was no athlete but working in Emergency meant being perpetually on my feet and I had missed the fitness which came without me having to even think about it.

There would be no excuses about being fit for work when my leave finished in three weeks time but I was giving it little thought, more concerned that every beep from the phone was Paige telling us to come and take her to the hospital. We had called in to see the newly decorated nursery when she started maternity leave the day before. Miniature hot air balloons, rain- bows, mint green and grey with splashes of sunshine yellow—

Paige had created a space that was both serene and joyful. I had cynically put her decorating mania down to nesting but when I saw the result, I could see all her love poured into that tiny space. Rob's handyman skills had been called upon to help with shelves and picture hooks and he had adored being allowed to help. Paige gently confided that she was glad the tasks had served a dual function, finishing the project and distracting him from fussing so much about her.

She had a point, I too had enjoyed my share of his considerate attention but we both knew that he had been an amazing support throughout the pregnancy, never too tired, always eager to go with Paige to an appointment. I wished I could have done more but at least enforced inactivity had given me plenty of time to finish knitting the baby blanket and a tiny outfit for when she was born.

There seemed to be babies everywhere. Cleo and Marco were besotted with little Sofia, their first grandchild. We had lunch a few days after the naming ceremony and Cleo joked that every Greek family in the city had been represented. The baby seemed to have given Marco a new enthusiasm for the world in spite of being tired from the big move to their rural retreat about three hours away. Country living was suiting them: Cleo had joined a book club and was playing tennis; Marco had taken up bowls. I had to suppress a giggle and an unkind if predictable quip as Marco started to explain it was a game of skill and strategy. They were both more relaxed once the hurley burley of selling and buying houses was over. There were a few remaining challenges with distributing funds to the three kids but most of that had been discussed and the worst of the outbursts resolved or weathered. Given his upbeat conversation over lunch it was a shock to see Marco walking so slowly back to the car. I turned to wave goodbye to see Cleo coming back towards me.

'I forgot to say, we're hoping you and Rob will come and visit us soon. Nothing like visitors to christen a new home', she called.

'Look forward to it', I started but Cleo interrupted as she reached me.

'Nell, I'm worried about Marco. Can I call you tomorrow?' and she hurried back to the car without waiting for an answer. She didn't call the next day or the one after and when she did days later there was a hesitation in her voice suggesting that she was choosing her words carefully.

'You know how a while back, I told you that Marco had been talking about having an exit plan if his illness deteriorates?' She paused and I thought I heard a cough or was it a sob?

'Well, when I was searching through the shed for some secateurs that I had misplaced in the move last week, I found this package. It hasn't been opened but it has come from Germany. I'm pretty sure he has already bought a kit to ... you know'.

'Can you ask him?'

'I'm not sure I want to find out the answer', Cleo's despondency was infectious.

Without letting myself think I offered, 'Do you want me to ...'

'Would you?' Cleo jumped in.

I knew I would regret that impetuous offer but what else could I do. Cleo must have anticipated my response because she immediately started planning for us to visit while I let the nausea swirl in my gut.

It was only mid-morning and I had already walked and done the exercises the physio insisted I keep up. Over the past week the mornings and evenings had been fresher as summer finally petered out but by midday it would be warm enough for a swim. Half an hour of laps at the harbour pool was time for reflection as well as a good workout. I swam inside the net, not too far from the shore where the water was warmer at high tide. The beach was quiet: a few people walking, a small child digging in the sand beside his mother and the calls of magpies interspersed with the lap of waves. Lost in the rhythm, four strokes one breath, I tried to imagine going back to the routine of work. Not much imagination was needed: seven o'clock starts, late finishes, weekend shifts, filling in when staffing was tight. My shoulders tightened and I stretched my neck and pulled back my shoulder blades.

A swim instructor had told be once that swimming was supposed to be relaxing and that having my shoulders up around my ears was one of the reasons my stroke was so inefficient. I could see him wagging his finger at me when I was twelve, pretty certain he would do the same today given the chance. That instructor had told me I would never be a sprinter, that I should focus on distance events that required stamina rather than speed. He insinuated that I was a plodder which had dissolved all childhood dreams of winning an Olympic medal. Smiling into my goggles made them leak but I felt the tension ease and a switch flicked in my mind.

I have always loved that peaceful feeling when a decision has been reached. The storm of weighing up the pros and cons, the to-ing and fro-ing between options, is torture. The visceral equivalent of nails scrapping down a blackboard. Sometimes, like on this occasion, it's as if the decision was made long ago and sitting in my subconscious until I was ready for it. The taunt of fear was eventually overcome by blessed certainty.

The phone rang as I was leaving the pool and I juggled the muddle of wet towel, swim bag, car key and phone that were all precariously clasped in my hands.

'Hi love, Paige just called me. Her waters have broken and I'm going over there now to take her to the hospital', Rob's voice was an octave higher than usual.

'I'll meet you there?'

'Yeah, sounds good. She sounded really calm but she said the contractions were strong when they come'.

'Drive carefully', I rang off not wanting to distract him.

When I arrived at the hospital Rob met me at the entrance. He was sweating and it looked like he'd been pacing the corridor waiting for news that we could see Paige, who was being assessed by the midwife prior to the obstetrician arriving.

When we were allowed to see her, it was clear this labour was progressing quickly. She was fully dilated, too late for an epidural, we could expect an early result. Rob clasped Paige's hands so hard he seemed to be willing her pain into his body. I fetched water, found a damp towel to wipe her forehead and held her legs when it was time to push. When he saw the little one's head, Rob cried and I tried to remind Paige to blow but her focus was all on the baby.

Paige had asked me to take a photo of the birth and I was afraid I was shaking so much it would be blurred. The very capable midwife took a backup shot. Before we knew it Paige was calmly holding her little girl who had come out pink and screaming, perfectly formed.

'Meet my lovely Maggie', she said, holding her up so we could see. 'I think my heart will explode with love', her smile was the happiest kind and there was a sweet ache in her voice.

Rob and I clucked and cooed until the midwife dispatched us with the suggestion of bringing tea and sandwiches while she and Paige dealt with the after birth.

'Oh my god, I have never been so proud of her', Rob's smile glowed like he had a light inside. 'When I was at her birth, all those years ago, I was so scared I couldn't really appreciate the sheer wonder of it. What an amazing gift to be here today'.

It was true. I had seen a lot of births in my early days of nursing but I had never been so affected as I'd been seeing little Maggie born.

'Do you like her name? I wonder if Paige was thinking of Marjorie when she picked it'.

'It suits her either way. She is so beautiful don't you think'.

A little later as he gingerly took his granddaughter for a first cuddle, I found myself having mixed feelings. I had never seen Rob look happier or felt the bond with Paige more warmly but a small part of me knew I had missed out on having that experience myself. That moment of grief was totally overwhelmed when I held Maggie myself, her own tiny person, she snuggled into my body demanding love and protection.

'Thank you Paige, for letting me here today. It has been truly one of the best days of my life', I said as I handed back Maggie.

'These endorphins are better than champagne', she smiled and her face was radiant as she studied the tiny replica in her arms. 'We should call Caro. I promised she would know the minute I could speak after the birth'.

In the midst of that family zoom call I knew I belonged to their tight circle more than at any previous moment and a tear escaped down my cheek before I could wipe it away. Rob noticed and smiled at me, assuming they were tears of joy which was almost true. They were tears of gratitude.

Chapter 18

We were both exhausted when we arrived home and I wondered if all the hormones were saving Paige from the same fate at least for a few days. We talked about Paige, the birth, Maggie and it seemed wrong to spoil it with anything less magical. But the next morning I was up early to make Rob breakfast, a rare event that made him raise his eyebrows and regard me quizzically.

'I thought after yesterday, you might need some sustenance', I tried.

His brows were now fully arched.

'Okay you are right. I have an ulterior motive', I attempted humour. He was still not buying it.

'Yesterday, I finally reached a decision about work, provided you agree...', my voice trailed off as I admitted to myself that he should have some say in this. 'So the thing is, I want to resign from the hospital. I know you warned me that getting a new job won't be easy', I stopped not sure how to go on.

'I have been expecting you to say that for weeks', Rob sounded surprisingly relieved. 'I thought you had some terrible news to tell me'.

'Well it would mean we only have your salary, at least for a while'.

'What do you think you will do?'

I took a deep breath and crossed my fingers, 'You'll think I'm mad but I have an idea for a business'. I stopped because Rob was shaking his head. I knew he would think I was a fool.

'That is so great, you amaze me, Nell. Of course I will support you, what sort of business are you thinking?'

'Well you know how you and Paige ran around after me when my ankle was broken? All that stuff made such a difference: the washing and ironing, taking me to appointments, making sure I could reach everything I needed, cooking, shopping. You were both amazing but there must be lots of people who don't have friends or family who can help out especially during the day'.

'So you are thinking some sort of service that would fill that short term gap?'

'Exactly, and because it is short term I bet many people wait it out and that would be miserable. I had the idea when I met Sonia. I'm not sure if you remember, I met her at the hydrotherapy pool and she needed a lift a couple of weeks when her son was interstate for work'.

Rob was nodding eagerly, 'I can imagine there is a big need and providing something local and responsive on a casual basis would be very attractive to people who are normally independent'.

'I thought that I would start small, just me, and advertise at a couple of rehab centres to see if I get any bites. It would be low risk financially and if it flops no harm done'.

'I'm impressed. You told me you wanted to leave the hospital but I didn't believe you'd actually do it. Go Nell!' Rob rarely showed enthusiasm so effusively and I wondered if the emotion of the past day was partly responsible.

'Thank you', another wave of gratitude. 'I will tell work today and hopefully I won't have to go back after leave. I'll need to work through the business end of things, set up a company and some sort of online presence. Do you think I can ask Paige to help?'

'She'll be pre-occupied for a while but I'm sure she could steer you in the right direction'.

'What do you think of *Neighbour-On-Call* as a name for the business?'

'Captures the idea well. Let's do a quick search and see if the domain name is available', no procrastinating with Rob.

Kate agreed to see me at four o'clock the next day which gave us time to call in on Paige. Maggie was feeding so we only stayed ten minutes but even that brief visit helped calm the butterflies that had begun circling. Babies and puppies, they demand all of you, right then, right there.

Emergency was relatively quiet and I managed to arrive at Kate's office with only a few waves to colleagues. She was working on the computer when I arrived, probably entering data for one of the endless reports that I had grown to despise.

'Nell, come in. You are looking relaxed. How's the ankle?'

'Thanks, good now'. It had occurred to me to claim some ongoing pain as the reason for my decision to leave but in the end I felt I owed Kate the truth'.

'I read your article in the nursing journal. Very insightful'. She paused for only a second, 'Would I be right in guessing that line of thinking is why we are meeting?'

Wow, this was going to be both easier and harder than I expected. 'Well yes, I suppose that is true. The reason I took leave was because I was burnt out and it has given me time to think about what I want'.

'And you don't want to work here?'

'Ah, yes, that's right', my voice broke as I stumbled on the words. 'Don't get me wrong I have loved nursing and this department is amazing. I feel like I have given it all I can but I don't want to keep doing that'.

Kate watched me, arms crossed, mouth a tight line.

'I'm sorry Kate, I have decided to resign from the hospital and try something else for a while. I was hoping that the remaining three weeks of leave could be my notice period...', my voice trailed away as she frowned and stood up.

An enormous hug was not what I had anticipated and tears welled up as she said, 'I've been half expecting this Nell and as much as I will hate to lose you, you are making the right decision'. Was I responsible for the rare weariness in her voice or was she wishing she could walk away as well? True to her words, she had the termination forms at hand. My hand trembled as I completed and signed the paperwork and I couldn't tell if that nervousness arose from second guessing my decision or fear of not following through with it.

As I got up to say goodbye, she smiled warmly, 'You will have to come back for at least one morning so that we can have a proper farewell for you'.

'I would like that. There are so many people to thank and lots of memories to laugh about'.

'Not to mention a roast or two', she warned, referring to the usual ribbing that departing colleagues could expect.

I was halfway down the corridor, heading back to the car when she called out, 'Nell, I almost forgot'. Kate was holding out an envelope, 'That mail I told you about a few months ago'.

'Oh, I had forgotten all about it. Rob was going to pop in and collect it but it must have slipped his mind. Thanks'.

A hand addressed envelope, so unusual these days. I tore it open as I walked to the car, thinking it would be a grateful patient's note of thanks. It was short, written in a small, tight script, all the words cramped at the top of the page. The letter was from someone called Gill Meadon who said she knew me in the early eighties and could we meet up for a coffee sometime to catch up about those times. There was a mobile number and a street address on the other side of the city. I had no memory of her, maybe Cleo or Pippa would know who she was but what harm could a coffee do. I sent a quick text message: *Sorry, only received your letter recently as have been on leave. Happy to have coffee. I am based in the Inner West if that suits. Look forward to hearing. Nell Saunders.*

The response was instantaneous, setting up a time for the following day at a place not far from home. I'd have to do some internet stalking in the meantime.

Chapter 19

Gillian had already been at the coffee shop when I arrived although I was a few minutes early. Sitting at a window table, eyes on the street, she gently tapped a teaspoon on the napkin that protruded from the empty cup in front of her. She was about my age, possibly a few years younger, significantly over-weight but with a beautiful face and immaculately dressed. As I walked closer, I could see the sheen of perspiration that gave her face a glow from a distance but up close looked sticky and uncomfortable.

She smiled as I approached the table, 'Nell, you haven't changed at all', she stood, her face alight with welcome and something else, perhaps relief. 'I'm so pleased we could meet up after all this time'.

'Gillian, hello', I extended my hand but she drew me into an awkward half hug. 'This is embarrassing but to be honest Gillian I don't really remember you?' my voice rose a level, inviting her to answer the implied question.

'Yes, of course, of course. I shouldn't have assumed', she waved her hands and I regretted having been so direct.

'I have the worst memory. I'm sure when you remind me of when it was...'

'We were student nurses at the same time but we didn't work on the same wards. I was mostly in theatres and from memory you were on the medical wards. I met you a few times because you were friends with my housemate, Neil'.

A picture began to form in my mind: a tall athletic girl wearing jeans and denim shirt, bouncing around the house, to whatever was coming through enormous headphones that precariously perched on her head. I had hesitated in the doorway, not sure if Neil meant for me to follow him or wait outside. He'd said he was rushing in to get his sunglasses. The girl had yelled out hello and I'd half-heartedly waved no idea that she recognized me from work.

It was the third or fourth time that Neil and I had gone out. We were heading to the cinema, some tediously long action film that Neil had chosen. He'd vaguely waved a hand towards his housemate and then me, 'Gill, Nell—Nell, Gill'. Then he'd grabbed my hand and hurried us down the stairs, calling out that we were running late. As far as I knew I never saw her again. I only went to his place a couple of more times and I'm pretty sure she was out each time.

'Now I remember you although not from the hospital. I think Neil briefly introduced us once when we were on our way out. I came to your place a few times but Neil was never overly keen for me to spend time with his friends. I always had the feeling he was embarrassed by me'.

She responded to my grimace and raised eyebrows with a shake of her head, 'No, he was like that; protective, private. We lived together for over a year and I hardly met any of his friends'.

Not sure where this was going, I offered to order coffee, pleased to have a few minutes at the counter to scan my memory banks, not that it helped. Gillian had moved her chair when I returned and was sitting beside me rather than opposite. I found myself pushing my chair further out from the table, re-drawing my personal space.

'You must be wondering why I asked you to meet me', she began. I sipped my coffee, noticing her hands trembled slightly as she raised her cup. 'I wanted to ask you about the time you were with Neil', the rising inflection, asking if she should continue. I nodded.

'I'm not sure how to say this but...was Neil...well, was he ever violent with you?' Nausea rose and I felt my neck flush.

'You mean did he hit me? No, nothing like that'.

'Or assault you?' she probed.

I didn't answer for an uncomfortably long moment. Gillian bit on her thumb nail. 'This is something that I haven't even told my family. The first time I met Neil, he pressed me to have sex but we were in a public place and nothing happened', I took another mouthful of coffee.

'I see, so normal behaviour for pretty much any horny young man'.

'I guess but then he came to see me a few weeks later. It was late, he'd been drinking and when we went to my room, he forced himself on me even when I begged him to stop. He just kept pushing me down and pulling at my clothes, there were bruises next day. He was surprised that there was blood, it was my first time and it happened on the cold wooden floor which added to the violation. He only stayed for half an hour afterwards and all I wanted was to shower, to wash away the bad feeling. You know I could still smell him on me the next morning at work, it was like he'd stamped me with his odour'. I needed some air all of a sudden but settled for gulping down water.

'Oh my god, I knew it. I knew I wasn't the first woman that he'd raped', I flinched at the word and at the venom in her voice. That was when she had described her own experience, so much more violent than mine, more callous.

'I literally couldn't stop myself crying. He kept saying to me, "Your perspective is really mucked up. Has anyone ever told you that you have a problem with intimacy, that you are cold—I really hope you get that together". My self-esteem was at an all time low, in that moment I might have accepted what he was saying but then he said, "If you'd said *no* louder the second time, I might have taken more notice, taken you seriously". She finally stopped for breath'.

'I was struggling mentally already. You see I had finally admitted to myself that I was gay. It had taken a long time to face the truth and I had been preparing to tell my family. I'd come out to a girl at work who I thought was a lesbian'. Gill gave a self-deprecating snort, 'She wasn't, but she was so supportive and accepting. She was really helping me come to terms with... no, be happy about... my future as a gay woman. And then Neil had to go and do that to me'.

'I am so sorry. I can't imagine how violating that must have been. Did Neil know you were gay?', I asked.

She nodded, new tears on her cheek, 'I thought he was my friend, that I could trust him. I had told him the night before but his response made me sick to the stomach. He told me that lesbians turned him on', the sadness in her eyes after all these decades broke my heart and my loathing of Neil roared up the scale.

'Disgusting!' my breathing was loud, fueled by the vehemence of reaction and shock. Gillian gave an ironic smile but said nothing for a minute.

'A year ago, I reported the historic assault to the police. I expected them to laugh at me but actually they were terrific'.

'God, that is gutsy. I could never be that brave'.

'It took a lot of time, a lot of counselling sessions', that same snort half humour, half despair, 'and the love of an amazing woman who has helped me see what a grubby prick Neil was'. Gillian's composure floored me. Part of me wanted to walk away, the better part knew I had to hear this out.

'When I made my statement, the policewoman said that she doubted they would be able to press charges given how long ago the assault happened. The best she could offer was to call Neil in for questioning and ask for a statement from him. Not much but knowing he would be outraged was almost enough...almost'. As Gill paused, I raised my brows, waiting.

'Anyway, long story short. I was telling a lawyer friend about it and she said that if the police had several reports of similar crimes, there was a chance that he would at least have to go to court. She was still skeptical that it would succeed but the allegations would be public'.

'And he has a family, a big reputation as a businessman and philanthropist, basically a lot to lose', I finally understood why I was here and my heart lurched.

'Exactly, so I contacted his two ex-wives and any old girl-friends I could dig up. I had no idea where you were but then I saw your article about burnout'. Of course, the cryptic message I'd received.

'Did any of them agree to make a statement to police?' It was hard to admit even to myself that I hoped she would say no and so it was all over, nothing more to be done.

'One of his ex-wives made a complaint but that seemed to be more about causing trouble for him than anything she actually experienced. A work colleague, he had an affair with has said she will...but her gripe is about how their inappropriate relationship ruined her career but she agrees everything was entirely consentual.

'So you want me to tell them what happened to me', time slowed down. 'I'm not sure I can'.

'I'm not here to pressure you. I understand it's not for every-one—the publicity, reliving feelings, ransacking the life you've created in spite of that episode. For me, it was deeply neces-sary. For the ex-, it's about retribution after a pathetic divorce settlement...' her voice trailed off, inviting me to reflect on my own situation.

All I could think was that the abortion would become public, a sacredly private act that should never be linked to the sordid crimes of the father. 'I'll think about it but I don't have your courage. I wish you well, though, you deserve justice'. I was sweaty, clammy with rage and fear. I needed to breathe. I needed to get out of there.

An hour later I was still in the car, staring at the waves, not seeing them. My mind was full of those brave young women on every current affairs program who held men like Neil to account. I tried to make sense of how it had affected my life. For a long time, I had believed that Neil found me dull and that was why he was so inattentive during our brief relationship. Lately, I'd acknowledged that he had seen my shyness as evidence of a submissive nature. Closer acquaintance had dispelled that idea and he had quickly extricated himself.

Having the abortion had been an obvious choice but what I hadn't resolved was how it had coloured my view of who I was. For reasons that made little sense, I had internalized the notion that I no longer deserved to be a mother. It must have been Catholic guilt convincing me that repentance was my just deserts. Why had I not understood this years ago? I had been so set on moving on from the experience that I hadn't processed its impact, hadn't allowed time for forgiveness.

Tears were blurring the crashing waves and sobs drowning out the screech of seagulls. Gillian's honesty stood in stark contrast to my own obfuscation. The conversations I'd had with Rob and Paige had been a start but easy compared to what I knew came next. I recalled the draft email to Neil that I had never sent with relief. This was a matter that required eye contact, not something that could be swiftly sent to trash without being read. That little girl in the nursery deserved a grandmother who would love her one hundred percent. Resolving my baggage would ensure I could be that person.

As I told Rob about my meeting with Gill, I broke down all over again. He was wonderful as I knew he would be, gentle and thoughtful as he asked, 'Did you ever think about reporting this guy before?'

'No, never. This will sound hopeless but I blamed my own lack of experience for what happened rather than him. I feel so stupid saying this but I didn't see it for what it was, I didn't call it out as rape. My way of dealing with the shame was to try to have a real relationship with him and to be honest I think the only reasons he kept seeing me was a mix of convenience and guilt', I stopped for a moment knowing I needed to speak the truth, 'Guilt and a belief that I wouldn't be demanding, would bow to his needs and for a while I did just that'.

'But you said you didn't introduce him to your friends'.

'I knew Pippa and Cleo would see straight through him. They would never have liked him, would have told me he was all wrong for me. And they would have been spot-on. What is most devastating and the thing that I have never thought about before is that if I had reported him, Gillian might have been spared. In all these years it never occurred to me that there were others ...'.

'Don't be too hard on yourself. You were very young and your mother had just died. You were vulnerable and trusting; those are wonderful attributes that he took advantage of'.

I knew Rob was right and I wished I could be as angry as I ought to be but mostly I was sad. Maybe that was why when I woke in the middle of the night it was with the lingering images of a dream that my friends had all gone out without me, that I was alone and that everyone had been laughing as they tried to leave without telling me where they were going. They were all having a great time, at a party, dancing and drinking and I was standing alone outside in the garden, not able to find a door or a window that would let me join them.

Tossing and turning I found myself replaying the one time Neil had invited me out with his friends. It was someone's wedding, a university mate, and we drove the two hours north with other friends. One guy I recalled as tall, heavily built, crumpled, with more stubble than was fashionable at the time and the other was shorter with tight curly hair and wire rimmed glasses. We must have gone to the wedding ceremony but I don't remember it, actually I don't remember much until about an hour into the reception. Neil and his buddies disappeared on the pretext of decorating the wedding car, presumably with cans and toilet paper and left me at a table with five other women. They knew each other well and soon tired of trying to include me in their conversation. One, two, almost three hours went by and still Neil wasn't back. I knew I was drinking too much but after a while I stopped caring, I had never felt so out of place. So it was no surprise that I was pretty drunk when it came time to farewell the happy couple, by which time Neil had resurfaced from his own drinking session out the back. I had trouble standing up, must have been slurring. Suddenly Neil was in a hurry to leave, such a hurry that we left my bag behind which would have been bad enough but it had our room key in it. It can be a challenge to find someone in a country motel after midnight to replace your key and I've no idea how long I sat in the corridor while Neil tried to raise someone. Next morning the drive home was silent with his fury which like everything else I told myself I deserved.

Chapter 20

The following morning I had a call from Paige to say she and Maggie could come home later that day, probably mid-afternoon and I gratefully brushed aside all remaining thoughts of Neil and focused on their homecoming. Rob had a meeting that he couldn't change and so I arrived at the hospital alone, packing all the gifts and bags into the car while Paige settled Maggie in the car seat we had installed the day before. It had been Rob's idea so that we could help Paige out as much as possible and now as I gingerly navigated out of the carpark I wondered if he'd thought about how nerve wracking it would be having such precious cargo. Paige sat in the back seat calmly watching her daughter sleep, both of them oblivious to my anxiety.

'Do you want to go straight home or come to our place for a while?' I asked as I spiralled around the final tight turn to exit the carpark.

'Home please. I've missed being in my own space but if you can stay for a while that would be great. I might need a hand getting organized and ...', she met my gaze in the rear vision mirror, 'I was hoping you might be able to stay tonight'.

'Of course', I was annoyed with myself for not suggesting it, I should have realized that the first few nights would be daunting even for someone as confident as Paige. 'Rob can collect a few things for me when he finishes work and pick up some dinner as well'.

'Thank you. The nurses have been amazing, teaching me all this stuff in the last couple of days but I'll feel better once I've done everything a few times on my own'. I concentrated on the road for the remainder of the short trip while Paige made cooing noises to her daughter. Attempting to put myself in her place, I could imagine how deeply she was missing Marjorie and I was ashamed not to have said so earlier. 'Your Mum would be so proud of you and how well you are coping. You must wish that she had met Maggie and that you could ask for her advice'.

'Of course I'm beyond sad that Maggie will never know her. And, yes, she would have had lots of suggestions for looking after a newborn, both helpful and irritating no doubt. Caro and I discussed the other night how we would both love her to be here now. How happy she would have been to be a grandmother but we also agreed we are happy that when Mum needed us, we could give her our full attention and neither of us would have been able to do that now that we are starting our own families'. Our conversation was interrupted by a crescendo of demands from Maggie.

'Obviously she is agreeing that she will be needing your undivided attention', I laughed.

Silver linings were all very well but sometimes they wear thin, I thought as we arrived at Paige's place and unpacked the car. Paige took the baby inside and when I joined them she was gently helping Maggie latch on and start to feed. Her greedy gulping and grunting were the only sounds for a while. Paige was monitoring her every suck and breath. I was beguiled by that tiny creased brow that suggested deep concentration or great effort.

'She seems to be feeding well', I eventually said.

'Yesterday and today it has been mostly every two or three hours but last night there were a couple of times when it was hourly'.

'Would you be comfortable expressing milk and letting me do a couple of the night feeds?'

'I haven't tried her on a bottle but that would be amazing if I could have a longer sleep. I don't think I should try it tonight but maybe in a few days time I will take you up on the offer'.

And so my new routine began, every evening I arrived at Paige's place and stayed until after midnight, giving her a chance to sleep, sometimes for as much as six hours. Those hours became the focus of my day, holding Maggie while she fed, her finger grasping mine, her snuffling breath, those windy smiles that squeezed my heart. Some nights Rob joined me but more often I was alone in the semi-darkness, a serene space until she cried softly demanding more milk or needing to be burped. I sang her old songs, half-remembered from my own childhood and made up stories about a beautiful girl who was loved by all in her kingdom. My nonsense seemed to soothe her when she had become worked up and the deep peace I felt as she settled again was like nothing I had experienced. As the pale blue of her eyelids slowly closed, I told her how much her Mamie adored her and what a lucky girl she was to have such a fantastic Mum. I told her that her Papi was missing her when he wasn't there and that her aunties would be having their own babies soon. I told her that she was a delight, that I rejoiced in being part of her life, that it was impossible to imagine the world without her.

Yet in spite of an overwhelming pull to stay in the moment with Maggie, there were many nights when I found myself thinking of Gillian, of Neil, of what might have been if circumstances had been different. I'd had a message from Gillian after our meeting, thanking me for listening to her story, telling me that the second woman had decided not to go ahead with a report and asking if I had thought any more about it. Her undemanding message made me feel more guilty than any direct accusation could have. Soon I would have to act but for the moment I wrapped myself in Maggie's milky sweetness, an unlikely but effective shield.

During the days I worked on a business plan for my company and with the help of our accountant put in place the boring administrative and regulatory necessities. My plan was to start advertising after we had been to visit Cleo and Marco the following weekend. It would be the first night that I hadn't been with Maggie for two months and I had mixed feelings: happy to be back in my own world; worried about Paige not having any help. Paige on the other hand was very definite— she would be perfectly fine, in fact for the future we should plan on me only helping out one or two evenings each week.

'Nell, you'll be busy with your new business. Maggie and I can manage now, she is sleeping better and I've become an expert at taking catnaps during the day when she sleeps'.

'I know, you're amazing. And I need to see if I can make a go of this but I will miss spending time with her. You have been incredibly generous letting us have so many hours together. It has been so special: every tiny change, even the threads of terror that creep in when she's distressed and I can't work out what is wrong'. My smile was rueful, self-deprecating and Paige hugged me for a long moment. I meant it when I said she was amazing, I had been worried that she would struggle with the lack of control that motherhood seemed to foist on most people but she had embraced those unpredictable, unstructured days and nights that were dictated by Maggie's needs. Some evenings, Maggie would want to feed almost constantly, cluster feeding Paige called it. Those days she looked as though more than her milk had been sucked dry.

Thursday night was my last six hour shift with Maggie before we had our weekend down south. Lately she had been feeding well for me and going down in her crib without too much fuss. I had been telling myself, now she was older and bigger, she would start to be easier for Paige to do overnights alone. Maggie had other ideas.

She had fed as usual just before I planned to go home at midnight but was clingy and wingy when I tried to put her back to sleep. None of my usual ploys were having any effect, she cried the minute I put her down, only stopping when she was safely back in my arms. Every time I thought she was asleep and attempted to transfer her, she woke instantly. One-handed I found the thermometer in the bathroom, no fever. Maybe being swaddled in the muslin wrap would make her feel more secure? I didn't want to wake Paige. Another feed, she could be still hungry? The darkness, the late hour, my own weariness were starting to play with reason when she finally allowed me to place her in the crib, only for Paige to appear in the doorway of the nursery.

'You should be on your way home', she whispered, rubbing one eye.

'Just going, she's been very clingy for the last couple of hours. Had trouble putting her back down but she's finally set-tled', I crossed my fingers but it was too late, she had roused at the sound of Paige's voice. 'Oh dear, you could have a long night still ahead', my voice was apologetic but Paige shrugged, and pulled her wrap tighter before picking up her now crying daughter.

'We'll be fine. You go home'.

'Call me if there is anything...' I had a premonition that sleep could be elusive as I tried to shake the low level anxiety that clenched my stomach.

Paige sounded surprised when I called her early the next morning to make sure they were okay. 'Maggie's good. She slept almost as soon as you left and she seems to be in her usual routine this morning. Nothing to worry about', she reassured. Grandparents weren't supposed to feel separation anxiety, I reminded myself as I turned my thoughts to enjoying our weekend away.

There had been a lot of rain over the summer and the highlands were obscenely, iridescently green as we wound up and around the rolling hills, strewn with dairy cows. Deep ocean blues appeared randomly, reminding us how close to the coast we were. Rob was playing a favourite blues album, singing occasionally under his breath while I gave my attention to the landscape, determined to soak up the bucolic calm in preparation for the whirlwind of Cleo and Marco.

I had been to Milton once or twice, years before and remembered it as a quaint village so was surprised by the modern development on its outskirts. Sea changers or tree changers I assumed. Signs at the showground still welcomed us to the Annual Show although it had been held in March and we were sorry to see we had missed the Scarecrow Festival the previous weekend as well. The main street was already busy with locals stocking up for the weekend, chatting over coffee or just enjoying the early winter sunshine. The bakery, clearly the hub for news and gossip, was doing a roaring trade in coffee and cakes and there were more than a few tourists wandering in and out of small boutiques full of goods that were as unnecessary as they were delightful. Cleo had warned us to bring plenty of warm clothes but the morning was brilliant if brisk when we stepped out of the car in front of their new home.

'This place is so gorgeous', I knew I was gushing but everything about it was perfect. A near-naked oak tree dominated the front yard and half a dozen hens were pecking at the ground around it, oblivious to our arrival. Not so the tiny puppy who barked from the wide verandah, contained by a child's play pen for the time being. The house itself was built of narrow, rough bricks that had seen many coats of white paint over the years but the corrugated iron roof was new and the back section of the house appeared to be a modern addition. The garden had already seen a frost or two and the rose blossoms were brown and shrivelled. Behind the house there were more trees, neatly planted rows of apples and pears.

Cleo appeared from the side of the house, 'I thought I heard Sammi bark. Welcome to our new home—it's so exciting to have proper visitors'. Sammi was jumping madly, determined to free himself from his enclosure and meet Lucca who was showing mild interest at best in the crazy baby.

'What a great house! You two have the best taste'. Their house in Sydney had been thoroughly modern but unlike all the other open-plan cubes of concrete and glass it used divided spaces, colour and garden to create intimacy and warmth. This new place was nothing like it except for that immediate impression of welcome.

'We were lucky to find it but yes, it's exactly what we were looking for. Somehow moving to the country made us want to go back to simpler times and this house...well, it's a constant reminder of that. Come and meet our latest addition' Cleo gestured for us to follow her to the verandah. 'This is baby Sammi; isn't he the sweetest boy'.

'So cute. How long have you had him?'

'Only a week. We picked him up from the breeder last Sunday and he has settled in so well'. Cleo ruffled his ears and picked up the squirming tangle of legs which quieted his yapping momentarily and I remembered Lucca at that age, along with the three hundred dollar pair of shoes and pieces of furniture he had chewed. I must have been frowning because Cleo's next words were to reassure me that he was ninety percent toilet trained and she would keep him in his crate overnight.

'Come around the back, Marco is trying to patch a hole in the chicken coop'.

'You two sure are taking this country living seriously', Rob walked up to join us, laughing at Cleo pout of objection.

As we followed her to the backyard her face became more serious and her voice was quiet, 'It's been the circuit breaker we needed. Let Marco show you all the clever things he has been doing'.

Marco was wearing headphones which presumably was why he hadn't heard our arrival. In fact he started as Rob clasped his shoulder in greeting, pulling them off but still shouting slightly, 'You're here! Fantastic. Sorry didn't hear the car. Listening to music and trying to mend this break in the netting. Our neighbour', he nodded to his right, 'says there are foxes around and we don't want to lose the girls'.

'Ha, yes, we saw them as we came in, the girls I mean. Can I hold that flap up so that you can tie it?'

'Thanks Rob, that would be good. I've been trying to prop it up with my knee and I'm starting to get a cramp'.

The two of them stayed outside, stooped over with heads close together, an occasional expletive the only conversation to be heard as Cleo and I walked into the house. I was expecting the house to be a work in progress but there wasn't an unpacked box in sight as we passed through the kitchen and living room to deposit our bag in the guest bedroom.

'This is your room and the bathroom is here opposite', Cleo said opening the door on a very modern bathroom across the hall. 'Our room is here and there's a third bedroom that we use as a study at the back'.

'This room is gorgeous', I said as we stood in the master bedroom, a huge picture window looking down through the orchard to rolling hills. 'You must love waking up to this'.

'It is spectacular, isn't it and this morning we had a fog that only lifted an hour or so ago. Marco described it as mystical; it was like being in a romantic nineteenth century painting'.

Back in the kitchen I was drawn to the old fashion cooker, 'Goodness is this Aga an original?' I asked touching it to feel the warmth but finding it cold.

'No', Cleo laughed. 'Thankfully it's a new reproduction of the old Aga but with modern features. There's still three ovens, though and the plate on top is the old traditional type'.

The kitchen was sunny with a big oak table at its centre and an armchair in the brightest spot under the window. Everything about it screamed, *this is home*, from the wooden cabinetry to the slate floor with its underfloor heating.

'Was everything already renovated when you bought it?' I was ready to move in myself.

'The kitchen and bathrooms were done. We painted the bedrooms and the sitting room because we wanted some colour but all the hard work had been done. Marco is still finding small things to do but there's nothing too big to sap his energy'.

'But enough to keep him busy?'

'Exactly', Cleo turned to put the kettle on and I sat at the kitchen table, admiring the branch of rosemary that she had arranged in an enamel jug. 'I bought that at the local bric-a-brac place. We'll go this afternoon. I love poking about in there, mostly it's rubbish but there are a few treasures that keep me going back'.

'Have the kids been down much? Oh and how is the baby?'

'Sofia is beautiful, we saw her when we were in Sydney a couple of weeks ago. They haven't been down, not ready to decamp with the little one just yet. Theo and Alice have only been down once, it would be a month ago. They are super busy with the restaurant and planning their wedding so it will be a while before we see a lot of them. Theo calls every few days though to ask advice about the business and Marco gets a real kick out of being able to help'.

'And Bella?'

'She has been magnificent—helping with the move, the cleaning, unpacking, everything. She made it so much easier for me and because she was here Marco was content to let us get on with it. That was the thing I was most worried about, that he would exhaust himself with the move and get sicker but in fact he has more energy than he's had in ages'.

'You guys have done so well. I would never have imagined either of you in a country town but you absolutely fit in'.

'Country hicks you mean', Cleo laughed again. It was a long time since I had heard such lightness in her voice and I felt a lump forming in my throat.

'Well very sophisticated country hicks', I laughed with her.

'Do I smell baking?' Rob asked from the doorway as he and Marco were removing their now muddy shoes.

'That's Marco's doing. Cinnamon scrolls are waiting in the warming oven. Tea?' Cleo nodded towards them.

'Yum, now we feel even more spoilt'.

'Marco's been showing me the orchard and his garden. I'm not sure which is better, the apple trees or his patch of cabbages and cauliflowers. Wish I had your green thumb, mate', Rob seemed to be taking to this country living a little too enthusiastically.

'Now where are the photos of the lovely Maggie. I've been expecting you to whip them out at every minute', Cleo said as she picked up the fluffy ball of Sammi.

'I've been controlling myself', I grinned while I fossicked for the phone. 'Here she is earlier this week, she is so tiny but I'm sure that's a smile'. There were lots of oohs and aahs as I flicked through the many images of our granddaughter, until I thought I had probably exceeded my audience's interest.

'Cleo said you've been spending nights as well?' Marco said.

'Evenings really. I'm usually home by midnight after I do a feed about eleven o'clock. Until Thursday she has been going down in the crib perfectly but that all changed this week so we'll see how it goes from now on. Paige said she doesn't need me as often which is a relief but also I will miss seeing her every day'.

'And what about this new business you were telling me about on the phone', Cleo was following my line of thinking.

'The business plan is finished. Rob's been terrific helping me with some of the nitty gritty and I think I'm ready to start next week. Trudy has designed this amazing simple logo and letterhead and the one useful thing I did on long service leave was teach myself to set up a website. So it's all systems go for, what do you call it—a soft launch?'

'That's fantastic. How will it work?' Marco was immediately interested. His business sense would be a useful reality check I thought as I described the concept to them and my plans to start off with just me and just build it slowly if there was enough demand.

Cleo wanted to know about the logo and how I was going to advertise. 'It's a red square that has a black circle and a square side-by-side across it'.

'Like the SOS flag? That's clever!'

'Yes, I really like it and I'm impressed that she came up with the idea all by herself. She is very creative, like my Mum, must have skipped a generation'.

'One thing I would say', Marco seemed to be choosing his words carefully, 'Don't be too low key in your ambitions. Sometimes you need to be a certain size to make the business work, you know so that you can respond to demand of different types and all at the same time'. I nodded, understanding he had a fair point. My soft launch probably was more like a feasibility piece and I would then need to invest earlier than I'd planned but that could wait a few weeks.

'Nell', Cleo was suddenly serious, 'Are you sure you won't miss the hospital and nursing? It's a big change after all these years of identifying as a nurse'.

'You told me once before that you'd had regrets but the time is right for me. You remember how burnt out I was before taking leave and as the end approached my anxiety levels were building higher every day. I can't go back to that combination of pressure and being sure I am doing a poor job because resources and time are so scarce. It empties you from both ends'.

Chapter 21

As promised after lunch, Cleo and I went to explore the local shops, making the vintage store our first stop. There had been a time when I would have arrived at the cash register with a pile of pretty plates, teapots, maybe a small piece or two of silver cutlery but I was more restrained these days. Happy to browse I saw with amusement that Cleo was not been burdened by any such moderation.

'What will you do with that?' I pointed to the slightly rusty enamel urinal she was holding.

'I thought for the garden. What do you think? Too quirky?'

'I'm sure you will make it work', I hoped I sounded more confident than I felt.

'The shopkeeper said, it's french', she expounded: reason enough to assume all would work out.

As we strolled and window shopped, Cleo told me about Marco's ups and downs and her voice and manner had lost much of the frenetic quality that had so worried me in the months before.

'Like I was telling you that day on the street, he has bought something in a big box that he is keeping in the shed where he thinks I won't look. I found it by accident but I can tell from the post mark he has had it a while. I'm pretty sure I know what it is but at least for the moment he seems happy and I've stopped worrying he will do something impulsive'.

'I know you want me to ask him about it but honestly I'm really uncomfortable.

'Of course. I shouldn't have asked; that wasn't fair. I was panicking that day. I'm not so scared now. Don't say anything; he would likely get angry anyway'.

'Thanks, that's a relief'. We had made our way to a coffee shop and were sitting looking down the valley and warming ourselves after being out so long. 'You see I've been dealing with some other emotional shit and I'm just not sure I am in a head space to deal with Marco's as well'.

Cleo looked more intrigued than worried as she moved her chair closer and leaned forward waiting for me to go on. 'Are you still worrying about Paige and Caroline accepting you. I think you pretty obviously have that sorted'.

I could tell she was giving me space, knowing that I was not talking about the girls but uncertain where to go next. 'Do you remember back when we were students, in that first place we rented in Glebe?'

'The place that always smelt like old boots? It was such a dump'.

The three story terrace in Glebe had lingering details of a more glorious past but it was rundown when we lived there. The basement was rented by two guys who were at university up the road. I can only picture one of them: Sean with his shock a black hair, heavy rimmed glasses and English accent was into the seventh year of a four year law degree and he was often around, ready for a chat. Pippa, Cleo and I had the middle floor which was better than the dark space below street level but we had tape on the windows where the glass had cracked and landlords in closer proximity than was healthy on the top floor. The fence was propped up in three places, paint peeled in reams from the outside walls and the creaking gate ensured everyone knew when visitors arrived or left.

'I drove past there, probably two years ago and it has been totally renovated. It looked amazing, all the wrought iron filigree and the frieze at the top had been replaced or repaired. It was beautiful. Anyway...a few months after we moved in, I still didn't know you and Pippa that well and we were all working crazy hours'.

'Those nights and the double shifts—do you remember how tired we would be when we finally got home in the early hours of the morning. And that bloody neighbour who used to complain about all the noise, if only we'd been partying instead of collapsing into bed'.

'I think I finally became an adult living there with you two. All those long talks, what did we call them? Dee and Ems'.

'Oh yes, deep and meaningfuls. We were into that big time. That was when we got to know you better, at the beginning you were so quiet I thought you hated us'.

'It was difficult after Mum died but I loved those conversations, developing our own views and our boundaries. You and Pippa were so much more interesting than me. And... I had some other stuff going on: a short relationship with this guy called Neil. Relationship is probably too grand a description for what it was. He wanted casual sex and we occasionally went out, there wasn't much more to it'.

'I can't remember him but a lot of people passed through that house'.

'You never met him, I made sure of that as far as I could'.

Cleo's eyebrows threatened to collide with her hairline but she didn't say anything. I appreciated how much resolve that must have taken.

'I knew you and Pippa would see him for the weak, using bastard he was. I wanted to believe I was a little in love with him and I wasn't prepared to reveal how fake the whole thing was...', I was concentrating on keeping my voice strong but I could hear a quaver as I uttered the word *fake*.

'Lots of us were into pretty casual relationships back then, he wasn't Robinson Crusoe. I didn't have many one-night-stands but there were at least two. Can't say I'm proud of them but hardly embarrassed either'.

This was harder than I expected, 'Cleo the thing is, Neil raped me the first night he came to our place. It was my first time and I wanted it to mean something'. Cleo's mouth dropped open but she said nothing, only covering it with her hand when I started to speak again. 'He wasn't exactly violent but he was more than insistent if that makes sense. In the end though he wasn't really into me'.

'What do you mean not violent, he raped you', Cleo's slammed her hand on the table making the couple at the next booth look up, puzzled, clearly discussing what they thought was going on between us. It was a relief when they got up to pay the bill a few minutes later, leaving us as the only customers still in the café.

'Did you report it?

'It never occurred to me. I know that sounds ridiculous but...and this is mortifying...I was kind of grateful that someone was interested in me. I hadn't had a boyfriend and I had wondered if there was something wrong with me, if I was unlovable in that way'. Cleo waited for me to go on, 'Trouble was, in the end I felt more unlovable than ever'.

'Nell, this is crazy. You had heaps of friends, your brother, so many people who relied on you'.

I nodded, not sure how to explain that there was a hole in me that all that love couldn't filled. I knew it had started when Dad died and Mum became emotionally removed and it had taken years for me to recognize that I was the only one who could fill it. Not even Rob's love had been enough—yet when he had loved me it had become easier to love myself. 'Anyway, there is more to the story. You may not remember but I had a holiday in Melbourne for a couple of weeks, my first big trip'.

'Vaguely. Pippa and I thought you were strange going off by yourself but neither of us could take leave. You sent a postcard of a tram, it was on the fridge for ages'.

'I broke up with Neil just before and needed to clear my head. Besides I hadn't been anywhere and Melbourne sounded romantic. One of the other nurses at work came from there and she used to talk about it all the time. You know, the Greek and Italian restaurants, the gardens, the coffee shops and wine bars. I told myself it would be a trial run for travelling in Europe but what I didn't admit to myself was that I was putting space between Neil and myself so that I wouldn't weaken and see him again'.

'Hang on, you know I think I did meet him. Pippa too. There was a guy who came and asked for you a couple of times when you were away. We thought it must be a secret fling but when we asked you about it you said you had no idea who it could be. I was creeped out by it at the time. Did you see him again, after Melbourne I mean?'

I shook my head, 'But not because I used the time to galvanise my willpower'. I stopped for a long minute and I could feel Cleo's impatience as her thumb tapped the table lightly. 'Three or four days after I arrived in Melbourne, I started to worry I was pregnant. My period was late, which wasn't unusual but I noticed that my breasts were tender and then I vomited one morning. I did a test; it was positive'.

'Nell, you never said anything?' Cleo's eyes creased with concern and a hint of reproach.

'I found a clinic and had a termination the same week. Nothing felt real. Afterwards I couldn't bear to think about it let alone tell people'.

'You must have still been recuperating when you came back to Sydney? I remember you seemed sad. Pippa and I thought you might have met a boy in Melbourne and then not been able to keep seeing him. Have you told Pippa?'.

I shook my head, 'You are only the fourth person. And that's the last part of the story—this woman Gillian, contacted me out of the blue. I asked you about her, remember but you didn't remember her either. Well turns out she was Neil's house mate and he abused her as well. She has reported the rape recently as a historical case and she was looking for other women he went out with him to see if...you know...'

'She wants you to report him as well? Is that a good idea after all this time'.

'Part of me thinks I should but I'm not brave. I buried that time so deep, the wound may never heal if it's exposed to air and light for a second time'.

Cleo reached across to hold my hands. I had been hoping she would leap up and hug me and I anticipated her next words would challenge me at best, disappoint and hurt at worst. She kept her voice low and measured, staring over my left shoulder as she searched for words. 'I'm not sure what exactly you are afraid of after all this time but I can see you hoped never to have to face it. Seems to me, you are more than halfway in, you can't undo it now; there is no path back so I don't see you have a choice'.

Cleo was the lawyer giving her closing argument and I was the guilty prisoner in the dock wiping tears, making no pretense of being in control. As though reading my mind, she went on, 'You have no reason to be embarrassed or ashamed about any of this. I can understand that you may regret your decision to not have your baby but it was another time, you were a teenager...'

How to explain the warped logic that had told me all these years that having the abortion was the right thing and yet at the same time meant I was not fit to be a mother? I told her that I carried that sadness as self-reproach, as evidence that I couldn't be trusted with that sort of joy. I admitted that I had misread Paige and Caroline; the prism of the confessional window distorted their words so that I heard barbs that were rarely intended. The whine of self-pity was threatening at every minute.

'Nell this is ludicrous! Listen to yourself. This is not you, not your life. Yes, it was one incident but it hardly defines you'. She stood up, apparently impatient with my nonsense and walked to the counter to pay, still shaking her head. As she walked back to our table, I prepared myself for the home truths her serious expression forewarned.

'If you had your time again, do you think you would make the same decision?'

'Almost certainly, I can't see how at that stage of my life I could have raised a baby without any support. I would never have asked Neil to help because the affair with him was tainted; it made me feel dirty. I suppose that came from all those nuns telling me that my body was my temple and sex for it's own sake was demeaning. It took me another ten years to properly let go of those twisted ideas'.

'Catholic education has a lot to answer for', Cleo agreed.

'And my Nanna—because I idolized her and she was always warning me to be careful that boys only wanted one thing. I feel ridiculous saying this out loud, like some sort of naïve thirteen year old. My niece would be rolling on the ground in hysterics at the very thought'.

'There might be a message there, you know. And at the risk of being crass, weren't you on the pill'.

'Of course and I was careful but I'd looked after a patient with meningitis and the doctors said I should take antibiotics to prevent infection. I think that's why I still got pregnant. For a long time I used to think I must have forgotten a dose but then one day we had an in-service with the ward pharmacist and she said that the antibiotic I took can make the pill less effective'.

'Wow, you couldn't take a trick'.

'I know bad luck was stalking me but that's not how I saw it at the time. It took me the longest time to realise I had to forgive my nineteen year old self for a lapse in judgement and now I need to forgive Neil too but that doesn't mean I shouldn't report his actions as well'.

'Good girl. That's more like the Nell I know. It's getting late and the boys will be wondering where we are'.

The walk home was hurried as a cold twilight blew in and we kept our heads down in the collar of our jackets. Talking to Cleo, more than Rob or Paige or Gill, had brought me to a better understanding of my feelings about Neil and those few weeks of pregnancy. For the first time since Paige had asked me to go to the clinic with her, I felt an inner calm. I had been procrastinating for months, avoiding anything that appeared risky but now those deliberate decisions and actions opened up as opportunities I should embrace.

Later that evening, Rob and Cleo volunteered to clear up after dinner and disappeared into the kitchen. My slow cooked casserole had been perfect for the early winter evening and together with the red wine that Marco produced had left us mellow, our conversation hushed. I was surprised then when Marco gestured for me to follow him onto the verandah. The sky was bright with stars and the only sound was the far away howl of a dog that had had his sleep disturbed.

I wrapped my arms around my shoulders, 'It's freezing out here but this sky is amazing'.

'It is one of the things I love most about living here, the night sky is vast and pitch black unless it's a full moon. You miss that in the city. Oddly, I am loving the cold as well. Since the MG diagnosis I have been cossetted from so much, it's a relief to feel something raw and honest and...yes, freezing'.

'I am so pleased the move has worked out for you both. I admit I was skeptical but the two of you seem to have found your niche'. At the back of my mind I was thinking this would be the moment to ask Marco about his longer term thoughts as Cleo had requested but his next words took us in a different direction.

'Yeah, now that we are settled and while I'm still well I wanted to ask you a favour?'

'Sure', my voice must have revealed my doubts.

'Only if you are comfortable. You see I want to send Cleo on a holiday as a thank you. She has been incredible, I wouldn't be here without her you know'.

'What a lovely idea'.

'And well, I thought maybe the two of you could go together so that she would have company. You could visit Pippa and live it up in France for a couple of weeks'.

'Funny, Rob and I have been talking about when we'll go to Paris to see Caroline so I could easily go with Cleo and then meet Rob in Paris for another week or so. I'm not sure how this will all fit with the new business but I'm sure we can work it out'.

'Great. I want to tell Cleo in the morning and then we can all discuss the best timing for flights and all that. Thanks Nell, this means a lot'.

'You're asking me to take a holiday, to a place I love. Hardly the worst thing...' I laughed off his gratitude. 'She'll be worried about you of course. What if she says no?'

'I thought the same so I've arranged for Bella to come and stay with me for a short holiday in the country. She likes it down here. In fact, she has even mentioned moving to somewhere nearby, probably on the coast'.

'To be closer to you?'

'Yeah, but she is also sick of the rat race and she mostly works from home. Her acting roles have dried up but the kids books are going gangbusters. Down here she could afford a house, more than you can do in the city these days'.

'You have it all covered. How exciting, a holiday with the old gang. It will be like old times, only better because we aren't so poor these days'.

Chapter 22

Next morning Marco was already in the kitchen making break-fast as the rest of us slowly emerged, yawning, demanding coffee, muffled in our winter woolies although Marco had already lit the fire.

'You're very perky this morning', Cleo teased.

'It's a gorgeous, sunny winter's day and I wanted to make everyone breakfast'.

'That's nice', Cleo looked as if she was about to offer to help but then sat down and let Marco serve her.

Following her lead I warmed my hands on the coffee cup and sipped appreciatively.

'I have missed your trademark coffee; it's as fantastic as ever, thanks'. Rob nodded his agreement but unable to stay still he was fiddling with the fire.

'I've made us a special treat, hope you all like eggs benedict'.

'Are you kidding, that's my idea of heaven', I didn't need to exaggerate, 'I've always said it will be my last meal'.

'Ha-ha, well hopefully not today'.

Once the eggs had been served Marco disappeared into the other room. Cleo was immediately suspicious, 'What's he up to? He's probably tired himself out doing all this'.

Before Rob or I could respond, Marco reappeared, both hands full. He had a bottle of champagne in one hand and an enormous box in the other. The box was still in its postage pack although it had obviously been slit open at the top.

'I have a special presentation that I would like to make', he announced.

We looked from one to the other, quizzical, amused at the dramatic breakfast interlude. Marco busily found glasses and handing Rob the bottle gestured for him to pour.

'Champagne for breakfast, must be a very special occasion', Rob played along. Cleo hadn't said anything and when I turned to catch her eye expecting a mischievous glint she was picking at her nails and staring at her coffee cup. Looking more closely at the parcel beside the table I could see it had been sent from Germany and I remembered Cleo's concerns about what it contained.

Marco cleared his throat, 'When Cleo suggested we down-size to the country a few months ago I thought she was bonkers and now I couldn't be happier. It has been the circuit breaker that let us start a new phase. My health is better', he tapped his head to simulate touching wood, 'and Cleo and I have so much time together. But there is one thing that has been bothering me'.

'Here it comes', Cleo's murmur was almost inaudible.

'Cleo has given up everything she loved for me and it is time for her to have some fun. Overseas travel has always been your passion sweetheart and it's going to be hard for me to do those long haul flights now, so...' he drew out the moment, 'this is for you'. With a flourish he brought the parcel to Cleo and kissed her brow. 'For you my love'.

Cleo shook her head, not understanding and began peeling open the plastic wrapper to reveal a cabin-sized suitcase, a retro design in the most extraordinary orange. 'Open it,' Marco was impatient.

Tears filled her eyes as Cleo found the envelope inside, 'Two first class tickets to Paris! Oh Marco this is so thoughtful'.

'It's all arranged', he looked positively smug. 'Nell will go with you and you can catch up with Pippa as well. Rob and

Nell were already planning a trip to see Caroline so they can continue on when you come home. And Bella will stay with me, suits her as she is looking for a place down this way and it will stop you worrying about whether I'm alright'.

'But you should come as well. Surely you would be okay going first and...', Marco didn't let her finish. 'My travelling days are over Cleo, I am perfectly content here and besides who would look after Sammi?'

'Marco, you can't buy my ticket as well as Cleo's. I told you, Rob and I were already planning a trip'.

'Nonsense and anyway, too late. You have been marvellous to us Nell and it's the least I can do to say, thank you'. Marco was hugging his wife and now I was the one in tears. Rob looked on bemused yet unconcerned, ready to work through all the details later but letting everyone else ride their emotions for now. 'Well let's cheers that', he said raising his glass.

The champagne must have gone to our heads because it was a lazy morning, feeding the chickens, playing with Sammi and trying to convince Lucca to play as well. Marco and Rob wandered down to the orchard to investigate the fruit trees, discussing the pros and cons of various natural pest control options.

'When did either of them become expert horticulturalists', Cleo laughed.

'I know, who would have thought?' I joined in her gentle mockery.

'We can hear you, you know', Marco called out.

'He is so happy this morning. It has given him so much pleasure to surprise you', I observed absently.

'Yes, and there I was thinking the worst'.

'I realized that when I saw the parcel, seems you have been jumping to conclusions'.

'I feel ridiculous now but I was so worried; well you know how worried I have been. I was thinking we should take a drive this afternoon—there are some old quince trees out at 'the two mile' that should have fruit on them. Might be full of moths but I do love quince tart'.

'Sound good. I know what you mean about the moths, I remember from when I was a kid, we'd cut them open and there would be this big black centre. Same with apples. At least we knew they were organic I suppose'.

Cleo went inside to see to a light lunch and I stayed in the weak sunshine, determined to enjoy it for as long as possible. I was still uncomfortable at Marco's generosity but there was excitement as well, a holiday with my friends, an adventure. In a moment of lucidity I acknowledged that a good part of the excitement was the prospect of escaping all expectation and (mostly self-imposed) commitment.

The conversation with Cleo the previous afternoon had sapped my energy and I had blotted it out as much as I could. Sitting quietly now, it crept back, persistent but benign. There was finally an inevitability to what I would do and my mind gave permission for tranquility. Closing my eyes I wondered how Paige was managing with little Maggie. I was missing my cuddles with her.

*

As we drove, Cleo pointed out historic landmarks and big properties. I was particularly taken with a homestead on the outskirts of town, an enormous gothic-style house, tree-lined drive, imposing stone gates, even a tiny gate house. 'It used to belong to a local family but it's been bought by a big corporation', Cleo told me. 'It's rented out for functions but as far as I know no one lives there permanently. Seems a shame'.

A while later Cleo pulled onto the side of the road. An empty paddock with quince trees along its perimeter, just inside the fence.

'Is it okay for us to climb the fence?', I asked. Cleo's response was interrupted by the sound of trail bikes as two girls appeared at the top of the hill. Cleo called out 'hello' to them but they skid to a stop and disappeared from view again.

'It's okay, I called Jenny, their Mum,' she nodded towards the hill, 'to check before we came that she didn't mind us foraging for the quinces. She's in my book club and she'd already mentioned that we were welcome to help ourselves'. Negotiating the barbed wire was more difficult than it had been in our younger days but by holding it down for each other we managed to reach the trees.

'Oh, I do love the smell of quinces', Cleo said. I on the other hand was rubbing my face as the furry skin made everything itch.

'They taste amazing but truly quinces must be the ugliest fruit'.

As we were picking, Cleo turned to me suddenly, as though she had finally remembered something important. 'Nell, can I ask you a personal question?'

Well that was a first, Cleo had never shied away from anything personal, she was all about the most intimate details. I nodded, intrigued about where this was going.

'Do you ever wonder why none of us had children: you, me, Pippa? Pippa was different—Gary's girls were so little, she was the only mother they knew—and you had that bad early experience but we are still odd'.

I didn't respond immediately trying to order my thoughts. I started slowly, 'I suppose we are all pretty self-confident and we had each other when we needed emotional support. Work was fulfilling, we travelled, we did all the stuff that young families can't do; music festivals, theatre, hedonistic weekends away...'

'But I wanted to have a family, I was so clear about that: four kids, big house, the lot', Cleo had given up all pretense of picking fruit. 'The obvious answer is that none of us met the right person at the right time. Do you think it's because we expected too much or were we too selfish?'

'Or in my case, not as mature as I liked to pretend', I said as it occurred to me for the first time that this was why I had not dealt with Neil's behaviour and with the pregnancy properly all those years ago. Closing things down, erectly walls had become my superpower.

'I'm not sure if you remember my dad. I idolized him and I measured every boyfriend I ever had against him. Marco was the first one to come close', Cleo was speaking slowly as if she too was revising her views of the past.

'Your Dad was special, so tall and, my word, such strong opinions. I made the mistake of having a discussion about politics with him once'. I laughed at the memory, 'made some inane comment about unions and not being sure if I would join the nurses union'.

'And you signed up the next week', Cleo enjoyed the memory as well. Her gaze shifted up the road in front of the car, 'Oh look'. A woman and small boy were walking towards us. The woman was tall, athletic-looking, wearing the standard cocky's weekend attire of linen shirt, jeans and riding boots. Her thick dark hair was dragged around over one shoulder and her eyes hidden behind sunglasses. I guessed she was in her early forties but unlike Cleo and I she had been careful of the sun and her face was free of freckles and lines. The boy was about four. His were knees were scraped and he had bruises on both shins; he would be a handful I thought.

'Jenny, hi. We took you up on the offer of quinces', Cleo gestured towards me, 'This is my friend Nell, she has promised us quince tart for dinner'.

'Lucky you. Hi Nell, lovely to meet you'.

'I assume you saw my eldest two terrorizing the cattle on their trail bikes up there. This is Matty'.

'Hello Matty, the girls appeared and disappeared just as quickly', Cleo smiled, her eyes crinkled against the sun that was low in the sky.

'Typical teenagers! They have been on those bikes all afternoon but I'm sure not a single one of their chores has been done', Jenny was distracted by her son stomping in a puddle he had found on the side of the road. He stood in the middle kicking up water and then bending to retrieve a pebble.

'Matty Hollows, get out of there', she called as the boy lost his balance and sat down with a cry in the muddy water. She and Cleo fussed, lifting him up and wiping him down, alternating between chastising and cuddling him. Tears flowed but soon he was running back up the road towards the homestead, his mother following and calling for him to slow down. Cleo called her thanks and waved at Jenny's retreating back. I said nothing, a brick had landed in my stomach.

'Such a nice family', Cleo said as we climbed into the car to head home. 'Matty is the youngest and according to Jenny, a gentle demon. There's an older boy as well who has just gone away to boarding school. He would only be ten, can't imagine what that's like'.

My voice was croaky as I asked, 'Do the girls go to boarding school as well?' I knew I was putting off my real question.

'No, there's a good private girls school about half an hour away, they go there. The boy is at his dad's alma mater in Sydney, not sure which one. Family tradition apparently'.

'It will be Riverside', I said.

Cleo gave me a sideways glance, 'What makes you say that?'

'It's where Neil went to school', my voice was flat. 'He was very proud to be the third generation to go there—a Hollows family tradition he said'.

'You mean the guy you told me about yesterday. That's too much of a coincidence'.

'No it's him. I knew he had a property down this way, had even played with the idea of trying to find out where. I didn't expect it to be quite so easy...'

'Shit, are you okay?'

'Shaken. I never imagined I would meet his family'. Jenny had been warm, the sort of person I would gravitate to at a party. 'She is his third wife, I wonder how many kids he has?'

'I remember Jenny saying they had his two oldest to visit last school holidays, so at least six. Apparently one of the ex-wives is very difficult, still bitter about the divorce and unpleasant to Jen'.

Neil was connected to so many people who were innocent of the experiences Gill and I shared. I wondered if Jenny was safe. I fretted about the damage that the truth of Neil's past could do to his children. I tried to picture what it would be like if I came face-to-face with Neil. The whir of thoughts was so loud that I was unaware I had been silent for so long.

'Are you coming in?' Cleo sounded amused and worried that I hadn't noticed the drive home or that we had arrived. I appreciated that she was giving me time to deal with all this new information but she wouldn't let me get away scot-free.

'Sorry, gathering my thoughts', I shook my head and exhaled loudly. 'I had better get started on the quinces so they have time to go that dusky red colour. My Nanna once scored me a five out of ten when I cooked them for her and only managed a pinkish, orange. She was like that, called a spade a spade no matter what'.

Chapter 23

Marco had had a nap and was full of energy when we arrived home. 'I bet I know what you two have been up to', he sounded pleased with himself. 'You have probably planned your whole holiday by now'.

Cleo laughed him off, 'Psychic, are you? We went to pick some quinces at Jen's place and I gave Nell a tour of the district'.

'Ah, playing the rustic tourists. One of the locals told me this week that you can forage for mushrooms in the forest about twenty minutes from here. He went last weekend and the season is just about finished but we should go next year'.

'What sort of mushrooms?' Cleo cocked a skeptical brow.

'No nothing that exciting', Marco laughed off her implication. 'The guy in the butcher shop just called them pine mushrooms. He was buying steak to eat with the ones he'd picked'.

'I remember picking mushrooms with my dad when I was a kid', I turned from peeling the quinces over the kitchen sink. 'It was of my favourite things. We'd go to the golf course, not far out of town, and pick these white field mushrooms that were pinkish brown underneath and then come home and have them grilled on buttered toast for supper'.

'Weren't you worried they might be poisonous', Cleo was dubious.

'People seemed to know they were okay, no one ever mentioned they might be poisonous. Different times'. I recalled

Stephen and I vying to fill our baskets first as Dad led the way up hills, one stride for every three of our galloping steps. I could see us so clearly: Stephen in his corduroy trousers and the mustard jumper that Mum had knitted, the arms slightly too long; me, in a red skivvy and plaid slacks. I'd worn those slacks until the two old crease marks from being let down were no longer sufficient to hide my ankles and a portion of shin.

'Penny for them', Marco said.

'I hope our grandkids have carefree moments like that', I said pulling myself back to the present.

'That's our job. To spoil them and show them the simple pleasures we loved'.

'It's a big responsibility'. I laughed but Marco was serious as he responded, 'I've realized that lately. I want to be here for them as long as I can'.

Cleo caught my eye but it was Rob who braved the truth, 'That's good to hear mate. I've been worried since you got sick that you'd lost some of your spark. Good to hear you back on form'. Marco made a small nod in acknowledgment, not needing to fill in the gaps.

On cue his phone beeped, 'Oh look it's a video of Sofia doing tummy time on her play mat. She is growing so fast. It's the only downside of our move—that we can't see her every day'. Marco gestured for me to join him at the kitchen table to see the video.

I though of all those precious evenings with Maggie. 'You know I had heard lots of gushing grandparents but until I spent those nights with Maggie, I had no idea. I wanted to protect her, love her. When she cried, I wished I could absorb whatever was worrying her so that she would be comfortable and happy'.

'Oh Nell, you old softie', Cleo teased me while Rob rubbed his hand roughly across his eyes. 'Nell is amazing with Maggie, she is so lucky to have such a wonderful Mamie', his defense sweet if unnecessary.

Cleo threw me a quick glance before turning to the men, 'I asked Nell today why she thought neither of us had had kids even when we really wanted them'.

'And what was the verdict', Marco asked.

'You first, tell me what you think'.

'You're both smart and independent. That's scary for some men', Marco offered. 'And I suppose your careers took up a lot of time when you should have been settling down although from what you have told me you had plenty of boyfriends, just not one you wanted to marry'.

Rob didn't appear ready to answer but finally said, 'I can't say for you, Cleo, but when I met Nell, I had to work to gain her trust. Me being married at the time didn't help. I suspected she had been burnt once too often...'

Marco went looking for glasses for a pre-dinner gin and tonic and Cleo followed quickly to assist. 'I think they are giving us a moment', my smile was rueful and sad at the same time. Rob didn't say anything else but sat beside me and together we stroked Lucca and his brown eyes watched us both with such sensibility that I had to wipe away my own tears. Finally he asked, 'And what did you say?'

'I said, I may not have been emotionally ready for that responsibility'. I looked at the floor not wanting to see Rob's expression but when I did look up, he was scratching his forehead trying to understand what I meant. I walked back to the quinces searching for the right words, 'Stephen and I used to say that we were orphans after Dad and Mum died and I became hesitant to commit to friendships let alone relationships. Even Cleo and Pippa thought I was stand-offish when we first all moved in together'.

Thankfully Cleo decided we'd had enough private time and she bounced back into the room with an energy I had not seen since Marco's illness. 'Now this holiday...have you thought about where we should go?' She had come to stand beside me while I cut the dry hard fruit ready to cook.

'Not really and anyway it's your treat. I'm just the chaperone'.

'Penelope Saunders you are no such thing. This is a treat to share', Cleo exaggerated her disapproval only to immediately change tack. 'Remember the big road trip we did with Pippa just before she married Gary. It was someone's wedding in Byron Bay, forget whose and we drove up after work on a Friday night'.

'It was Helen's wedding, I haven't seen or heard from her since. Weird how that happens'.

'And we had three cassettes that we played on rotation. It was so hot and humid I thought I'd melt before we arrived'.

'Oh God, I'd forgotten that. Hours of listening to Olivia Newton-John and Billy Joel. Was our taste in music really that awful?'

For the next hour or so we debated the merits of the south of France, the Loire and the dark depths of the Dordogne. Marco recommended the region around Sancerre for its beauty and its wine. Rob thought we should think about walking in the Pyrenees or around Lake Annecy, provided the weather was good. Cleo said, she'd heard about an island off the coast of La Rochelle that was idyllic and famous for its potatoes. At this rate we would need a year, not a few weeks to see everything. Leaving us to whittle down the long list, Rob and Marco escaped to put the hens in their coop before playing ball with Sammi in the garden. It was almost dark when they rejoined us in the kitchen and opened a bottle of wine.

'Looks like you need a refill', Marco laughed and I was embarrassed to find I had almost finished a glass while everyone else had barely touched theirs.

'It has been a big day,' I started not knowing if I was ready for this conversation. I told them about our how we had met

Jenny and some of her children. Rob looked at me intently as I explained that Neil Hollows was their husband and father—he made the connection immediately and came to stand behind where I was sitting at the kitchen table. Marco looked from Cleo to me to Rob and not finding any answers sat down opposite ready to hear more. And so yet again I recounted the story of my short affair with Neil and the pain of how it began and how it ended. Unlike yesterday, Cleo had tears in her eyes and I hated that her outrage had turned to pity.

Marco stood up slowly, the sound of him biting his thumb nail audible in the heavy silence. 'I know Neil Hollows or at least I have met him'. He looked at Cleo, 'You remember that fund raising lunch I went to a couple of weeks back for the local politician, he was one of the guys behind it'.

'He and his family have a lot of influence', Cleo backed Marco.

I nodded recalling what I had researched previously. He was rich, connected, respected; not someone who would take Gil's accusations lying down. Suddenly I was clear about the true reasons for my own hesitancy to report him and they weren't concern for his family or fear of reliving and exposing my own past. They were more visceral. Only a fool puts herself in harms way without the stakes being enormous. For Gil, I understood the stakes, for myself it was less clear.

As much as I may have wished for it, there was no way I could escape the rest of the evening without a forensic debate about what I should do now. Rob and Marco were inclined to caution against going public, not seeing much would be achieved and it would be unpleasant at best. Cleo was on fire, determined to convince me to make a report to the police. I sat back, the detached observer for as long as they let me but eventually, I needed to bring the conversation to a halt.

'So what I've decided is...' as I drew breath, the other three held theirs. Sammi's yapping breached the silence but no one paid it any heed, not even Lucca who had come to put his head in my lap.

'I've decided to contact Neil and ask him to meet. I'm not sure what I will do after that. Not even sure what I want to say to him right now but it's important for me to own this. Can you understand?' I searched Rob's eyes and found the validation I needed to continue. 'For me, this is more about me than him. I need to find my peace and whether he is hurt or spared in that is not my main concern. I'm not looking for justice or vengeance, it's too late for that'.

Nods. Silence. A collective assessment of the words I had not known I would say.

'Don't go alone', Marco's brow was creased. 'Take Rob or Cleo'.

'I guess you're right', I hadn't thought this through. It made sense to have a witness, another set of ears when anxiety and distress started to roar in my own. But who? I would dissolve, trying to have the conversation in front of Rob. I couldn't imagine Cleo not interrupting before either Neil or I could say what we needed.

'Do you think Paige would come?' I asked Rob.

Chapter 24

Back home Monday morning I threw myself into promoting *Neighbour-On-Call.* The website went live, I posted my offering on social media and drove over to the two nearest rehabilitation centres to drop off brochures. Taking Marco's advice, I also called two colleagues who'd recently reduced their hours at the hospital to ask if they would be interested in doing occasional days if I became busy. Surprisingly both jumped at the offer and so there were police and working with children checks to sort out.

The first call came at four o'clock; an elderly man who needed someone to take him to two medical appointments at either ends of the city later in the week. By six o'clock when Rob came home my week was booked out: a woman recovering from a knee replacement who had a physiotherapy appointment; a daughter asking if I could help her mother with some light shopping every Monday; several people who needed transport to hospital for outpatient appointments and weren't mobile enough to catch the bus; even a young mother, isolated at home because she couldn't drive who wanted a lift to the shopping mall—that child seat would come in handy.

My head was full of logistics, for the following day when Paige called. 'How was your first day in the new job?' she joked, although her voice was unusually husky.

'So busy. I am full up for the next week, so hopefully my other ladies will be able to start fairly soon. You know I did my research but the pent up demand is amazing. At this rate I will need someone to take phone bookings while I provide the service before the end of the month'.

'That's so great. I knew you were on to something', she broke off coughing. 'Sorry I have a miserable cold and now I feel bad because you are so busy but do you think Mamie-On-Call could drop over for a couple of hours tonight. You don't need to stay late but if you could give me little break...', she sounded terrible.

'Absolutely no problem. I will come in an hour or so, unless you need me sooner. Rob will be home, he might want to come as well'.

'You're an angel, thank you. Why don't you have dinner here? The home delivery people know me well these days'.

As predicted, Rob needed no second invitation for an evening with Maggie and a short while later we were giving her a feed while Paige tried to sleep.

'I have an idea I want to run by you', I watched Rob who was fully focused on the little girl. 'If today is typical of what's coming, all but one person phoned to book me, the website and social media may not appeal to a lot of my clientele. I was thinking about what Marco said, not to start too small and I can see I am going to need office help with bookings and scheduling the casuals. Provided today wasn't a flash in the pan'. Rob had turned to me waiting.

'The police checks for Mary and Ellie will take a week or so and then I can start to book them for jobs. But what I'm thinking is, well, what about I ask Brian to man the phones and respond to web enquiries. He obviously can't have direct physical client contact with his history but I can't see much risk with him doing admin. What do you think?'.

'You're still worrying about him but yes, I agree I can't see much risk. Maybe check in with Paige as well, she'll have a better idea if you're opening yourself up to any legal liability or if it will affect your insurance'.

'Good idea, that's two things I need to ask her'.

'What two things?' Paige wrapped her arms around her body to warm up as she came into the room. 'How is my little Magpie? Did she feed? I can see Papi has been conned into letting her sleep on him instead of in her sleeper'.

'She's been perfect', Rob smiled and kissed the top of Maggie's head.

I explained about Brian and Paige agreed it was good idea but suggested I clear it with my insurer. 'The second thing is more complicated so please say no if you're not comfortable. I have decided to ask Neil Hollows to meet me and the consensus is that I shouldn't go alone. I wondered if...'

'I would come with you', Paige finished for me.

'Sorry it's not the time to ask when you are feeling so rotten but yes, would you'.

'It will be a privilege Nell', the sincerity of her hug made me teary. I seemed to cry an awful lot these days.

Brian sounded strange when I rang three weeks later. There was a hesitancy, a crackle of tentativeness that made him sound older. When I asked how he was he immediately started telling me about his five hundred hours of removing graffiti and sweeping streets. 'Community service was demoralizing but everyone keeps telling me I should be glad I didn't go to prison. They're right but people treat you differently all the same'.

'Have you finished it?'

'A month ago. I went to Centrelink last week so at least I have some money coming in now. I suppose you heard that Rox left me almost as soon as I was charged. Shacked up with another bloke, a lawyer but from what I hear she is going to need his services professionally, not just in the bedroom'. The mix of defeat and venom in his voice shocked me and I had second thoughts about my proposition.

'Well nice of you to check in on me Nell. Give my best to everyone at work'.

'Wait', I sensed he was about to hang up. 'The reason I called was to feel you out about an idea I have. You see I've resigned from the hospital'. I cut across him as he started to exclaim surprise, 'I have started a new business, it's very new but so far its doing well'.

'You in business, I'd never have guessed that, thought you'd die in your scrubs'.

'I took leave and eventually I decided I didn't want to go back to Emergency. I was burnt out, tired, over it to be honest. So now I have this little business that provides casual services to people in rehabilitation after strokes or surgery, that sort of thing'.

'You mean like home nursing?'

'No, much more low key. We drive people to appointments, do errands, shopping. The stuff you would ask family to help out with if you are lucky enough to have them around. Turns out there's a huge demand from older people who want to retain some independence from their families or don't have anyone'.

'And what has this got to do with me?'

'I have two other women, you remember Ellie and Mary from work, helping with clients but I need someone to manage the office. You know scheduling bookings, web admin, not exciting but I think you would be perfect'.

'I don't know, my case was all over the papers. If someone puts two and two together it could ruin you'.

'There is a small risk, I know but I am comfortable with it or I wouldn't have called you. Why don't you think about it and let me know in a week or so?'

'Yeah, okay. Don't get me wrong, I appreciate the offer but...well...we'll see'.

When I told Rob about the conversation later, he was not surprised. He explained that if Brian did come to work for me, I would need to think about how to support his anxiety and feelings of guilt. He was vulnerable in a way I had not antici-pated but with hindsight made sense, the future would be full of unknowns. Rob suggested a trial period might be a better option for both of us but also that I shouldn't rush him. Good advice, especially as my first inclination was to immediately send a text suggesting the trial period idea. I would wait until the end of the week and then message him.

Being so busy with work and the occasional night with Maggie made it easy to find reasons not to contact Neil. It had waited thirty years, what was a few more weeks? I might have gone on procrastinating if not for Paige. It was a Friday evening and I was doing my old six o'clock to midnight shift for the first time in ages. It had been a long day filled with clients, four regulars and three new ones.

The regulars took the most time, wanting to chat about everything from politics to the footie. Over recent weeks it had become evident that a good part of my service was reliev-ing social isolation. It had also struck me that an inordinate number of older people watch parliament on television in the afternoons—it was the new *Days of Our Lives*, at least among my clients. Today, for example Mrs Simpson had booked me to take her to a hair appointment. She went every week for a wash and comb up and monthly for a cut. It was a fastidious schedule that taught me some lessons in the importance of grooming for healthy ageing. Almost before I could start helping her into the car, she was telling me about the terrible behaviour of our elected representatives, yelling at each other, cutting across and interjecting, refusing to answer questions. 'They were like ten year olds squabbling over a game of marbles', she said.

Paige came to find me about ten o'clock with my eyes closed. 'Oh Nell you look so tired, why don't you go home now. I'll do the next feed'.

'No its okay, just resting my eyes', I said, yawning in spite of my words.

'I'll make us a cup of tea and then you go home', she insisted. I followed her into the kitchen and perched on a stool while she filled the kettle. 'I had a call from work today asking if I will go back in two days a week from next month'.

'So soon, Maggie is too little and you are too sleep deprived!'

'Exactly, that is what I told my boss but he was super pushy about it'.

'Don't they have to let you take a year of maternity leave if you want?'

'Two years actually. He implied that if I didn't come back my career path would plateau at best'.

'At least in the hospital, managers understood the importance of supporting women to come back into the workforce, although they never had enough staff to make the conditions family friendly'.

'Some law firms are progressive but unluckily not ours'.

'So what will you do?

'Not sure, I'm definitely not ready to go back. I probably need to go in and meet with my manager in person. It would also be a good chance to introduce little Magpie to my work friends but that is also a challenge'.

I frowned my response and waited. 'You asked ages ago if Maggie's father would be involved in her life. The thing is, he is a work colleague and he hasn't met her yet. It seems wrong that the first time he sees her is with everyone else although he has made no attempt to contact me since she was born. I sent a short message telling him her name and that she was healthy and he sent a smiley face in response!'

'You could offer to meet him for coffee first and then see everyone else. That would keep it low key but respectful. I'm surprised he doesn't want some involvement, most men would at least be curious'.

'It's complicated. He is one of the partners, he has a wife and two daughters, a big house at the beach. He told me when the affair ended that any trouble I made would be career-limiting'.

'What a hide. Surely, he knows you better than that. You are the last person I would threaten in that way'.

'True but he did and I said nothing. If I'd made a complaint, even if it had been upheld, I knew it would colour how the bosses viewed me. I wasn't prepared to test them. Anyway this is about Maggie having a relationship with her biological father and provided I don't make any demands, the door to that stays open'.

'You won't ask him for financial support?'

'No, I'd rather not. If he wants to make payments into a trust account for Maggie that's fine but I can do without his money'. The tea was hot and we both warmed our hands around the mugs, glancing at the baby monitor to check that Maggie was still asleep. 'Have you thought anymore about contacting that guy, Neil?'

'The business has been so busy, I've not had time to think about it'.

Paige put her mug down, her eyes met mine with obvious questions. I stalled, taking a sip of tea but her gaze was steady. 'Okay, so yes, I have been putting it off. I have moments of being full of resolve and others of utter cowardice'.

'I'll make you a deal. Next week I'll meet Peter for coffee and you'll contact Neil to set up a meeting. Yes?'

'Alright, you're on' I said but my voice was tired and flat.

Chapter 25

Tuesday morning I had a text from Paige confirming that I would come that evening to look after Maggie and saying she was going into work Thursday morning and that Peter had agreed to meet. The subtext was that she would grill me tonight about what progress I had made. The answer of course was none and the dullness that had been threatening all morning became a tight band across my temple. I flipped through old messages until I found the one from Marco with Neil's contact details. He had them from the fundraiser and sent them to me a few days after our visit. Biting my lip, I typed out the email I'd been rehearsing in the middle of the night:

Dear Neil

It has been a very long time since we were in contact and this email will seem to come out of the blue. I was hoping I could meet you for a coffee sometime to talk about the brief time we were together. I have been resolving some issues recently and it would help to hear your memory of that time. A friend who lives in Milton gave me your contact details after I serendipitously met your wife Jenny. I hope you will agree to meet but realise you may not even remember me—the eighties are a lifetime ago.

Best wishes

Nell Saunders

I read the message a third time and hit the send button with the faintest niggle of guilt. I was giving him an easy excuse, partly hoping he would take it up. Luckily, I was fully booked for the day before I had to rush over to Paige's place so there was no chance to dwell on what might or might not happen. Maggie was grisly from teething and insisted on being held rather than put down in her cot as usual. I was happy for the cuddles and she eventually settled enough for me to check my messages. A few reviews for *Neighbour-On-Call* and a note from Cleo with pictures of Sofia who had been visiting with her parents. For now I could unclench my teeth and relax my shoulders.

Two days later as Rob and I were alternatively pacing the kitchen and checking the street for Paige and Maggie to arrive, his phone rang. 'Ah left the phone upstairs', he muttered as he took the stairs two at a time. A moment later he was coming back down and my phone rang. 'Missed it', he said as I said hello to the unknown number on mine.

'Nell, it's Cristiane. I tried to call Rob but he didn't answer. We are at the hospital'.

'Is everything okay?' I asked distractedly calculating that Caroline was only thirty four weeks while trying to switch the phone to speaker so that Rob could hear.

'We are good. Caro is in labour and the doctor says everything is going well. I'll let you talk to her'.

I handed the phone to Rob. 'Caro sweetheart how are you?'

A sharp grunt was followed by a long silence before Caroline responded, her voice an octave higher than normal, 'Dad I'm okay. The contractions started two hours ago and I am waiting for the doctor to put an epidural in. The nurse said I'm not fully dilated yet so we don't know how long it will be. The babes are doing well though so hopefully we can stick with the plan for a natural birth'. She broke off then with another contraction.

'Those contractions are pretty close together', I said, worried it would go faster than she expected.

'Is that Caro?' Paige was struggling with the back door, clutching Maggie and the nappy bag in her rush to join us. Rob nodded handing her the phone. 'Good luck little sis. You'll be great. So wish we could be there with you'.

Cristiane was back on the phone, 'The anaesthetist has arrived, have to go. We'll keep you posted'.

Paige stayed longer than usual as the text messages from Paris kept us all by the phone and between messages she told us about her day. She had met up with Peter as arranged and Rob was quick to clarify that he hadn't said or done anything too terrible. She told us that he had held Maggie for a short time and he had offered to contribute to her education through a trust fund. He did not want any regular contact at least for now as it would put his marriage in jeopardy—his wife had given him an ultimatum about his affairs and he was desperate to try and save the relationship. There was plenty of snorting in disbelief from Rob and I about that statement but it seemed that Paige had brokered an arrangement that would work for now and then when Maggie was older it could be revisited. After all she had two half-siblings who she may want to know in the future as well as her father.

For now though she was sleeping after an enormous feed, making up for being off her food while she was teething. Rob stroked her head and told her she was the most beautiful girl in the world. I had never seen his protective instincts kick in as fiercely as when Paige was telling him about the meeting with Peter. His arms were crossed, he looked angry and he spat our expletives at regular intervals like a pressure valve at its limits.

'Why don't you hold Maggie Magpie for a while', Paige offered, sensing his instinct to keep her close.

'No, I'll wake her', his self-conscious grin evidence of our usual calm Rob returning.

Finally, close to ten o'clock we had another call from Paris. The messaging had gone quiet for a while and we were all so on tenterhooks that the ringing made both Paige and I cry out in alarm and anticipation.

'Dad, Nell, Paige, meet the two tiniest most wonderful boys. We are all well, the boys will have to go to the neonatal intensive care for a few days because they are early but the doctor said that everything is fine'.

Caroline's announcement was interrupted by Cristiane telling us how strong her partner had been, Paige asking for more details about weight, names, how long the labour was and Rob blissfully telling Caroline how proud he was. Animated words fell over each other, laughter gurgled in sinuous streams, seeking out every tiny space between their words. The two boys were indeed tiny, not quite two kilos but they were perfectly formed and their scores were all good. Cristiane was given the honour of telling us that they would be called Jean-Luc and Remy which started off the exclamations all over again.

After they rang off, Rob went to the kitchen in search of champagne, returning with three glasses in spite of Paige saying she was driving. 'Here's to our precious family. We are so lucky to have each other and to be blessed with cousins for Maggie. I miss having Caro close but we'll make sure we are part of their lives. Won't we?' this last addressed to me. What else to do but nod, my mouth stretched with joy.

'Maggie's excited too. She shouldn't be awake yet', Paige said hearing her daughter wake. 'I'll feed her and then go if that's alright with you. I know it's late but I hate driving with her when she is hungry and crying. I'm so distracted I could easily have an accident'.

'Of course. And we are too excited anyway to sleep'.

'I'm hoping that champagne will kick in. It's been a very long day, so many emotions'.

'Why don't you stay here tonight. You have enough milk and nappies and then you can have a few hours while I give Maggie the early morning feed'.

'Actually Nell, that would be amazing. Do you mind? I know you are super busy as well'.

'Nell, you are a genius. Of course she must stay', Rob was already unpacking the nappy bag and taking the expressed milk to the fridge. 'You can wear one of my enormous old t-shirts like you used to when you were ten or twelve'.

'Ha, I'd forgotten that. I did love wearing your t-shirts to bed, the old ones were the softest. I'm not sure what sort of fashion statement I imagined I was making, showing my androgynous side or something...'

By morning we had been inundated with photos of the baby boys being held alternatively by each of their mothers. I wondered at the love they would know, that Maggie knew, it was the best start possible even if there were no dads. Rob after all would be a fine male figure in their lives and there would be others, Cristiane's father and brother, my brother, Marco and perhaps eventually a partner for Paige.

For once I was pleased that I had no early clients because as predicted sleep had not come quickly. Rob had filled his wakeful hours planning our trip to France and in his enthusiasm stymied whatever sleep I might have managed by sharing his ideas. He was not so lucky, having an early meeting and so it was Paige and I sitting over a coffee and marvelling at each of the many photos.

'I didn't like to say it before', she admitted, 'but their faces are a bit swished and wrinkled. I'm sure they will look better in a day or so'. I giggled my agreement, knowing as she did that Rob had seen only perfection.

'But they do have a lot of black hair. I wonder who that's from?'

'It will be so nice exchanging stories with Caro. Since she moved to Paris, well since she and Cristiane got together really, we haven't talked as much as we used to. She has always been able to read me, better than Mum and Dad could. I miss the way she brings me back to earth, reminds me of what matters instead of whatever I'm stressing about'.

'I know what you mean. Stephen has been that person for me: the one who knows me better than I know yourself. I wonder if as the younger sibling it was a matter of preservation', I laughed, 'Work out your older sister to survive'.

'Ha, you could be right. I was awful to Caro, playing psychological games, telling her she was adopted, calling her a copycat when she wanted to be like me. Truly vile but it made her stronger'. We both laughed but also knew there was truth in funny stories.

Paige was getting ready to go home and I was flipping through my emails in case any last minute requests had come in from clients. A strange noise rose from deep in my chest as I saw there was a response from Neil.

'What's up', Paige looked worried.

'It's Neil. He says he would love to meet for a coffee, of course he remembers me and that actually he had been thinking he'd like to catch up for a while. He has offered to come to Sydney or else to meet near his work in Wollongong. What do you think?'

'Well, always better on home ground'.

'Maybe but I'm not sure I want him on MY home ground. I like the idea of keeping him at arms length. Does that make sense?'

'Absolutely. So say Wollongong and then maybe we can drop Dad and Maggie with your brother's family for a few hours and you and I can do the meeting'.

I nodded, a plan starting to form and the clench in my stomach squeezing tighter.

Chapter 26

'Guess who I signed up this week?' I had turned to Paige who was in the backseat with Maggie.

'An ageing celebrity?'

'Not a client, a new employee'.

'No idea. No, of course, you mean that guy you asked me about. What was his name?'

'Brian, yes, he has agreed to be our administrative support and he is doing really well. Rob has been super helpful as well, telling me what I should look out for as he makes the transition back into work. I had presumed because he avoided gaol, it was unlikely he would have so many issues but it seems I'm wrong'.

'You mean like feeling confident or mental health problems from what he's been through'.

'Yes', Rob interjected, 'but its more than that, his life and everything he knew about himself and his future have been destroyed. He has to create a new narrative and that's scary, not everyone can do it'.

'Hmm. It makes your offer to him even more important Nell. I can see you don't want to mess that up, or let him mess it up. It's a remarkable gift and a risky one for him. But if anyone can make this a positive experience it's you Nell'.

'Not so sure about that but so far so good'.

'Don't underestimate your compassion and empathy. I've seen and experienced your ability to literally heal people with kindness. We all love you for that'.

I coughed pretending an irritation as a stifled sob closed over my throat. Rob glanced at me from the driver's seat but said nothing.

The minute we arrived at Stephen and Melody's place, everybody was wanting to hold Maggie, see photos of the twins, tell Paige she looked amazing so soon after the birth—typical Saunders pandemonium. Trudy held Maggie gingerly as though expecting her to break and came to sit beside me where I was avoiding the unpacking and general hubbub.

'She is perfect. Look at her little pink ears and those finger-nails are so cute'.

'Sharp too. Yes, she is special. Paige calls her Magpie some-times, her pet name'.

Trudy held her away a little, studying her gurgling face, 'It suits her. She is watching us all the time with her head tilted to the side, just like a magpie'.

'The inspiration was more her squawking, but we'll take that. Thanks Trudy', Paige joined us on the verandah. Seeing her Mum, Maggie screwed up her face and made good on Paige's explanation for her nickname.

'It's time for her feed. Here, I'll take her inside and give her some boob if that's alright'.

'Trudy why don't you take Paige into the living room. She can feed in the there where it is warm'.

'You can stay and talk to me if you like', Paige said as Trudy turned to leave.

'Are you sure? I thought you'd want privacy'.

Paige laughed, 'I got over all those niceties when she was born. It was pretty undignified and now I'm so focused on her I hardly notice how other people react. If they're embarrassed or offended, I'm sorry but I don't need to feel that way'.

'Exactly', Melody said coming inside to join us. 'When you were a baby, I used to be relaxed about feeding in public too but I had one friend who thought it was rude. Do you remember Helen, she used to teach with me? She was older so I suppose when she had her kids in the sixties breast feeding in public would have been frowned upon'.

Trudy was more interested in seeing Paige position the nipple guard and latch Maggie on than on what her mother was saying. 'Does it hurt?' she asked.

'Sometimes, when she starts it can hurt but it's more like a tugging feeling'.

'She makes a lot of noise', Trudy was intrigued so I was unprepared for her next question. 'Aunty Nell, do you wish you'd had babies?'

'Yes, part of me does but it was never the right time and besides I have the best niece in the world, two stepdaughters and three grandchildren. I've been blest', and I knew for the first time that I meant it with all my heart.

'Has she tried to pass on her family secrets to you?' Trudy directed her attention to Paige again.

'What sort of secrets?'

'Oh all sorts of old fashioned things. She makes this amazing sponge cake that she taught me to make last time she was here and she knits. Oh and she has this weird way of folding sheets that requires two people and a long corridor...'

'Trudy Saunders, are you mocking your old aunt', I grimaced with pretended outrage.

'I'm laughing with you, not at you', she said, mischief in the creases around her eyes.

'Well it might be old-fashioned but it keeps me connected to people I love, to my Mum and her Mum. It takes me back to being with them; I can hear Nanna's voice when I darn a sock, reminding me to keep my stitches small and Mum, telling me to fold not stir the egg whites for the sponge. Tiny gestures but they are my way of keeping our history alive'.

Paige gave me a sad smile, 'And Maggie has a beautiful rug, thanks to those skills. I know what you mean, though. Mum had a particular way that she folded clothes in the dresser drawers and last week I found myself using her method with Maggie's clothes. I had never given it any thought until then—it was part of me without me knowing'.

Maggie finished feeding and Paige bundled her up, ready for a cuddle with Melody. 'I've missed that smell', she said inhaling the milk cloud. 'It takes me straight back to those long winter nights when Trudy was a baby and we were too poor to have proper heating so I devised a blanket tent to keep us warm while she fed'.

'You used to wear a beanie as well. Do you remember?' Stephen said as he and Rob came back inside.

'Goodness, I had forgotten that detail. I must have looked a sight'.

'Never more beautiful', he dropped a kiss on her forehead and then on Maggie.

'You two had better get going', Rob said, charging the room with a new tension. 'Maggie has a team of people to dote on her, she's in good hands', he reassured Paige before coming to put his arm around my waist. 'Good luck and remember this is for you, you don't owe anyone'.

Trudy watched us closely not sure what was happening but her instincts told her there was drama afoot, 'Can I come?' she asked.

Floored, I grasped for words as Melody intervened to say that now wasn't a good time, that I had an important meeting to go to. On autopilot I followed Paige to the car but at the last minute I turned back, 'If it's okay with your Mum and Dad you can come with us. You'll have to wait in the car but I can explain what it's all about on the way'.

Melody looked dubious and Stephen was shaking his head, 'Are you sure?'

'I think it will help and Trudy is a young adult, I value her opinion'.

The three of us drove the twenty minute route to his office in silence until I had structured my thoughts more clearly and started to tell Trudy about my relationship with Neil as a teenager not much older than her. I tried to explain my self-doubt, having never had a boyfriend and feeling less sophisticated than him. She listened with an intensity that made my neck burn, deepening her frown when I told her about him forcing himself on me, the first time we had sex.

'You asked me once, what my first time was like and I avoided giving you a proper answer. I hope your first time with a boy, if you choose to have one, is something to celebrate'. She nodded but gave no sign of being ready to comment so I proceeded to describe the brief affair and the end result before her incredulity finally overcame all reticence.

'Really, you actually had an abortion? Didn't you feel guilty that you were...you know...?' her voice trailed off but I knew how that sentence ended.

'I felt sadder than I ever have before or since, ashamed as well that I'd messed up. I never used to think that I felt guilty because sometimes you need to take hard decisions but lately I've been wondering if that's true'.

Trudy waited for me to continue although I could see she was longing to ask more. 'You see, there was this little voice in my head that told me that I wasn't cut out to be a mother. I used to think it was because my Mum was not there for Stephen and me in her last years but now I wonder if I conflated that with terminating my only chance at motherhood'.

'Like mother, like daughter', Paige expelled a loud breath. 'Nell, you just shone a light on a dark hunch I've been trying to ignore. I've been telling myself that I'll be no good in a long term relationship, that Maggie will be enough, that I can do it alone'.

I gave Paige a tight smile, thinking of Marjorie's bitterness after the divorce and wishing I had been more aware of how that must have affected the girls. The side windows of the car had fogged up and I wiped mine clear with a tissue, needing to see the outside. It was all still there, the ocean a strip of blue on the horizon, suburban streets with Italianate Mcmansions, ugly flyovers, the garish green of the escarpment. A renewed intimacy settled on the three of us bringing a peace I had not felt for a long time.

Trudy waited in the car, Paige was on a plastic chair near the door, I faced Neil across his desk. His secretary had brought us into the office while he finished off a meeting somewhere else but fortunately the wait was brief. I had worried that nerves would overtake me, that I would 'chicken out' as Stephen would have said when we were kids. Instead I felt my shoulders brace against the high backed chair and my hands sat firmly on my crossed knee. Neil had made a half-hearted gesture to kiss me on the cheek in greeting which I pre-empted by quickly offering my hand.

'Nell, it's so good to see you. It must be, what, thirty years? You haven't changed a bit'.

'Closer to forty actually and we're all older', my lips tightened in the semblance of a smile. 'I recently met up with a mutual acquaintance, Gillian Meadon and as I said in my email, it's raised some issues for me'. Paige's advice had been to get straight to the point and it felt good to take control of the conversation though out of character for me.

Neil covered his mouth with his hand and ran his thumb down under his chin, 'I been half-expecting you to contact me for months. It was almost a relief when you did. I assume Gill told you what happened between us'.

'She told me what happened to her and honestly I was shocked. Slowly I've been coming to terms with the negative impact our short relationship had on me as well'.

'Was it so bad? I really liked you Nell but I always had the feeling that you were somewhere else, or would like to have been'.

'I was very shy and you know, I hadn't been with anyone before. I think that's why when you forced yourself on me that first time and later when you only turned up after a drinking session, I kept seeing you'.

'It's true. I didn't behave well, I realise that, the callousness of youth and all that. Besides, I was intimidated by you, you were smart and doing something worthwhile while I was just working in one of Dad's businesses. I'd dropped out of Uni —it's not an excuse but I was a failure in Dad's eyes and after he met you that first time, he told me that you were too good for me'.

'I felt like a country bumpkin around your family. You were all so worldly wise and business orientated, I didn't know any-one else like that'.

'You said before, I forced myself on you. You mean...why didn't you tell me to stop?' Before I could answer he continued, 'Because the thing is, and it's a terrible thing to say, I don't have much memory of that night'.

My earlier courage was failing. How could an evening that turned my world upside down have meant so little to him? I swallowed hard, the last thing I was going to do was cry in front of this man.

'Not that I don't believe you, I do. And if you decide to join Gill in making a police report I respect that, I only ask that let me tell you what was going on for me'.

I leant back, so here we go, now I have to hear why he is the real victim, I thought.

'So I was twenty two and as I said, I'd dropped out of Uni. I let you believe I had already graduated, in fact that's what most of my friends believed. When I was at Uni, I lived at one of the all male colleges and the best way to fit in was to drink and to be successful with women. I wasn't very good at the second, so heavy drinking became my fall back position. By the time we met, I was an alcoholic but mostly I could cover pretty well and I was even doing okay in Dad's electronics store in the city'.

'You had all these plans to be involved in computers', I said trying to recall what I had known back then.

'That was my dream. Anyway, after we broke up I took up with a girl I'd known at school. She was working in a big bank and we had some wild times. She was the one who introduced me to cocaine and soon it replaced alcohol as my drug of choice. I was using coke the night with Gill. I'll never live down the shame of that night. I was brutal, entirely out of control, I wanted to hurt her'.

'She was your flat mate, your friend'.

'She had her shit so together and I was literally falling apart. When she told me she was gay it was like she could see her path, like all of a sudden, the world made sense to her. Meanwhile I was staring into a dark tunnel that had no end'.

'So what, you were jealous?'

'Crippled with self-loathing more like. And nothing I did could make that any worse, at least that was what I thought'.

I waited, seeing Paige shake her head from the corner of my eye and I wondered if it was in sympathy or disbelief because so far, I wasn't feeling a lot of sympathy. Neil took a sip of the water on his desk, 'The day after the incident with Gill I had a car crash on the way to work. The car was a total right off and I blocked the harbour bridge for three hours. Found out later the woman in the other car almost died from her head injuries. She survived and Dad intervened to make sure there were no charges on the proviso that I went into rehab. My sister knew about the extent of my drinking and drug use and as it escalated, she had decided to tell Dad'.

He paused again but I had no inclination to validate his story, 'Anyway, long story short, I eventually got clean, went back to Uni, finished my degree and became a respectable businessman, father and husband—the son Dad always expected me to be'.

Meanwhile Gill and I had not been able to break free of that history so easily. 'Have you ever apologized to Gill?' I asked.

His grimace was an ugly slash on his otherwise handsome face, 'The lawyers said I shouldn't speak with her now that she's made a complaint to police. They are negotiating with her legal team to see if we can reach an agreement on what compensation she might need to convince her to drop the charges'.

'You're trying to buy her off', I was surprised at how angry I sounded.

'That makes it sound like a bad thing, no I want to offer her compensation, to make amends'.

'For all those years in therapy, for the trauma, for smashing her self-esteem...' I stopped before I dug any deeper into that pit of contempt, knowing I had a confession of my own.

'Sorry, that's none of my business and there is a bit more to my story. After we broke up, I went to Melbourne for a holiday'.

'Yeah, I tried to see you a couple of times but your house mates said you were away. I thought if I could see you, we could get back together. I know I didn't treat you well but I loved the idea of being with someone so principled, so decent'.

Why had I not understood all these years? In spite of my better self, I gave in to him and he took that to mean the attraction was stronger than my good sense. He had won. I pulled my thoughts back to what I had been saying, 'In Melbourne I discovered I was pregnant and knowing there was no future for us, I decided to have an abortion'.

He had the hide to look wounded, 'I would have married you'.

I cut him off before he could go on, 'We both know that would have been a disaster. I was still a teenager and you were unpredictable, not to mention uninterested in anything serious. For goodness sake, you've just told me you were an alcoholic'. I couldn't stay in the room any longer and I turned towards Paige and nodded to the door.

'Look don't go yet, I spoke with my lawyers before you came and they suggested I offer you financial recompense for any pain or suffering I unwittingly caused'. So much for his earlier claim that he had little memory of that night.

'Goodbye Neil, thank you for seeing me and no I do not want your money. Save that for your legal bill'. Paige held my arm as we walked down the long corridor our heels loud on the wooden floor, the sound of a rushed retreat or a deliberate march forward? I decided it must be the latter as Paige held up her phone to show me it was recording.

Chapter 27

No one spoke as Paige drove out of the grounds but as we pulled onto the highway, Trudy could not contain herself any long, 'So, what happened?'

My brain was a scramble of fury and squeezing my eyes closed only partially cleared it. 'It was grueling, different to what I expected but just as bad. Neil admitted some of his behaviour was wrong and he said it was because he was addicted to alcohol and other drugs. He said he would have married me if he'd known about the baby. Like that would have made everything all right. Like I would even have wanted it', my voice was rising as recounting his words made the implications starker. 'Then he offered me money, ostensibly for pain and suffering but I'm not stupid! It was so I wouldn't testify if Gill doesn't drop her charges'.

Paige nodded, 'Yes, he probably realized he had said too much and thought if you were compromised by taking his money your testimony would be invalid. That was some sob story he gave you about his father and drinking, using cocaine, almost like he was the victim'.

'Exactly, until then I was prepared to believe I had misjudged him but in the end it was all about him'.

'Typical man', Trudy's cynicism brought me up short.

'No sweetheart, typical Neil. Not all men are like that, look at your dad, he is kind, honorable, trustworthy. Look at Rob who looks after all of us, never thinking of himself. Most men are good but there are some people, men and women who don't have a good moral compass. The best thing is to learn to spot them early so that you can stay out of their way'.

'Why are they like that?'

I was grateful when Paige responded, 'Lots of reasons but in my experience, I'd say it's two main things: they've had bad things happen to them like maybe they've been bullied and they had a problem with self-esteem. If they treat you badly, make you feel small, they can pretend to be more important and impressive than they are'.

'Neil's Dad certainly was tough on him and I think a lot of his behaviour was rebellion against that. Also his sister was uber smart and hard working so he was always being compared to her. I remember him saying that he had a higher IQ than her so I supposed when he flunked his course that was a blow to his ego'.

'His ego has clearly recovered if today was anything to go by', Paige snorted.

'A lifetime of building it up eventually pays off', my turn to be cynical.

'And yet, you know, he still wanted you to say you understood that he'd had issues'.

'And all I wanted was for him to say sorry, without justification, without rationalizing'.

'And he had the gaul to imply the reason he was such an awful boyfriend was because he was in awe of you. That part really was too much. Not to say you aren't amazing Nell but you are hardly intimidating'.

'Actually that was one point I kind of understood. I can be stand-offish especially when I'm not sure—you and Caroline told me that, remember. With Neil I was way out of my depth and I would have said shy but he may have seen it as being aloof. The thing is, his story about being intimidated by me is absolutely the opposite of what I experienced. I would have sworn that he thought I was submissive early on and then when he discovered I wasn't, he lost interest. You would think at my age I would know that it was never about me, it was all about him and his inner demons'.

'Did you take the money?' Trudy was sick of our amateur psychology.

'What do you think?'

'I hope you didn't because then you would owe him. Like he can buy whatever he likes and doesn't have to live with the consequences'.

'Trudy that is a very grown up way to look at it, I'm really impressed', I said and hoped that it didn't come across as patronizing.

She was quiet for a while and I could see that her mind was busy solving a problem. 'Remember how a while ago I asked you to talk to Mum about the pill, Aunty Nell?' She continued without waiting for a response, 'I told you there was no one special and that I might like a girl but the thing is a bit after that, I got with this boy called Trent'.

Paige must have recognized my frown as lack of comprehension, 'She means they kissed, not that they had sex'.

'I see. Are you and Trent together now?'

'Nah, I liked him but he lied to me all the time. Like he'd say he had to do something with his family and then I'd hear he was out with his mates. He just wasn't that into me and so I dropped him'.

'Good girl, I wish I'd had the good sense to do the same with Neil but we learn from our mistakes as well'.

'Like what?'

'You mean, what have I learnt?'. I stared out the passenger window wondering if I had anything of substance to say. I had learnt that my own actions could be misinterpreted; I had learnt that people are mostly driven by their own insecurities; and, I had learnt that it was okay to be sad and that it wasn't the same as regret. Grief and shame did not have to cohabit but for a long time I had forgotten they were separate things.

Finally I tried, 'I learnt that I shouldn't measure myself against other people's actions or expectations and also that decisions made in good faith should not be relitigated later in life'.

'Relitigated, you mean judged?'.

'Precisely, less judgment more tolerance because the hardest person to forgive is always yourself'. A wave of exhaustion broke over me and I rested my head back against the car seat. Behind closed lids I saw Neil sitting there still confident that he could manipulate me after all these years. He was wealthy, important, and he would be accustomed to people giving in to him.

But Gill hadn't given in, well at least not yet. Would she settle for the compensation given the uncertainty of her case? I could understand if she did. Or like me, did the offer galvanise her to take a stronger stand. Neil had helped me reach a firm conclusion.

Paige's deep exhalation roused me enough to open my eyes, 'Everything okay?'

'I've been thinking about Maggie's Dad. Trudy is right, people can't buy their way out of problems they don't like. I am going to insist that he recognize Maggie as his daughter. I don't want his money but I do want Maggie to have a choice about her own identity. That's her right to decide, not his, or his precious family's.

'Will that be difficult given he is a partner?'

'Sitting listening to Neil this afternoon brought the facts into stark reality for me...finally. Staying there will compromise our lives as well as my career so next week I will hand in my resignation'.

'That's a brave move but I agree it is the right one, not that you need my approval'.

'Appreciate the support and I am taking inspiration from you'. I tweaked my left brow in query and Paige continued after a well-staged pause, 'When you were setting up your business you needed advice about the best way to do it, the legal pitfalls, how to set up insurance so that you wouldn't default. More and more women are starting their own businesses and I'm guessing that there is a huge need for legal advice but provided on their terms because a lot of these women have young families and are busy. So instead of working nine to five I could have an evening service or include home visits that would suit me and them. I need to do the research but I think the idea has legs'.

'Not just women with businesses either. My clients are all house bound to a greater or lesser extent and they are finalizing or changing wills and bequests as well as navigating social security traps. I imagine they'd welcome a more flexible service offering'.

As we parked at Stephen and Melody's place, Rob appeared at the door with a sleeping Maggie in his arms. Stephen and Melody were close behind crowding the doorway.

'Aunty Nell was amazing', Trudy pronounced as soon as we were within earshot giving Paige a moment to whisper, 'So you are going to do it, aren't you'.

I nodded. I would call Gill on Monday and tell her I would be a witness if the case goes to court. I did not need to have my own experience affirmed but I would support her quest to find the justice she needed. We all have our own way of dealing with painful pasts and so long as they brought peace, I had no qualms about my choice or hers.

Paige rushed to cuddle her daughter who immediately demanded a feed. 'Here hold her for a moment can you Nell while I get the nappy bag'. I kissed the top of her head and in my mind's eye pictured those two Parisian-born boys. Maggie burrowed into me and I knew no matter what went before or after that second chances were the best of gifts.

Acknowledgements

My thanks to those who have supported me in this endeavour, especially my husband Iqbal who has patiently endured me plotting in the middle of the night and being unresponsive while writing in the day. This story is entirely fiction but a small number of incidents are inspired by past experiences. Thanks to the friends who came with me on that first cross-country ski trip from which Cleo recalls sore, stiff muscles and those in earlier years who endured a joint family picnic that mixed cuisines and cultures in ways that were a surprise to all. My own mother and grandmother were keen bakers, knitters and sheet folders and memories of their no nonsense approach to life is never far from me. Finally, an enormous thank you to those who read *Grafted. A Novel* and were so encouraging with their feedback.

www.ingramcontent.com/pod-product-compliance
Lightning Source LLC
Chambersburg PA
CBHW020405120726
47904CB00002B/713